ALSO BY A. J. BANNER

The Good Neighbor

THE TWILIGHT WIFE

– A Novel –

A. J. BANNER

TOUCHSTONE
New York   London   Toronto   Sydney   New Delhi

Touchstone
An Imprint of Simon & Schuster, Inc.
1230 Avenue of the Americas
New York, NY 10020

First Touchstone trade paperback edition December 2016

TOUCHSTONE and colophon are registered trademarks of Simon & Schuster, Inc.

For information about special discounts for bulk purchases, please contact Simon & Schuster Special Sales at 1-866-506-1949 or business@simonand schuster.com.

The Simon & Schuster Speakers Bureau can bring authors to your live event. For more information or to book an event, contact the Simon & Schuster Speakers Bureau at 1-866-248-3049 or visit our website at www.simonspeakers.com.

Interior design by Jill Putorti

Manufactured in the United States of America

10 9 8 7 6 5 4 3 2

Library of Congress Cataloging-in-Publication Data
Names: Banner, A. J., author.
Title: The twilight wife / A. J. Banner.
Description: First Touchstone trade paperback edition. | New York : Touchstone, 2016.
Identifiers: LCCN 2016025793 (print) | LCCN 2016028854 (ebook) | ISBN 9781501152115 (softcover : acid-free paper) | ISBN 9781501152122 (ebook)
Subjects: LCSH: Women marine biologists—Fiction. | Memory disorders—Fiction. | Amnesia—Fiction. | Psychological fiction. | BISAC: FICTION / Suspense. | FICTION / Mystery & Detective / General. | FICTION / Contemporary Women. | GSAFD: Suspense fiction. | Mystery fiction.
Classification: LCC PS3602.A6665 T95 2016 (print) | LCC PS3602.A6665 (ebook) | DDC 813/.6—dc23
LC record available at https://lccn.loc.gov/2016025793

ISBN 978-1-5011-5211-5
ISBN 978-1-5011-5212-2 (ebook)

In loving memory of
James Robert Machcinski

Yesterday is but today's memory,
and tomorrow is today's dream.

— Khalil Gibran

CHAPTER ONE

This morning, I know the scientific term for the vermilion star, *Mediaster aequalis*, but I have trouble remembering my name. I reach into the icy water to touch the sea star's bumpy exoskeleton, and I feel like a child full of fascination, not a thirty-four-year-old marine biologist recovering from a head injury. They say I taught freshman classes at Seattle University, but I have no memory of those days. I wonder about the moments I've lost, the people I loved. We surely must have laughed together, lifted our glasses to celebrate weddings, birthdays, anniversaries. I used to have a life. But now I have only this island, the husband who stays by my side, and a peculiar recurring dream.

I came down to the water's edge today, to see if I could conjure a memory, but instead I found this rare, healthy sea star, untouched by the mysterious wasting disease ravaging sea stars along the west coast. Here is this bright orange miracle, all five arms intact. I suppose I'm a miracle, too, still alive and intact after fracturing my skull in a diving accident three months ago.

These islands haunt me, but I have no conscious memory of this area. No memory of my decision to move here to study the rare Tompkins anemone. No memory of buying these pajamas, my sweater, my running shoes.

And I don't recognize the jagged scar on my right thumb. A thin white line. My husband, Jacob, said I cut myself on a barnacle-encrusted rock while diving.

I once knew how to assemble a scuba unit, but I don't trust myself to even put on a mask anymore. I don't recall learning how to dive. Last thing I remember, I was thirty years old. And after that . . . the boat trip to this island two weeks ago. Jacob thinks the beautiful forest emerging from the fog and the rocky coastline of this special place will help restore me. All I can think is, what am I doing here?

I long to reclaim the four years I've lost. After my recovery in the hospital, we came here to Mystic Island in the Pacific Northwest, where the wind blows in cold from the sea. On this remote outpost, emergency responders can be slow—if they even get the call. The locals pride themselves on staying "off the grid." Our landline goes out so often, we might as well not have one.

Jacob follows me everywhere. He worries I'll forget where I am. He won't like that I've wandered down to the beach alone. I could become disoriented, lose my way. My husband watches over me like a guardian angel.

And I barely remember him at all.

"Kyra! What are you doing?" His voice drifts toward me on the wind. He's racing along the beach in graceful strides.

"I found a healthy sea star!" *My name is Kyra Winthrop. I dropped my maiden name, Munin. I've been married to Jacob Winthrop for nearly three years.* I have to keep reminding myself.

When Jacob reaches me, breathless, he pulls me to my feet. "You scared the hell out of me." His T-shirt is on inside out, and he's in jeans and hiking boots. He's striking in a Nordic way, with blue eyes, strong features, and a blond buzz cut. If I could talk to my old self, I would congratulate her for making such a wise decision to marry this thoughtful man, who clearly loves me.

"Sorry I scared you," I say, looking toward the sea. "I needed to get outside, that's all."

"You walked a long way. I got worried." He looks around in a panic, as if some malevolent force might try to steal me. But there is no other human on this beach, only the seagulls riding the updrafts.

"You shouldn't worry. You need your rest. Taking care of me is wearing you out." I touch his cheek, rough with the beginning of a beard. His fatigue shows in the shadows beneath his eyes. I wish he didn't insist on cooking for me, tidying up after me, doing the laundry. He patiently answers my questions, but I hate having to ask them.

He pulls me into a hug. "Tell me the truth," he says. "What's going on? Was it . . . ?"

"Yeah, the dream again," I confess. It's always the same. I'm diving in murky, churning waters, struggling against the current. I wake in a cold sweat.

"That nightmare won't leave you alone." Jacob steps back and rests his hands on my shoulders. They're heavy hands, as if his bones are made of concrete. "Maybe you need to talk to someone."

"I'm sorry the burden has been all on you."

"You're never a burden. That's not what I meant." He lifts my hand to his lips, kisses my fingers. His breath is warm on my skin. "You could've woken me. I would've come down here with you."

"But you looked so peaceful."

He scratches the stubble on his chin. "I'll be more peaceful inside by the woodstove. Come on, you're shivering. You should've put on a coat."

"My sweater is good enough." But he's right. My teeth chatter as we head back along the beach, picking our way across kelp and shells. I imagine how we must have carried our scuba gear across a similar beach at Deception Pass, the day of the accident. We thought the amazing marine life in the pass would outweigh the risk of diving in such rough waters. He has shown me pictures of the area where we dove, several miles south of Mystic Island. But I don't remember the Deception Pass Bridge, its span of nearly 1,500 feet rising 180 feet above the narrow strait that separates Whidbey Island from Fidalgo Island. Apparently, we consulted the tide tables, which we thought were in Pacific Standard Time. But they were in Pacific Daylight Time. We were diving earlier than we thought, through strong currents instead of in calm waters at slack current.

I turn to look up at Jacob. "How did we survive?"

"What?" He looks at me with confusion in his eyes.

"We made it to shore east of the bridge. But how?"

"We swam. I told you already." He can't hide the touch of irritation in his voice.

"I don't remember every detail of what you tell me—"

"I know. It's just . . ."

"I'm sorry you have to repeat yourself."

"It's okay. I don't mind."

But I know he does. He tries so hard to be patient. "I want to go back to the pass," I say. "I want to see where we dove. Maybe I'll start remembering on my own."

He interlaces his fingers with mine. "We'll go back, okay? But not yet. You need some time."

"Fair enough." I know he's the one who needs time. He remembers everything, and now he suffers from post-traumatic stress, while my brain simply blacked out.

I follow him up the steps toward our sprawling cedar bungalow with its plethora of windows and a small garden cottage. Vines of ivy climb the western wall of the main dwelling. Rosebushes cling to the south-facing side. Jacob's mother planted the first roses nearly forty years ago, when his father built the house as a refuge from city life. It's the kind of house that might harbor a fugitive or someone in witness protection—or a weary soul seeking a retreat, a sanctuary surrounded by forest and the sea.

Despite its sprawl, the one-story structure feels unobtrusive, as if it has grown naturally from the landscape. Many times in recent days, I've stood in the garden or on the beach, staring at the house from different perspectives, trying to remember the last time we were here. I imagine Jacob chasing me up the stone steps, both of us laughing. I know we loved this place—he has shown me the photographs. How lucky I am that his parents left him the place. He hired contractors to remodel the rooms, add the solar panels, and build the garden cottage, where he types away on the Great American Novel. He left his lucrative software business in Seattle to take care of me. He stocked the pantry and rigged a spotty satellite Internet connection in my study, but the island has no cell phone service. It feels like we're light-years away from civilization, instead of a hundred miles from Seattle, across the Strait of Juan de Fuca.

If I stand on the deck, I hear the rush of wind, the rhythm of the surf, the muted chirping of birds in the underbrush. There are no cars on this dead-end road, no television, no neighbors. Since we've been here, I have not even heard the drone of a distant airplane. At night, far from the city lights, the stars crowd into a spectacular display in the inky dome of sky. The sheer wildness of this island leaves me breathless, a deep and unspoken longing rising inside me—for what, I'm not sure.

When Jacob and I reach the house, a blue pickup truck comes into view in the driveway. A woman I knew here before, Nancy Phelps, traipses toward me through the long grass. Last week, she brought over autumn squash and pumpkins from her garden. She's in jeans, pullover, and boots, her golden hair flying.

This time, a man has come with her, probably her husband. I seem to remember—she told me he runs a salvage diving company. He must've returned from his latest expedition. He's crouching to examine the broken solar panel in the driveway.

"Morning!" Nancy says, striding up to us and pulling me into an apple-scented hug. Her features etch delicate impressions into her face. Small nose, wide-set hazel eyes, and a scattering of freckles.

I look down at my damp pajamas, then I smile at her. "If I'd known you were coming, I would've worn my fluffy slippers."

"You look gorgeous," she says.

"You, too. But you're lying. I look like I just rolled out of bed."

"It was a gorgeous roll out of bed."

"Come in for coffee?" I say.

"Too much to do, but thanks. We were headed up this way to drop off some eggs. Thought Van might take a look at repairing the solar panel."

"He's our fix-it man," Jacob says.

Her husband strides over in a slightly bowlegged gait. He's handsome in a rough way, all stubble and thick, dark hair. He's in work boots and jeans and a flannel shirt. "Kyra," he says in a deep voice, shaking my hand. As his fingers touch mine, I'm struck by a lightning bolt of recognition. *He's gazing into my eyes, offering me a glass of wine.*

"You must be Van," I say, letting go of his hand.

"Good to see you again," he says. "Nancy says you won't remember me."

She gives me an apologetic look. "I had to tell him what happened, couldn't have you pretending."

"I'll be pretending if I say I remember you," I say. "I'm sorry."

"Nothing stayed with you, huh? Not a danged thing?" Van points at his right temple. "You hit your head, and now . . . ?"

"Van," Nancy warns him.

"Just sayin'. You got nothing of . . . how long?"

"Four years," I say.

"Damn." He lets out a low whistle.

Jacob pats my shoulder. "She knows how she felt about this place. Don't you?"

"Yes," I say. "I loved the island." I feel silly and cold standing here in my pajamas.

Van steps closer to me. "Any chance it could all come back?"

"No," Jacob says, while I say, "Yes."

"Maybe a few moments could come back," Jacob corrects himself. "But it's highly unlikely."

I bite back my response. *Highly unlikely?*

For a split second, the two men gaze at each other. The voices seem far away, traveling a great distance through the sludgy atmosphere.

". . . better take a look," Nancy is saying. "Van's a whiz at fixing things."

Jacob is suddenly jovial. "What's the prognosis, Van?"

We're all following Van to the solar panel. "Big one," he's saying. "Twenty-four-volt, two-hundred-watt . . . not sure."

Jacob nods. "Can you fix the broken glass?"

Van kneels next to the panel and examines it closely. "I could use some UV-resistant plastic. I could seal it for you. You're low on watts, but the voltage is okay."

"That'll work?" Jacob says. "You can't replace the glass?"

"Hell no. That glass is bonded to the cells. Could damage the thing. I would use heavy-gauge plastic. I know of some good waterproof sealant. Used on roofs. Not strictly green, mind you."

"That's okay," Jacob says.

"Got to make sure the panel is dry. There's a trick to the repair. I've done it before. You don't want to get wrinkles in the plastic, like—"

"No need to go into details," Nancy says, but not in a cruel way. It's a familiarity born of time and shared experiences.

"Go for it," Jacob says. "Name your price."

"We barter around here," Van says, looking at me. I look away, out across the sea. The wind is kicking up whitecaps.

"Not sure what I can barter," Jacob says. "I've got some oysters—"

"Van's allergic to shellfish," Nancy says.

"Wood," Van says, pointing to the wood pile. "A cord?"

"You got it."

Nancy pulls me aside. "How are you holding up?"

I watch Jacob and Van crouching over the solar panel, their backs to us. "I'm okay, but it's day by day."

"I told you I would help," she says.

"You and I. Were we close? Before my accident?"

"We did talk some." She squeezes my arm gently. "Give it time. And in the meantime, let Jacob take care of you. You're lucky to have a husband like him." She looks at him and tucks her hands into her jacket pockets.

"I worry he's getting tired of all my questions."

"I'm sure he's okay with it. He says you still have an amazing memory for facts . . ."

"If he says so."

"Have you given any thought to coming down to the school?"

"The school?"

"To talk to the kids, remember? Teach them about marine biology?"

"Oh, right," I say faintly. I don't recall this piece of our previous conversations.

"You could tell them about, say, the Portuguese man o' war."

It comes to me immediately. "The Portuguese man o' war is an ancient, foot-long purple bladder in the phylum Cnidaria, existing virtually unchanged for six hundred fifty million years . . ."

"You do remember a few things," she says, her brows rising.

When these facts come back to me so quickly, I surprise even myself, though I know I knew all of this years before the time I lost.

She gives me a peculiar look. "I bet you attracted Jacob with all those facts. He always liked smart women."

"Always? What do you mean by that?"

"I mean, since we grew up together, I know Jacob's taste in women. He must love your brilliant mind," she says, smiling.

"I'm not sure I have much of a mind left," I say.

"I'm sure you do. So, you'll give it a whirl? Teaching? We have only twenty kids, all ages."

A sleeping memory stirs inside me. "Yes, you teach in a one-room school. Now I remember being there, vaguely."

"You talked about delicate ecosystems and the way the warming oceans are destroying the balance of nature. You motivated the kids to make a difference in the world."

"I'm sure you inspire your students as well."

"I like to think I do," she says, hooking her arm in mine. "Let's walk a bit?" She's already steering me down the driveway.

"Where are you going?" Jacob asks.

"I'm taking her for a little stroll," Nancy says. "We're catching up."

He gives me an anxious look. "Don't be long. She needs to get some rest."

"I'll have her back soon." We turn right onto the dirt lane winding through a dense fir forest. When the men are out of sight, she says, "This road was a lot bumpier when we were kids."

"How long have you and Jacob known each other?"

"Since we were babies," she says wistfully. "Spring, summer, Christmas. He lived in the city, came to the island on holidays with his parents. But I told you all this."

"Sorry. I still have a little trouble—"

"Have you given any thought to seeing Sylvia? She might be able to help."

"Sylvia?"

"The therapist."

A familiar anxiety seizes me. "We talked about her, too, didn't we?"

"I asked you if you were seeing anyone, like a psychologist. You said your doctors in Seattle did all they could."

"They gave me memory exercises to practice at home, but—"

"I told you if you want to consult with a professional here, I know of one." She reaches into her coat pocket and hands me a business card embossed in blue text. *Sylvia LaCrosse, Licensed Clinical Social Worker*, with a telephone number and an address on Waterfront Road. The card looks familiar.

"Did you give me a card last week?" I say. She must have, and I've lost it. What did I do with it? My fingers tremble. I nearly drop the card in the dirt.

"No, I didn't give you a card," she says. "You said you wanted to think about it."

I breathe a sigh of relief. "She's not a psychologist."

"She's as good as one. She worked for Pierce County for a lot of years, family therapy. She got burned out in the city. Too many sad cases and not enough funding. She's semiretired, but she's still taking on some clients in private practice."

"You told me all this last week, too, didn't you?"

Nancy nods sadly. "You need to see her. Trust me, she's good at what she does."

"Thank you," I say, tucking the card into my pocket. Somehow, the possibility of talking to Sylvia LaCrosse calms me, like a soothing balm.

When we get back, Jacob gives me a searching look. "Are you feeling all right?"

"I'm okay," I say, although my legs are wobbly.

Nancy gives him a high-wattage smile. "We were talking about how you two have to come over for dinner."

Jacob looks up at me. "If Kyra wants to—"

"We would love to," I say.

Van is already in the truck, revving the engine.

"He's too impatient," Nancy says. She gives me a quick hug. "We'll pick a date for dinner. Don't forget about the school. So good to see you." But she's smiling at Jacob, not at me.

"And you," I say as she heads back to the truck.

Jacob takes my hand. "We don't need to go for dinner if you're not up for it."

"It'll be nice to be with friends. They can tell me things about my past, fill me in, so it's not all on you. And it sounds like Nancy might have some great stories about you as a teenager. I wouldn't want to miss out on that."

"I don't mind it all being on me." He kisses my forehead. "And I'll have to warn her not to give away any of my secrets."

Nancy climbs into the truck next to her husband. He says something to her, not looking at her, waving his arm in a dismissive motion. She shrugs and looks away, tapping her fingers on the passenger-side window. The wind scatters leaves across the garden as he shifts the truck into reverse, hits the gas, and peels out of the driveway.

CHAPTER TWO

In the spacious master bathroom, I run my fingers through my hair. My wavy mane is growing at a breakneck pace. I barely recognize my sunken cheeks, haunted expression, and the scar on my right temple, just above my eyebrow. But I am me. My features are mine—large brown eyes, thick lashes, full mouth, and high cheekbones. The slight indentation in my chin. But my left front tooth is chipped. How did that happen?

How did I end up here, in this spacious bathroom in a beautiful house, with such an attentive husband? Four years ago, I was a heartbroken, jilted woman whose boyfriend had just dumped her. I was renting a room in a drafty Victorian, my future unwritten. If I close my eyes, I can still hear the grating traffic, the screech of the Route 70 bus braking on the corner of 50th Street and Brooklyn Avenue. I can see my quilt bunched up on the bed, the glow of my alarm clock, and I remember my loneliness, my longing to escape the confines of city life. I can see the dim bathroom with its slightly moldy grout, chipped tile, and claw-foot tub, opening onto a view of a postage-stamp yard and surrounding houses crammed together in our Seattle neighborhood. I am almost there again—in my mind, I *was* there only a few weeks ago. I imagined eventually moving away from the crowds, but I did not anticipate meeting a man like Jacob—or living with him on this windswept island.

I have to remind myself that years have passed. I fell in love with him over a period of time. We came to this island after much planning and deliberation. Our relationship evolved. Nothing happened suddenly or by accident.

And yet, I still expect to hear my roommate's laughter, to find her towel thrown on the floor, her bra hanging over the doorknob. Instead, I have this tidy bathroom all to myself. Lined up on the countertop are my lotion, toothpaste, and the bottles of diazepam, alprazolam, and zolpidem tablets. Strange to be on so many medications, when I rarely took even an aspirin for a headache. But here I am, overloaded with pills like some kind of junkie. The zolpidem, brand name Ambien, is supposed to help me sleep.

But I don't want any more help. I finally stopped taking the pills a few days ago. Without chemicals circulating through my bloodstream, my mind is clearing.

I wash my face, which feels like an unfamiliar mask made of bone and skin. I brush my teeth and run a comb through my tangled hair. Each strand is four years older than I remember—maybe most of my hair is new, my old head of hair having gone through its life cycle of two to six years when I wasn't looking.

How much of my body is the same as it was? White blood cells live only a few weeks, red blood cells only about four months, but brain cells last a lifetime. When neurons die, they're never replaced. I don't recall where I learned all this, or how—but I know I'm only a shadow of my former self, as spectral as a dream.

I can't recall who I was in this house, or the nights I spent with Jacob in our corner bedroom overlooking the sea. I sleep in here alone now, while my husband has been exiled to the guest room. I don't remember gazing out these windows, which run along two walls, or painting the other two walls bluish-white. They're lined with bookshelves and a modern, mirrored dressing table. On the shelves, the books reflect my profession: *Principles of Marine Biology*, *Introductory Oceanography*, and more intriguing titles: *The Soul of an Octopus, Spirals in Time: The Secret Life and Curious Afterlife of Seashells*. There's a binder with a printed label on the front, *Kyra Winthrop, Instructor, Intertidal Invertebrates*. On the pages inside, I jotted notes for my lectures in bold strokes, unlike my writing now, which trembles across the page, shaky and insecure.

But I was once confident. My self-assurance shines out from a wedding photo on the shelf. I'm dancing with Jacob at the reception. My shimmering white gown fans out around me. I'm grinning in pure delight. Jacob looks impossibly dashing in his tailored tuxedo, his features rough-hewn. The way we gaze at each other makes my heart ache. He must be lonely, lying awake in the guest room down the hall, hoping I'll climb into bed with him. But I need time to get to know him again. To get to know myself.

I tear my gaze from the picture and search through my dresser drawers for a comfortable pair of sweats. I don't recognize any of my clothes, all in muted twilight colors. I pull out an unfamiliar gray cowl-necked sweater, the kind my best friend, Linny Strabeck, would wear. We often shopped in vintage boutiques together. I see her whipping a sweater off a hanger and pressing it against me. *Perfect,* she says in my mind. She has an eye for fashion.

If only Linny would return from Russia. She flew back to spend a week with me in the hospital before she had to return to work. I barely remember her there. I feel like I still need her support, her memories of the last few years. But she's pursuing her passion, studying orcas in a race to protect the species. She emails me when she can get to a computer, but her brief messages pale in comparison to her presence in person. I miss her dramatic stories, her impulsive nature, and her propensity to choose my clothes.

She would not approve of these baggy blue sweats. They hang loosely on my body, but they're comfortable. The act of putting them on requires concentration. When I get dressed, my fingers still fumble with strings, buttons, and zippers.

I take the business card from my pajama pocket, run my finger along the embossed letters. *Sylvia LaCrosse, Licensed Clinical Social Worker.* Her address is 11 Waterfront Road, Suite B. Five miles south of here. I could ride my bicycle.

I tuck her card under a T-shirt in my top drawer, and I go out to the living room, which opens into a dining room and kitchen. Everything is made of salvaged wood and river rock, from the floors to the ceiling beams. Bay windows offer panoramic views of the sea. I imagine Jacob as a child, laughing by the woodstove with his parents, when the house looked radically different inside, bare bones and furnished for the late 1970s. He was probably handsome even as a child, charming the socks off the grown-ups. Maybe he already had plans to become rich like his father, but not from an inheritance. He prides himself on being a self-made man.

He's in the living room making a fire. We rely on the woodstove for heat. He has put on socks and slippers, and his T-shirt is no longer inside out. He's carefully choosing firewood from the bin and making a perfect triangle of cut logs.

In the kitchen, I open the cabinet and choose a multicolored ceramic mug, squished on one side, as if it got skewed on the pottery wheel. Jacob says I chose the mugs at the Fremont Sunday Market in Seattle. I wish I could remember strolling the aisles with him, buying produce, ceramics, and locally made honey. He adds three tablespoons of honey to his coffee every morning, the only vice of an otherwise health-obsessed man.

I pour myself coffee and sit cross-legged on the couch, savoring the robust flavor of freshly ground beans. The pungent aroma fills me with nostalgia, for . . . what? The answer eludes me.

"What were you and Nancy talking about?" he says, fitting kindling into the stove.

"She said I taught the kids at her school."

"You did, for an hour here and there."

"I'd like to try it again."

"You have to be careful with her," he says.

"Why? She seems nice. Although, I think she may have had a crush on you when you were kids."

For a split second, his shoulders stiffen. "I've known her a long time. She can be a little strange . . ."

"What do you mean, strange?"

"Obsessive. She was into the Rubik's Cube for a long time, always playing with the thing. Then it was the Cabbage Patch dolls. When she hit puberty, she traded in the dolls for a Walkman. Then all she did was listen to that thing, all the time."

"Did you two have a thing? You and Nancy?" I sip the coffee, savoring the slightly bitter flavor.

"We were friends. I think she may have wanted more at some point, but nothing ever came of it."

"What about you? Did you have a crush on her?"

He looks up for a moment, out at the shifting clouds.

"She's a nice person. But no, I did not have a crush on her. It was a long time ago. A lot of years have passed. We're all grown-ups now. We've matured."

"Except me," I say. "I've regressed."

"You're recovering well," he says.

"But I can't believe this is all I am. This lost woman without her memory. I need to do something with my life."

"You are doing something. You're regaining your strength."

"And relying too much on you."

"Never too much." He jumps up and grabs his Nikon camera from the windowsill. "I almost forgot our picture for today."

"What was yesterday's again?"

His expression registers deep disappointment. "You don't remember, really?"

I press my fingertips to my temples. "Yesterday morning, you took a photograph of the sliced boiled egg on my plate. With all the salt and pepper on it."

He breaks into a bright smile of relief. "I printed it."

I pull the memory book from beneath the coffee table, a handmade, linen-bound photo album among the many others he created for me. But this album is special, a scrapbook to recreate our previous trip to the island. On the front, he pasted a photograph of the two of us sitting on the beach above the words, *Live, Laugh, Love.*

I flip to the first page, which shows a dreamy black-and-white photograph of me crouching in the sand, holding a perfect, closed clamshell in the palm of my hand, both halves of the shell intact. I'm grinning into the camera, my cheeks flushed. He took the photograph the day after we arrived, to reenact a moment from last summer. *You loved to find undamaged seashells, without any missing pieces,* he said. *I remember one time when you found a perfect clamshell, but it was much bigger than this one. Still, this one will do.*

The next pages show snapshots in time, re-creations of shared moments. I'm spearing a square of ravioli with my fork; a selfie shot shows the two of us smiling on a forest trail beneath a cathedral of fir trees; I'm paddling a two-person kayak in the calm waters of Mystic Bay, close to the shore, laughing as Jacob makes faces at me. He printed thirteen photographs for our thirteen days here so far, each image representing something fun we did here before. In yesterday's picture, the egg is sliced thinly. I'm grinning at Jacob across the table, the slanted morning sunlight in my hair.

"What should I do for the picture this time?" I say, putting the album on the table.

He stands back against the window. "Get naked?"

"Not a chance," I say, blushing. "Try again."

He grins. "All right. Before the accident, every morning, you got up and drank a cup of something. Usually it was orange spice tea."

"Coffee now," I say, holding up my mug.

"You were always reading a magazine."

I pick up a copy of the *New Yorker* from the coffee table, the Style Issue from last autumn. I open the magazine in my lap.

"You liked to fold back the page," he says. "Just like that. But you didn't sit all stiff and upright."

I look down at myself, then at him. "Am I stiff and upright?"

"Self-consciously so. You were carefree. You doubled up the cushions against the arm of the couch and lay down, sprawled out. That was more your style."

Carefree. Is that even possible anymore? I'm trying so hard to file away every moment into memory. To remember where I set down my mug, what I last read in my book on the nightstand, what I had for breakfast. I turn and lie on the couch, setting the cushions under my head. "Like this?"

He looks exasperated. "Not so staged."

"I can't help staging—I don't know who I was before."

"Just relax," he says, beginning to snap photographs. "Smile."

I laugh. "I'm self-conscious, I can't help it. You keep taking pictures of me."

"You're so beautiful," he says, looking at me above the camera.

"If this is foreplay, it's working," I say, my cheeks heating even more.

"Are you relaxed now?"

"This is definitely comfy," I say.

He comes over and squeezes onto the couch beside me, holding the camera above us and taking a selfie of the two of us lying side by side.

"You're squishing me," I say, giggling.

"That's my MO."

I shove him over and he falls onto the floor and snaps a picture of me at an angle, grinning down at him. *Come down here with me,* he says in my memory. He lay in just that spot, in the warmth of the fire. I tumbled onto the plush carpet and into his arms. We must have taken off our clothes . . . But I'm only guessing. Whatever actually happened next, and on all the days afterward, is lost to me.

CHAPTER THREE

"After I get some work done," Jacob says, "I thought we could visit more of the places we used to go."

"There are more?" I say, taking another sip of the coffee. We've driven the scenic routes, kayaked in protected bays, and hiked the bluff trails.

"The island is full of beautiful places."

"What about Nancy and Van? Did we go places with them? Were we friends with them as couples?"

He looks thoughtful. "We hung out with them last summer." He crumples paper and tucks it inside the pyramid of logs.

There's a beat of silence. "You and Van? You're friends?"

"He's a decent guy. A good fix-it man. His forte, not mine."

"But you're good with computers. You did a great job of rigging up the Internet. Nobody else on the island even has a connection."

"It's our secret."

"I won't tell a soul. You're an expert at making fires, too."

He grins at me. "I like to look at you in the firelight. We used to . . ."

A blush spreads through my cheeks. I'm thinking what he doesn't say. *We used to make love by firelight.* "You're a romantic."

"Speaking of which, we should go to the Whale Tale for dinner."

"A date," I say.

"No strings attached."

"You're my husband, we're attached."

"But I don't want you to feel pressured."

"You're not pressuring me." I run my finger around the rim of my mug. "I made a good decision, marrying a patient man."

"I try. But I've snapped at you more than once since we got here."

"It has to be difficult for you, living with Mrs. Rip Van Winkle."

"At least you didn't wake up speaking a foreign language, like that guy who lost his memory and wandered around speaking Swedish. The doctors couldn't trip him up and get him to speak English. But he'd never learned Swedish. How could a guy who never knew a language start speaking in only that language?"

"That is weird," I say. "Did they ever find out who he was?"

"Some American guy with major problems. His ex-wife had remarried. He'd lost his job. Everything was going wrong. One theory is his brain reset itself. Wanted to start over."

"The brain is a mystery," I say, looking down into my coffee.

"Yours is a beautiful mystery."

I feel another blush coming on. "This coffee is good . . . What is it?"

"Peet's Gaia Organic." He adds kindling, lighting a match to the crumpled paper. "But you stopped drinking coffee about two years ago."

"Because we were trying to . . . ?"

"Yeah. Start a family. You were off caffeine." He takes a

cloth from the firewood rack next to the woodstove, wipes the soot off his hands. He puts the cloth back on the rack.

"And now?" I grip the mug so tightly I'm afraid the handle might break. I wish I could remember wanting a family with him, but even sleeping with him would be like picking a random man off the street. A handsome, caring man, but a stranger.

"We'll take our time. We can talk about it when you're ready."

"What if I'm never ready? What if I'm a different person now?"

"You're not different. You just don't remember who you really are."

I peer into the dark liquid in my cup, but I see no answers there. "Thank you for filling me in."

"I hope the pictures help, too."

"More than anything."

He sits beside me and reaches for one of the photo albums on the shelf beneath the coffee table. He tried showing me images on my computer, but if I stare at the screen too long my brain turns to mush. Dizziness slams into me, and nausea—the aftereffects of a head injury. Jacob assures me that these symptoms will subside over time. My inability to concentrate makes me want to throw the computer across the room.

I've gone through the printed photographs a few times since we arrived, dwelling on my childhood with wistful nostalgia, on images of my parents. My father, slightly chubby when he was young, sported a handlebar mustache, which he later shaved off. My mother was delicate-boned and perpetually cold, even in California. We fit squarely into the middle class in our modest stucco home on the Riviera in Santa Barbara. My mother taught high school math; my father mechanical engineering at the university. In an instant, their lives ended on that stormy night on Highway One, when their car skidded off the cliff and plunged into a ravine. They were heading north to Mendocino for their anniversary.

My parents are gone, but I remember them. I remember my childhood, my teen years. But when I flip to the pictures of Jacob and me, the ground slips away beneath me. I remember nothing. I do know the smell of him, a mixture of subtle, spicy cologne and his own indefinable scent. When he's close to me, my heart beats faster. My nerve endings come to life when he places his hand on my arm to steady me. I love the way soft wrinkles form next to his eyes when he smiles. His habits echo with familiarity. He cracks his knuckles when he's preparing to take on a task, like cooking a meal or going for a jog. He clears his throat when he's thinking hard or trying to decide what to say. If I ask him to relate a particularly difficult emotional memory, he squints off into the distance before answering.

Here we are in Pike Place Market, perusing a produce aisle. A stranger must've taken the picture. We first met in front of the famous flying-fish counter. He caught a frozen salmon as it sailed through the air, almost hitting me in the face. Jacob to the rescue.

Even the pictures of Linny and me feel distant, since they were taken in these last foggy years. In one photo, she wades into the water at Alki Beach in West Seattle, releasing a giant Pacific octopus into the Puget Sound. I must've been the photographer cheering her on.

At least she keeps me sane by email. Her encouraging words are a breath of fresh air. *You'll be okay. You'll rediscover your love for Jacob. Trust me.*

I flip through an album of wedding pictures and mementos. I don't recognize the guests in their formal attire, only Linny and Jacob. I taped a silver key onto a page, and I wrote the sentence below: *You hold the key to my heart.* Jacob did the same on the opposite page. I pressed dried white rose petals into the album, printed a wedding invitation, and included a delicate lace coaster from the reception dinner. Our wedding cake was a three-tiered affair with ocean-blue icing, covered in vanilla sea stars.

In another album labeled "Our Adventures," Jacob printed photographs of us on hikes, dives, and outings in the city. On the second-to-last page, I stop at a photograph of Jacob and another man. I don't remember seeing this one. But I must have. I've flipped through this album before. The two men are standing on a bluff trail with the sea stretching out behind them. Jacob's in rain gear, but the other man is in a thick black turtleneck, hiking pants, and lace-up boots, as if the weather doesn't bother him.

"Who's that?" I say.

"That's Aiden Finlay, buddy of mine. The three of us were hiking at Ebey's Landing, on Whidbey Island. You took the picture."

I took the picture. Aiden Finlay. The name echoes in a far recess of my mind. He looks vibrant, alive, with his ruddy cheeks, tousled dark hair, and a carefree expression. *That expression. He's offering his hand to help me down from a steep embankment.* I see it now. I slipped in the mud. His hand felt warm, firm, steady. I fell into Aiden's arms. He held me, and I could smell the damp wool of his sweater, the fresh soap on his skin. The fleeting image is so vivid it's startling. *I wanted him to hold on to me.* A shot of adrenaline rushes through me, an interior tremor like the beginning of a tectonic shift.

CHAPTER FOUR

Jacob inches closer to me, sending the memory skittering away. A headache claws at my temples. I get up and turn to the map on the wall, my back to Jacob. I'm afraid if he sees my face, he'll know my secret. He'll know I was attracted to Aiden. It's as if my guilt is tattooed on my cheeks. But am I guilty of anything, really?

I focus on the map showing the archipelago of islands. San Juan Island lies at the southwest corner, Orcas Island to the northeast, surrounded by the other islands. Mystic Island is barely a dot just north of Patos and east of Saturna. It's as if I'm looking at the constellations, and we live on a tiny star far removed from the others.

Jacob comes up next to me. "You're not seeing all the islands on this map," he says. "Not even all the named ones."

"There are more?" I say.

"One hundred and seventy-two have been named, but there are four hundred and fifty islands in the San Juans."

"Easy to get lost there."

"People do. Especially when they're looking for buried treasure."

"You're a fountain of information."

"Mostly useless trivia." He traces a line on the map between the islands, following a circuitous route. "That's the ferry passage. The boat stops here and here." He points to San Juan Island and Orcas Island. "A small ferry runs to Mystic. You have to take your own boat to the other islands."

"And we wanted to have a family here in the middle of nowhere?"

"Nobody has to lock their doors here. We're safe. Our children will be safe."

Our children. What a peculiar thought. Did I want safety for them? Or did I want to step off the grid to escape reminders of Aiden? To arrest my own tendency to stray, the way an addict might enter a monastery? But that's a stretch. Falling into Aiden's arms does not mean I slept with him.

"How did you and Aiden meet?" I say.

"I knew him in college."

"When did you introduce him to me?"

"I think it was about six months after you and I started dating—"

"You and I met at Pike Place Market. You bought me roses."

"That was after I intercepted the fish. I told you." His voice tightens.

"Sorry, right. You intercepted the fish. *Then* you bought me a bouquet of roses."

"Your face lit up when you smelled those flowers. I fell in love with you instantly. At first sight."

"There's no such thing," I say.

"All I had to do was look at you. Then I couldn't get you out of my mind."

"Did I play hard to get?"

"You were cautious, yes. But I knew I wanted to marry you. The moment I met you, I planned to spend the rest of my life with you."

"But you didn't even know my personality."

"Sure I did. I could see your personality in your intense gaze, your focus, your spontaneity. You burst into laughter when I bought you the flowers. But then you looked sad. You said you would rather see blooms on living plants. You hated seeing them wither and die. So I brought you a potted hydrangea on our first date."

"I lucked out. You're so romantic."

"We had living plants at the wedding, too. Hydrangeas everywhere."

"How lovely! Linny was my maid of honor, right? Aiden was your best man."

He rubs the bridge of his nose. "I told you all of this already."

"Thank you for being so patient. I'm trying to retain it all." I want to scream at my faulty brain, but I sit on the couch again, feigning calmness. "I wish I could remember our wedding." I know this weighs on him, my inability to recall the most important ritual in our history together.

"We could, you know . . . get married again," he says.

"You mean go through the ceremony?"

"As best we can, here on the island, with our friends. A renewal of vows."

"You would do that?"

"Absolutely. When you're ready."

"Tell me more about what we said to each other. We could repeat exactly the same things."

"I recited a poem by E. E. Cummings." He sits next to me and kisses my cheek with tenderness.

"'I carry your heart with me,'" I say. The echo of a voice tickles my memory. *i carry it in my heart . . .*

"More like, 'i like my body when it is with your body.'"

The heat rises in my neck. "We didn't recite erotic poems at our wedding, did we?"

"No, but I wanted to." He whispers in my ear. "'I like your body. i like what it does.'"

I see the words the way they appeared on the page. I see Jacob handing me the paperback copy of E. E. Cummings erotic poems. *An early birthday present,* he says. The gift was charged with meaning. I'm flushed all over now. Flushed and flustered. I reach under the coffee table, grasping for a distraction, for the powder-blue baby album. I flip through the pages labeled, *first words, first steps, weight, personality, handprint, footprint,* and on and on. Empty pages, waiting to be filled. Inside the front cover, Jacob wrote in his neat script: *The story of our child.* He places his warm hand over mine. "We don't have to look at this now. We have plenty of time."

A tight ball of panic forms in my chest. "I want to know what we were planning. For a family. You say we tried to get pregnant."

His lips turn down, and he looks off into the distance. "For several months."

"But we didn't succeed. I couldn't, or you couldn't?"

"There's nothing physically wrong with either of us, if that's what you mean." *Us,* as if we are one person.

"When did we make the decision to try?"

"A couple of years ago. We talked about it a lot." He smiles, and an endearing dimple appears in his right cheek. "We talked about everything. We both loved our jobs, so we decided to compromise. We figured I would work from home at least three days a week."

"But how would that have been possible?"

"I'm the boss. I can make anything possible."

"I don't doubt it."

"I was so ready to be a stay-at-home dad. I love children. I was so ready to . . ."

"What?"

"To make a baby with you."

I can't deny the electric charge every time he touches me. *But I was also drawn to Aiden.* I don't yet understand the implications, or where the attraction went, if anywhere. But the photograph burns into my mind.

"I don't remember." My breathing is fast and shallow, and the tingling returns to my fingers.

"Hey, just breathe." He takes the album from me and puts it away. "I knew we were rushing this."

"I'll be okay." I take deep breaths.

"You should take up yoga again. You were good at it."

"Yoga." *Here, let me show you the downward facing dog,* I said to Jacob. He tried to imitate me, but he couldn't push his heels down on the floor. "I remember teaching you a pose."

He squeezes my hand. "That's amazing. We should celebrate. What else do you remember?"

"Nothing else right now."

He lets go of my hand. "I'll make your favorite mushroom omelet. How about that? Go and take a long, hot shower. Forget about any worries." *We'll go away and forget about all this,* he whispered in my ear, long ago. Forget about all what?

In my room, my refuge, my breathing slows. The seashells I gathered on beach walks are lined up on the windowsill. They bring me comfort. Finger limpets, the elongated shell of a bivalve, the Northwest ugly clam. *Entodesma navicula.* The Northern slipper snail, which resembles a slipper when turned upside down. These are the former exoskeletons of living beings, remnants made of mostly calcium carbonate and only a little protein. These mementos hold silent reminders of my past, as does my purse in colorful printed seashells on pleated cotton fabric.

As I've done before, I turn the purse upside down and empty the contents on the bed. Sometimes I forget what I've found inside. Maybe I'll discover a new clue to my past. *The objects in a woman's purse reveal a lot about who she is.* Where did I hear that, or read it? I find natural lipstick. A small hairbrush. A tiny tube of lotion. A small bottle of hand cleanser. A gel pen. A keychain with no keys attached. The logo reads, *Not all stars belong to the sky,* with an image of a sea star. A slip of paper with a list: *Haircut, Lingerie, Print ticket, Get you know what . . .*

Why would I be so cryptic?

Inside my wallet, I find my driver's license, three twenty-dollar bills, a debit card, some coins, a local library card, and my PADI Open Water scuba diving certification card. The logo on the bottom right shows a blue globe with a red diver swimming across the bottom in scuba gear. Birth date, certification date, and diver number. I've successfully completed the training to become an open water diver. Jacob, on the other hand, is a Master Diver. He's qualified to teach.

I slip my fingers into the pocket behind the card holders. There's another pocket, one I missed, hidden behind the first pocket. I reach inside and touch a flat, square package. It's difficult to extract. But when I pull it out, I stare at it for a minute, confused. It doesn't compute in my mind, and yet here it is. The shiny blue package is a Durex brand ultrathin latex condom.

CHAPTER FIVE

The expiration date is three years from now. The package is unopened. But we were trying to get pregnant. Why would I hide a condom in my wallet? I couldn't have used the condom with Jacob, if he wanted a child and I didn't. A condom would require his complicity. If I wanted to prevent pregnancy, I would have gone on the pill or used a diaphragm or . . . what? What if I used the condom with another man? With Aiden? What if I had an affair? Or planned to have one?

If Linny were here, she would know what to do. I can hear her bossy advice in my head, across the miles. *You were taking care of yourself, woman. Go with it.* Linny, fiercely independent and adventurous, never married. What makes a woman so sure of herself? She has to know who she is, and to know who she is, she needs knowledge of her past. She remembers falling in and out of love, making a decision to marry or remain single. She remembers the choices that define her. But I don't have that advantage.

This condom was a choice I do not recall. I drop the offending evidence into my purse, take off my wedding ring, and put it on the dressing table. Maybe I have no right to wear it.

Outside, the sky has clouded over. In the sudden rush of rain, the expansive view disappears, and the world shrinks to the size of this room. A rhododendron branch scrapes the window like a fingernail scratching the glass. Jacob whistles softly in the kitchen. Pots and pans clank, water runs from the faucet, and the refrigerator door swings open and closed.

In the bathroom, I strip off my clothes. My body looks unfamiliar, thin and frail after weeks in rehab. As I turn on the shower, a vague image materializes through the mist, the faint, muscular outline of a man. He turns toward me—he's Jacob, inviting me in. The thrill of anticipation soars through me.

I step into the shower, holding my breath, reaching for the memory, but he dissolves. As the hot water runs over my body, I try to conjure him again, but he's gone. Through the translucent shower curtain, I can make out the vague shapes of the sink, the mirror, and the blue towels hanging on the rack. I pick up the soap, lather my skin, rinse off. The hot water soothes me.

"Kyra?" Jacob says, pushing the door half open. I can't see him on the other side.

"Hey," I say, my heartbeat kicking up.

"Omelet's ready." The door starts to close.

"Wait. Don't go." I turn off the shower.

"I'm still here."

"Hand me a towel?"

He reaches in and hands me a towel.

I dry off, wrap the towel around me, and push the shower curtain aside. The room tilts, the floor rushing up to meet me. Jacob grabs my arm, holds me steady. "Whoa, you okay?"

"A little dizzy."

He steers me to sit on the toilet. The air seems to ripple, the walls undulating. Nausea rises in my throat.

"Deep breaths," Jacob says. "In through the nose, out

through the mouth." His soothing voice envelops me, and the room settles around me.

"I'm better now. I had a memory of us."

I hear a catch in his breath. "What kind of memory?"

"I saw you in the shower."

"Were you with me?"

"You invited me in, and I got in with you. I wanted to . . ."

"We will. Right now, you need to get dressed and eat. I'll stay with you."

"I'm not an invalid," I say.

"I didn't mean it that way—"

"I know," I say. "I'm frustrated with myself, that's all. I'll be okay."

He nods, a look of consternation on his face, and leaves me alone.

Jacob has set the breakfast table in woven blue place mats, ceramic dishes, silverware, and napkins. He poured a glass of freshly squeezed orange juice for me, the usual energy shake for him.

I sit at the head of the table. "You've outdone yourself. This is too much." I'm aware of the condom in the back pocket of my jeans. Why did I bring it out here? I could've left it in my purse or thrown it away. Out of sight, out of mind.

"It's never too much." Jacob places a steaming plate in front of me, heaped with a fluffy omelet and hash browns. My nose fills with the smells of onion and mushrooms.

He sits next to me with a big plate of food. "Well, how is it?"

I taste a forkful of fluffy egg and smile at him. "Amazing."

"If I don't cook for you, you forget to eat."

"I'm a lucky woman." *So why would I sleep with someone else?* The image of Jacob in the shower returns to me—and a sudden awareness of his body. I remember what he looks like beneath his clothes, the tiny mole on his right shoulder.

Before I fully understand what I'm doing, I place the condom on the table between us. A river of blood rushes in my ears. My fingers are trembling. "I found this in my wallet."

He doesn't even blink, doesn't show any surprise. "Another one?"

"What do you mean, another one?"

"You found one before."

"But I just found it."

"You found one before and showed it to me."

"And put it back in my wallet?" My voice teeters on a high wire.

"I assume so," he says through a mouthful.

"But why would I do that?"

"In case we want to use it again?"

"So we used them before."

"Yup, why?"

I tap my fingers on the table. I don't know what bothers me more, knowing I hid a condom in my wallet, or not remembering that I found it before. "I don't know. It's just . . . What if I'm not the person you think I am? What if I kept things from you?"

He grins at me, disbelieving. "You think the condom is from an affair?"

I sit back, no longer hungry. "Could it have been?"

"I doubt it. We used those condoms." He stabs his omelet, cuts a piece, and pops it into his mouth.

"But the expiration date is three years from now. Don't condoms have a shelf life?"

"I never thought about it."

"I'm afraid I—"

"What? You're afraid you what?"

"I don't know." I press my hand to my forehead. My jaw tightens. The rain has stopped, but the gray sky still frowns in through the window.

"But I do know. I know your heart is with me. I'm certain of it."

I withdraw my hand from his. My omelet seems to deflate. I pick at the mushrooms with my fork.

"You don't have to finish the food," he says. "I won't be offended."

"It's not the food. It's me. What if I don't deserve you?"

"How can you say that? I don't deserve *you*. You've always deserved better than what you got."

A cold draft comes in from somewhere. "What do you mean? Better than what?"

He rubs his forehead. "Better than what you grew up with . . ."

"You mean my parents?"

"They were critical of you. Nothing was ever good enough for them." He scrapes his chair back and gets up, carrying his plate.

"Why are you bringing up my childhood?"

"You're a good person, and you deserve to be loved. That's all I'm saying."

"But did I? Could I have . . . ?"

"No—look, sometimes we used condoms, like I said. It's no big deal."

"I kept one in case we were in the mood, before we were sure we wanted a family?"

"Why do you keep asking all these questions?" He's still standing with his back to me, his shoulders hunched. "Can't you just . . . ?"

"Just what?"

"Can't you just *be with me*?" He turns to face me, his face crumpled in pain and irritation. "Can't you just *be my wife*? I'm trying my best."

"I know you are." My throat goes dry. "I didn't mean to start a fight. But I can't remember anything. I *have* to ask questions."

"But you don't take my answers at face value. You want to make up your own answers."

"You're right. I'm sorry, Jacob. You know I hope we can start again." Why do I push him to the edge? Deep down, I worry that he's giving me too much credit, pretending I'm a better wife than I actually was.

"We're out of firewood," he says. "I'm going to chop some logs. We'll talk about this later." He strides out into the blustery morning, the door slamming after him.

CHAPTER SIX

The fire has died in the woodstove. I scrape the remains of my omelet into the garbage beneath the kitchen sink, rinse the dishes, and load the dishwasher. Then I put the condom back in my purse. Was it so wrong to bring it out, to ask questions? Maybe I've asked all the same questions before. If I were in Jacob's shoes, I would storm out the door, too. He's consigned to a kind of hell, repeating the past to a wife who has forgotten him and who sometimes forgets what she even had for dinner.

I retreat into my study at the end of the hall. Painted soothing, pale blue, the room faces south, overlooking the garden and the cottage. I push up the cordless blinds and look out the window. Several yards from the main house, the small, cedar cabin nestles in a copse of Douglas firs and bigleaf maples. Its large bay window reflects Jacob's shadowy form. He's standing at the woodpile, his breath condensing into steam. I hear the muffled thud of the ax chopping the logs. He looks up for a moment, and I step back into the shadows, my heartbeat erratic. I have to work on remembering every moment of every day, or I could lose him.

But I don't remember this heavy desk, the drawers neatly stocked with office supplies, my computer on top. When the hard disk crashed, Jacob salvaged what he could, but little data remains. I sign into my email and find ads, *New York Times* headlines, and Linny's reply to my last message, which I sent to her when we arrived on the island.

Dear Kyra,

Mystic Island sounds like a dream. You wanted to live there, so maybe in a weird way, losing your memory was a gift. You finally got what you wanted. I envy you. Don't get me wrong. My research brings me joy. But you married the perfect guy and now he's whisked you off to paradise. Who could ask for anything more? I'm about to lose my connection. Signing off. Xoxo,

Linny

I click *Reply* and type:

Dear Linny,

I'm so glad you came back to be with me in the hospital for a while. I wish you never had to return to Russia. I need my best friend. Do you remember playing Bananagrams on my twenty-ninth birthday? You made me that collapsed vegan chocolate cake. But I know you remember many good times after that, including my wedding to Jacob. I wish we could sit and talk about everything for hours.

Jacob and our friends on the island are taking their time with me. It feels sometimes like more than I deserve. I can't shake this feeling of guilt, is it for being so dependent on Jacob? Or for something that I'm scared to remember? I remember falling into another man's arms—Aiden Finlay. Did I talk to you about him? Was I unfaithful to Jacob? Be honest.

I wish you were here.

Love, Kyra

I hit *Send* and sit back. I'm slightly dizzy from staring at the screen. My inability to concentrate makes me want to throw the nearest breakable object at the wall. *Why can't I remember four whole years of my life? Why only four years? Why not everything? Why not just the accident? Why do I forget conversations? Pieces of time?* The doctors called me an anomaly, an outlier on the spectrum of memory disorders.

I've conducted numerous Google searches for types of amnesia, news about my accident, my own history. But I can't read the results for long, before a headache knocks me square between the eyes. Often I'm about to hit upon an important tidbit of information, when the message pops up: *You're not connected to the Internet.*

The computer offers me a list of options for fixing the problem, but none of them ever work. *Refresh the page in a few minutes. Check that all network cables are plugged in. Restart your router.*

A cosmic joke, these options. Jacob always manages to fix the connection within a few hours, or the Internet kicks back on like a ghost flipping a switch in the machine.

After I log out of email, I type my maiden name, "Kyra Munin," in the Google search box for the umpteenth time. Nothing new. I've found my high school reunion photographs from years ago and a long-ago blog entry about resident Dall's porpoises in Puget Sound. My personal bank account, which I opened years ago, shows a balance of $641.52. Jacob takes care of the joint account and our bills, for now.

Yesterday, I entered his name, and I lost the connection. But today, when I enter "Jacob Winthrop," his biography appears on the Cascade Northwest Software site. He was a young computer genius educated at MIT. He read voraciously. He worked at various software firms until he founded his own company.

When I enter Jacob's name and "diving accident" the usual articles pop up:

> *The man who survived a diving mishap near Deception Pass has been identified as the founder of a local software company . . . His wife suffered a head injury and was airlifted to Harborview Medical Center . . .*
>
> *. . . Experts said the waters in Deception Pass are gorgeous but deadly. "The water is icy, atypical. There's a precipitous drop-off," said Tom Michaelson of Fire District 12.*

I enter "Kyra Winthrop," and the Internet crashes again.

"What did you find out?" Jacob says from the doorway, his tone neutral.

I nearly jump out of my seat. "I didn't hear you come in. How long have you been standing there?"

"Not long. I made reservations at the Whale Tale for tonight. Dinner. Seven o'clock." He seems to have recovered from his bout of frustration.

"Okay," I say, suddenly nervous about going on a date with him. With my husband. This seems absurd. Our argument about the condom has flown out the window.

"I'm going to work for a few hours," he says.

"I thought I might ride into town this morning." Does he detect the tremor in my voice?

"Wait for me, and I'll ride with you."

"But you need to work on your book." The only reason he would ride with me: to make sure I don't hurt myself.

"What if you get dizzy?"

"Then I'll stop for a bit."

"The rear tire looked a bit flat."

"It's fine. I want to ride alone for once. You can't always come with me."

His fingers curl into fists by his sides. "Stick to the main road. If you're not back in—"

"Give me a couple of hours. After that, you have permission to come looking for me."

CHAPTER SEVEN

We brought the Trek bicycles in the truck, after the movers had already transferred everything else to the house on the bluff, but I've forgotten our long voyages to the island. The old ferry, MV *Mystic*, runs infrequently and often breaks down. Only thirty cars fit on the lower deck. On the day we moved here, there were five cars on the boat and no other passengers out on the upper deck. I awoke from a long sleep, surrounded by mist and holding a strange man's hand. I gasped and yanked back my hand, as if I had touched a hot stove. I almost screamed—I know I was startled.

The tall, handsome stranger smiled down at me, his nose slightly crooked, a dimple in his right cheek. He seemed unperturbed, as if we had done this before. *I'm your husband, remember? We're on our way to our new home.* The images returned to me. I saw him leaning over my bed in the hospital. And before that, a walk by the ocean. I saw him kissing the back of my hand, squeezing my fingers, his eyes full of adoration. His deep voice comforted me, but the moments flashed by like fleeting reflections of light, there and then gone. I remembered my condition, that my short-term memory still faltered, leaving me disoriented, unable to easily hold on to what had occurred even ten minutes earlier. I stood in a cool mist, not alone, but alone with these thoughts.

Our new home, yes, I said. I looked at our matching gold wedding bands, shiny reminders of our union.

As the boat glided into the harbor, a thick mist enshrouded the shoreline, enveloping the town in mystery. Jacob led me down to the truck on the lower deck. The captain cut the engine, and we drifted the last several yards toward the dock. All the while, pieces of memory fell into place—Jacob bringing me a cup of hot tea from the galley, pointing out sea lions resting on a buoy, assuring me that I could recover in peace on Mystic Island.

A few quaint stores and brick buildings emerged from the fog—a yellow Victorian housing the library; the mercantile in a small brick building; and the only bed-and-breakfast on the island. *We stayed there when we first arrived last summer,* he said. *In the Gargoyle honeymoon cottage.*

I asked him about the rented house I remembered in Seattle, my roommate, my plants, my former life. It was all gone, he reminded me, four years in the past. My last few months as a graduate student were old news. I'd started teaching marine biology; I planned to conduct research at a satellite station in the San Juan Islands. *You hit your head on a rock,* he said. *We were diving two-and-a-half months ago. You spent a week in intensive care, then almost nine weeks in rehab. Physically, you're doing remarkably well. But we have to work on your memory exercises. The doctors thought you wouldn't get the last few years back, but if we work hard, you can build new memories.*

The truck vibrated as the boat hit the dock. The ferry workers scrambled to secure the moorings. A man in orange rain gear, his face ruddy from the cold, directed the cars to start their engines. In a moment, we ascended the ramp and into our new lives. As Jacob drove along Waterfront Road, I felt as if we'd entered a quiet, alternate world of dirt lanes, boutiques, hanging flower boxes, and iron streetlamps. He made a sharp right turn onto the main road heading north, a twelve-mile stretch traversing the island from bottom to top. Five miles up, he turned left and headed west on a winding, narrow driveway toward our secluded house on the bluff.

Our house. I still can't get used to the concept, although I'm growing accustomed to the play of light on the walls, the soft hum of the refrigerator, the distant, calming rhythm of the waves.

I call Sylvia LaCrosse from the hall phone. The line fills with static, but the phone rings at the other end. An answering machine clicks on. Her voice sounds soft and pleasant, like a lullaby. *You've reached the voice mail of Sylvia LaCrosse. If this is an emergency, hang up now and dial 911. Otherwise please leave me a message.* I give her my name and the time I'm calling. "I'll come down to your office—"

"Hello?" She picks up, out of breath.

"I was just leaving you a message. I'm Kyra Winthrop."

"Nancy mentioned you," she says.

"I'd like to make an appointment."

"Can you get here in an hour?"

So soon. "I'll do my best."

I dress quickly and find my bicycle in the garage, next to our scuba suits hanging on hooks. Our scuba tanks sit on a shelf nearby. My bicycle helmet dangles from the handlebars by its chin strap. I press the button on the wall to open the garage, and the electric door whirs upward. The wind has quieted; wrens and towhees take up their chittering in the underbrush. The blackberry vines twist darkly, but the tops of the trees glow in the slanted rays of autumn sunlight.

I consider telling Jacob I'm riding down to see Sylvia, but he'll worry even more. He'll insist on coming with me to talk to her. I see him in my hospital room, through my haze of memory, holding my hand while my neuropsychologist asks me to memorize various pictures. Her features elude me.

I'm still wobbly on the bicycle. Frustrating, not to have my strength back. The ride takes all my energy and concentration. I head south toward town, past dense forests and vast, empty fields. Occasionally, I pass a herd of sheep or cows in a pasture, but I don't see a single human or vehicle on the journey. Not one.

When I reach Waterfront Road, I'm out of breath and bathed in sweat, despite the cold. I'm fifteen minutes early for my appointment. The streets are deserted in late autumn. The shops huddle forlornly along the shoreline. Sylvia's office is on the second floor of a quaint, faded green Victorian. The bottom floor is a boutique selling homemade soap, Mystic Thyme. Surprisingly, the sign reads, *Open.* I'm about to go inside, when a man waves and calls out to me. He's in a black rain suit and boots, tying a boat to the dock.

He crosses the street toward me, stooping slightly, his handsome face weathered, deeply lined by time. "You're back," he rasps, his eyes wide and glassy. "It's been so long. But it can't be you. You're . . ."

"I was here last summer," I say. "Do I know you?"

His brows rise and he looks startled, then all the light goes out of his eyes. "Oh. I'm sorry. I . . . I thought you were someone else."

"I don't recognize you—"

"I'm sorry to have bothered you." He turns and walks back toward his boat.

"Wait!" I shout. "You're not bothering me!" I leave my bike propped against a lamppost and run after him. "I've forgotten your name."

"I mistook you for someone else." His eyes are haunted, and clearly, seeing me has shaken him.

"You recognized me. I need to talk to people I knew."

"I'm afraid you and I don't know each other."

"But can we talk, at least?"

"We could if you like . . . I live up off Windswept Bluff."

"Where is that?" I say.

"Road's not marked. Four miles up, turn left at the twisty madrone."

"That's not far."

"Everything's close to everything else here." He's already unwinding the rope from the dock, pushing off in his boat.

"When will you be back?"

"Not sure exactly when. Soon."

"What's your name?"

He mouths his name, but I can't hear the words above the roar of the motor. By the haunted look in his eyes, I can see that he did recognize me—or someone he thought I was. But he's pulling out into the bay now.

I watch him go, unbidden tears in my eyes. I feel silly, about to cry for no discernible reason. Maybe it's my feeling of déjà vu, with no way to recapture its source. The universe carved out chunks of my memory and threw them away, out of reach. Who is this strange man, and what did our encounter mean?

I'm bound to run into him again. Next time I see him, I'll explain my situation. But the last thing I want to do is reveal to every stranger that I'm deficient in the memory department. How do I know he isn't suffering from hallucinations or dementia? Maybe he goes up to everyone he meets and says, *You're back . . . Oh, I thought you were someone else.*

I want to shout at the top of my lungs, *Why me? Why?* But the self-pitying moment quickly passes, and I cross the street and go inside Mystic Thyme.

CHAPTER EIGHT

The scents of eucalyptus and lavender fill my nose, and I know I've been in here before. I was drawn to the window display, to the rows of soaps and lotions arranged on wooden shelves among sprigs of dried lavender, beneath a purple, hand-painted sign reading *Mystic Thyme*.

You and your sense of smell, Jacob joked, following me inside.

You know I can't resist lavender, I said. I see him like an apparition, picking up a bottle of aromatherapy massage oil. It was late summer, not the first time we'd been in the shop. He wore a T-shirt, shorts, and flip-flops, his sunglasses perched on top of his head. I was in a sleeveless summer dress and sandals. The dress, made of raw silk, shone in cobalt and swished as I walked. I loved that dress—brilliant blue has always been my favorite color. I collected cobalt bits of sea glass from the beach, cobalt ceramic pots for my plants, cobalt jewelry.

Where is the blue dress now? Is it hidden in a drawer, in a box of summer clothing in the closet? Maybe my memory is flawed, and I wasn't in a blue dress. Maybe I wore a different color. I could have been in shorts and a T-shirt.

Now all we need are candles and the Kama Sutra, Jacob said. A young woman turned to look at him. My face nearly boiled from embarrassment. I needed to tell him something, urgently, but he had been putting me off, saying we could talk later, that we should just enjoy ourselves now.

"Everything's organic, grown on our farm," a soft voice says, breaking into my reverie. A woman stands close to me, her wavy, bleached blond hair tied back. She's wiry, athletic, no part of her body wasted.

"The scents are wonderful," I say, smiling.

"I thought I recognized you!" She breaks into a wide grin, her lips pulling back to reveal her gums. "Welcome back!"

"Thank you. It's good to be back." The familiar panic crashes into me. I don't know who she is. I don't want to have to explain. These social pressures were the very reason we decided to recuperate here, with fewer well-meaning acquaintances to pretend I remember. I smile and hope she won't ask any personal questions.

"How long are you here?" she says.

"We might be here permanently."

"I'm glad to hear that," she says. "I'm tickled. How are you? It's been, what, a year?"

"A little over a year, yes. We were here last June through September."

"How has your year been?" she says, pushing back her ponytail. "You had a lot of plans, as I recall."

"Plans, yes. To come back here! And here we are!" I force a smile. Can she see how fake it is? How fake I feel?

"Here you are!" she says, but her smile falters. "You made it work after all."

"Made it work?" Did I discuss my personal life with her? Our marital problems? Did I come in here without Jacob?

"The move," she says, clasping her hands together, then

opening them in an expansive gesture. "You said it would take a lot of finagling to be able to move to an island. Finagling and maneuvering."

"We did a lot of finagling and maneuvering, yes," I say. "It all worked out."

"I bet you're looking for this." She hands me a small bottle labeled *Mystic Thyme Oil for Spiritual Healing*. "A housewarming gift. Your favorite."

I read the ingredients. Arnica montana, St. John's wort, lavender, essential oils. "I needed spiritual healing."

"I could tell," she says. "How are you doing now?"

"Much better, thanks."

"I hope you'll forgive me for saying so, but your aura was tightly closed in around you last time you were here."

"My aura."

"I see auras, remember? I see black auras when people are sick or dying—"

"But I wasn't sick or dying."

"No, but you said you were worried your life was out of your control."

"What about now?"

Her brow wrinkles as she assesses me. "Your aura is fuzzy and gray now."

"What does that mean?"

"You're here but part of you is not here."

"That sounds almost poetic," I say.

"If you want a reading, I can give you a more detailed analysis." She hands me a business card reading, *Eliza Penny, Owner, Mystic Thyme*. "Call me anytime. Or just come in."

"Thanks. I will. But right now I'm looking for the therapist's office. I'm going to be late in a minute."

She points back through the store. "You'll see the stairs to the second floor."

Sylvia opens her office door before I can even knock. She reminds me of Audrey Hepburn, clad in soft black slacks and beige cashmere sweater, her black hair tied back. Her office is all cushions, tissue boxes, and tall windows.

"Thank you for seeing me so soon," I say.

"Serendipity. I had a last-minute cancellation." She hangs up my raincoat on a hook by the door. "Would you like a cup of chamomile tea?"

"I could use some water. Thanks."

"Coming right up." She brings me a tall glass of ice water. An antique table clock ticks away the hour. "Have a seat anywhere you like."

I see only comfortable armchairs. "You mean I don't lie down on a couch?"

"Would you like to lie down on a couch?"

"No, it's just . . . I pictured you sitting behind me, taking notes while I lie on a couch and talk about my thoughts and dreams."

"That sounds very Freudian," she says.

"Freudian, yes. I talk while you analyze what I say."

She laughs. "Is that what you would like me to do?"

"Not really," I say truthfully.

"I'm glad. I practice a different form of therapy. More interactive. More . . . twenty-first century."

"So I can sit there." I point to a plush armchair.

"You most certainly may."

I sink into the comfortable cushion. There is something

safe about the room—its simple furnishings, the throw pillows, the leafy plants.

She sits in the armchair directly in front of me, a wooden coffee table between us. She crosses her legs, revealing black pumps with one-inch heels. I never liked high heels, but I owned pumps in a few different colors, for special outings. But in the last four years, I traded in the bold colors for muted browns and black.

"What brings you to see me today?" she says, clasping her hands in her lap.

I look out the window and focus on the distant horizon. "You have a great view from here. The vistas on this island take my breath away."

I expect her to say, *You came here for a therapy session, and you're avoiding the subject. Let's get to the point.* But instead she says, "It is soothing." She follows my gaze. Her expression is open, receptive.

"Must be different from where you were before. Nancy said you worked for Pierce County."

"In Tacoma, yes," she says, turning back to face me.

"She said you're semiretired. Why did you move out here?"

"I was trying to simplify my life." She rests a notebook on her lap, pencil in hand.

"Me, too," I say.

"Why don't you tell me more about yourself? Whatever you feel comfortable sharing."

"I'm not sure how much you know about me."

"Nancy told me a little about your accident. But I don't know the details."

"I don't really know them, either," I say, looking at my hands in my lap.

"What do you mean by that?"

I shift in the chair, unable to get comfortable, despite the softness of the cushions. "I don't actually remember the accident."

"Do you know what happened?" Her brows rise.

"We were diving and we were caught in the current out at Deception Pass and we were kind of . . . thrown around. There were driftwood logs and rocks hurtling through the water . . ."

"How frightening," she says, her eyes widening.

"I suppose it was, but I don't remember any of it. Something hit me in the head, probably a rock. I don't know exactly when, or where I was in the water. But Jacob, my husband, got me to shore and the Coast Guard picked us up." My words come out feathery and breathless.

"It sounds like there was incredible violence in the accident, a real assault on your physical being," she says.

"Yes, you're right," I say, nodding slowly. "I could have died."

"You could have," she says. "People have died in the pass."

"You know about the pass?"

"Deception Pass? Sure. The waters are violent there."

"I guess I'm lucky to be alive, but everything feels out of whack. As if I'm someone else and I got dropped here, but I don't know who I am anymore."

"How difficult and scary." I detect no trace of condescension in her tone.

"I wake up scared. I have nightmares. I forget things. The changes to my life in these last few years are subtle and dramatic at the same time, like a fast-forward fifteen minutes in a movie."

"Not like jumping from the beginning to the end," she says.

"Exactly. But I can't remember many experiences and conversations. The days and nights, birthdays, dinners, my thoughts moment by moment. My walks, the city, research, classes. Meeting my husband and getting to know him. If I think too hard about all of it, I can't breathe. I wonder if it's even possible . . ."

"If what's even possible?"

"To fall in love with him again. I can't tap into my emotions. Except . . ."

"Except?"

"I had a vivid memory of being in the soap shop with him just now. The smells."

"Smells can evoke memories in powerful ways. The smell goes to the olfactory bulb, which is directly connected to the parts of the brain involved in emotions and memory."

"I remembered wanting to stay here but knowing I had other obligations. But it's only a piece of the past. Like I'm looking through a tunnel and seeing a circle of reality." For a brief moment, I wonder why it's so easy to spill my thoughts to this sympathetic stranger, when I can hardly speak to my husband. Something about her manner, so calm and open, accepting, makes me trust her. Or maybe I've simply longed for a confidante, someone disconnected from my former life.

She leans toward me, her expression kind and caring. "Sounds like you feel disoriented and alone."

"I do," I say, blinking away tears. "I feel damaged, dependent on my husband. But I want to remember my own memories and not just what he tells me."

"We'll piece it all together as we go along—"

"But how? Other people have suffered from head injuries and lost their memory. How do they go on? I need a map or instructions."

"There isn't any map for recovery, except the one you create for yourself. With time, we'll get a handle on this. You're not alone."

"Thank you," I say. I find myself talking, the words tumbling out in a heap—about the accident, my nightmares, my dizziness and headaches. The years I've lost. Everything. I don't know how long I've been talking. She nods and offers encouraging sounds now and then.

"How overwhelming for you," she says, when I stop to catch my breath. "Of course you're feeling vulnerable and disoriented. Anyone would."

"Thank you for saying so." Somehow, I pictured a therapist as distant, assessing and analyzing me, but Sylvia LaCrosse is not like that at all.

"I'm glad it helps. But you've helped yourself by seeking me out. By not trying to carry this burden alone."

I nod, wondering about her, and about the client who canceled, leaving an appointment open for me. Maybe troubled souls sail in from other islands, drawn by the sign on the building, shining out at them like a lighthouse beacon. Is Sylvia married? She wears a plethora of rings on her fingers, but I can't tell if the white-gold one on her ring finger is a wedding band or merely decorative. Does she have children? Why did she choose to retire in the middle of nowhere? But I'm not supposed to ask her these questions. I'm supposed to focus inward, so I say, "I do feel really alone. I mean, I have my husband, but he remembers everything. He doesn't get dizzy or forget entire conversations. The gaps frighten me."

"Of course they do," she says gently. "They would frighten me, too. It might take us a while to figure this out, but we'll figure it out, okay?"

"I hope so," I say, feeling somewhat reassured. "I know the doctors told me why this is happening . . . but then I couldn't even remember what they said. I don't understand my own brain and what's going on with my head."

"I don't have a lot of experience in this arena, but I do know that people who suffer from a head injury might forget the accident itself and have difficulty retaining new memories afterward. This is called anterograde amnesia. Or they can't retrieve memories from before the accident—this is called retrograde amnesia. They might forget many years or only a few months, possibly only a few hours. Generally, the pivotal moment is the accident itself. But in your case, you've forgotten four years before the accident, the accident itself, and you had trouble forming new memories afterward, transferring them from short-term to long-term storage."

"Two kinds of amnesia."

"Both anterograde and retrograde. But it seems you're beginning to retrieve memories from before the accident, in pieces, and you can form new memories fairly well now, with some gaps."

"I seemed to start remembering new things all of a sudden. On the boat ride here, to the island, I woke up, almost as if I had been asleep for years. But at the same time, I knew I'd been here before."

"Sometimes it can feel sudden, when memories come back to you. This happens, even when the memories might be coming back gradually."

A stress headache pushes at my temples. "There are so

many strange things. I felt like I knew Van Phelps. I was attracted to my husband's friend in a photograph. It's all a jumble. Frustrating."

She looked thoughtful. "It does sound frustrating."

"I have a recurring dream. I'm diving in murky water. I'm swimming against a current. I'm wearing a scuba suit and a mask. But I don't remember learning how to put on all that equipment. I don't remember the dive in Deception Pass or getting rescued. Sometimes I wonder if I'll ever remember."

"It's possible," she says. "Generally speaking, in the case of traumatic head injury, the event itself rarely returns. But memories from before or after could keep coming back."

"You're saying I might never remember hitting my head?"

"When you jar your brain, all the neurons and synapses get shaken up pretty hard. Quite often, the trauma itself and events close to that time are lost forever."

I look out at the roiling sea, the whitecaps hurtling toward shore. "I'm not sure what happened out in the pass. I'm not sure what happened *before*. I'm not sure of anything. I don't remember what Jacob tells me about our plans. For a family. Children. I'm impatient to get back to what I wanted."

"What's important is what you're going through right now."

"I suppose I've wanted it all to come back all at once. I want to know everything, and it frustrates me that I can't. But maybe I don't need to know everything so fast. I don't need to be so impatient."

She gives me a reassuring smile. "Sounds like you put a lot of pressure on yourself."

"I've always been this way," I say. I tell her about my childhood, my high-achieving parents expecting perfection from me. Then my parents were gone, and their expectations no longer mattered. I was grieving, bereft, and adrift with only my Uncle Theo to console me. He helped me, supported me. "Now he's sinking into dementia. He's in a nursing home in Oregon. The only other person I'm still close with, who still knows me well, is in Russia. Her name is Linny."

"Are you in touch with her?"

"We email each other."

"Brothers and sisters?"

"None, and no cousins or aunts or uncles anywhere near here. No close friends that I can remember from the last few years. I was always a bit of a loner. Linny and I—we're similar that way."

"And what about your husband? Did you say his name is Jacob?"

"We've been married about three years. We dated for six months. Whirlwind courtship, apparently."

"Sometimes it happens that way."

"So we could've known right away."

"Sure."

"From what I understand, last summer, we visited the island for a few months, and we made a plan to move here. After that, we went back to the mainland. Then the accident happened. I was in the hospital and rehabilitation center for almost ten weeks. Then Jacob brought me here two weeks ago."

"Are you on any medications?"

"I was, but I stopped taking them."

"Do you remember what they are?"

"Two antianxiety medications and a sleep aid. Do you think I should still be taking them?"

"You made a good decision to *stop* taking them. Some medications can actually impede the return of your memory."

A sense of calm returns to me. "So you think it's okay."

"Yes, I think it's perfectly okay. In fact, I *recommend* you stop taking the medications."

"Wow, thank you." My shoulders relax. "But why would a doctor have prescribed the meds if they interfere with the return of my memory?"

"I can't answer that," she says. "Maybe your anxiety trumped everything else at the time."

"I have been anxious, so worried about everything," I say. "I would love to understand things, like the dream. I'm in churning waters. The current is strong. I'm disoriented. I don't know which way is up."

"Are you having trouble breathing in the dream?"

"I think so. But I'm not suffocating. I'm definitely scared. Worried . . ."

"Are you alone?"

"I don't know. I'm swimming, looking for someone. I don't know who it is. It must be Jacob."

"Do you know where you are?"

"No," I say. "What do you feel the dream represents? Could it be related to the accident? Could my dream have actually happened?"

"Yes, of course."

"But maybe it didn't. I used to be able to follow my intuition, but now my intuition is muddled at best."

"We'll get back to that intuition. This has been a difficult time for you."

"I don't have an internal compass to rely on. I can't help feeling my memories are still here, but my mind doesn't want to remember. Could that be the case?"

"Absolutely," she says. "It's possible."

"So even though the doctors said I would probably never remember everything, I could remember? They could be wrong? I mean, some moments are starting to come back. I'm remembering."

"You definitely are," she says.

"Is there a name for it, when your mind doesn't want to remember . . . suppressed or repressed memories?"

"Do you mean there could be a psychogenic component to your memory loss?"

"Psychogenic."

"Things your brain chooses to forget. Absolutely."

"Why wouldn't I want to remember? Could something bad have happened?"

"Something traumatic? Certainly—"

Someone rings her buzzer.

I glance at the clock. "The time went by so quickly."

"My next client is here. Do you want to come and see me again?"

"I think so," I say. "Yes. But I don't want to tell my husband . . . He's trying so hard to fix all this for me. Plus, I don't know, this feels like it's mine. Coming here."

"Sure, of course." The buzzer reverberates through the room again. She gets up, smoothing down her sweater. "We have so much more to find out. Don't you agree?"

"I do," I say, getting up, too. I'm oddly disappointed that our session has to end.

CHAPTER NINE

"Do you remember buying massage oil at Mystic Thyme?" I say in the afternoon, as Jacob drives us down the main road to explore our old haunts. I have not told him about my session with Sylvia. My talk with her feels like a special secret.

"The soap shop? We went in there a few times," he says, looking over at me.

"I was wearing a beautiful cobalt dress. What happened to it?"

His eyes sadden. "That was one helluva dress, but it's gone. You spilled tea all over the front. You were mad about that. It never came out."

"Not even with stain remover?"

"It was ruined," he says. "But wow, you remembered the dress."

"It was last summer. We were here on vacation. I loved being here with you. The island felt like a dream. But I also had an underlying restlessness, a strange pull to go back to the mainland."

"You were a workaholic." He turns left at a sign reading *Island Wetlands Preserve*.

"It felt like more than work. I needed to set something right, correct something."

"Like I said, work," he says, parking in the lot next to an

interpretive sign. "You were a teaching assistant. Professor Brimley expected too much from you."

"Professor Brimley. I vaguely remember him."

"He gave you too much to do for what you were being paid. You had to develop lesson plans, grade papers. You were pretty stressed out. Come on. Let's walk." He takes a pair of Audubon binoculars from the glove compartment, and we walk the trail through the wetlands. The rustle of grasses soothes my soul. *Nobody will come after us here,* he said to me, holding my hand.

"Who would come after us?" I say.

"What?" He gives me a startled look.

"You said nobody would come after us here. Were we fugitives?" I smile to lighten the words.

He laughs. "From city life, yes."

"Was I recovering from something?"

He gives me a sharp look. "What makes you say that?"

"I needed spiritual healing, according to Eliza at Mystic Thyme. She gave me a bottle of essential oils."

"Not that I remember."

"Nothing at all? There must have been."

"Trouble at work, maybe?"

"Trouble with us?" I say.

"You keep going back to that," he says. "I'm starting to think you *want* us to have been in trouble."

"I'm not saying that." But maybe I'm looking for cracks in our relationship, flaws that might have compelled me to stray from our marriage.

"Then what are you saying? I told you we were good."

"Okay, we were good, then." On the rest of the loop trail, I fight the urge to ask more questions. I focus on watching the blackbirds, towhees, and the mallards in the pond. In this wetlands reserve, Jacob and I could be the only two people on the planet.

After the hike, he drives me out to Windy Reef Park, where we view the sea lions congregating on the rocky shore. We hear them barking before we spot them. "Amazing lookout point," I say. "I had no idea."

"You called this the Magical Nearshore. You taught me that term."

"Nearshore, the volatile confluence of sky, land, and water. I love that you remember."

"How could I forget? The nearshore was always your favorite place to go."

My heart warms to this man who wants only to make me happy. "What about you? What's your favorite place to go?"

He looks into my eyes. "Wherever you are. That's the only place I want to be."

"Perfect answer," I say, as we climb the trail. I take off ahead of him, toward a high cliff bounded by a wooden railing. "That must be a spectacular viewpoint."

Jacob catches up, grabs my wrist, and pulls me back. "Don't go up there. You could fall."

"I'm not going to stand at the edge." His grip becomes tense and I look down, startled.

"You get dizzy," he says. "You never liked going up there. You were afraid of heights."

People have jumped off the cliffs around here, Nancy said. *I'm not going up there.*

We were here with Van and Nancy. The sun shone brightly on the water. Wild roses were in bloom, and tiny white flowers dotted the blackberry vines.

Half the people who jumped were probably pushed, Jacob said.

Drowning someone would work better, I said. *No way to prove it was murder.*

Did I really say that?

"Do you see the orcas?" Jacob says now, pointing out to sea. He doesn't seem to notice the shock on my face. He doesn't know I'm remembering. He must think I've been watching the fins gliding through the waves.

"Those are Dall's porpoises," I say faintly. "They're much smaller than orcas."

"You're the expert."

"I'm also cold. Let's go." I turn and rush back along the trail toward the parking lot, stumbling a little in my haste.

"You okay?" he says. "Dizzy again?"

"I remembered being on that trail with Van and Nancy," I say as we get into the truck. "You said most people who jump off cliffs here were probably pushed."

He frowns. "You're right. I did."

"I said drowning someone would be the perfect murder."

He laughs as he slides the key into the ignition and starts the engine. "Wow, what a weird thing to come back to you."

"Just that piece of the conversation."

"We all got to talking about ways to kill someone and make it look like an accident. You mentioned drowning someone. Van said Nancy could get rid of him just by kissing him . . . after eating a clam. The conversation got morbid. Hey, don't look so worried. It was all in fun."

"I'm not worried," I say, but on the drive home, I grip the door handle, my shoulders tense. Sylvia's words echo through the passing shadows. *Do you mean there could be a psycho-*

*genic component to your memory loss? . . . Things your brain
chooses to forget. Something traumatic.*

What if my brain is choosing to block out not trauma, but
something else altogether? Impossible. I have to dismiss the
thought. I have to believe what Jacob is saying. The conversation was all in fun. Just because someone talks about murder,
doesn't mean they intend to actually kill someone.

CHAPTER TEN

"Could you drop me at Nancy's school?" I say on the way home.

"That memory worries you," he says, glancing at me side-long. "I told you the truth about it, about what we were all talking about."

"I know you did," I say, forcing a lighthearted tone. "I just want to see if the classroom environment brings anything back to me."

"You're not trying to ditch me?" He gives me a pleading look, half in fun, half serious.

"I'm ready to divorce you here and now. Let me out and don't come back for me."

For a split second, he looks shocked, then my face breaks into a wry smile. His shoulders relax when he realizes I'm joking. "Jesus. Don't kid like that."

"Sorry," I say. "I'm not going to divorce you, okay?"

"Good. You nearly gave me a heart attack." He veers right, looping around back to town, pulls up in front of an old white church, the sign reading *Mystic Island Day School*. "I'll pick you up in an hour?"

"Make it two," I say as I get out of the truck. "Give me time to escape to the mainland."

"You'll need more than two hours to go that far."

"After I talk to Nancy I want to take a walk."

He hesitates, then nods slightly. I close the door and watch him drive off around the corner. I linger outside in the wind, wondering what I'm really doing here. I do need time to think, to regroup. I could keep walking down to the beach, bypassing the school altogether. But I came here for a reason, so I go inside, closing the door quietly after me.

Class is in session. The students are a mix of ages between maybe six and thirteen. The walls are a pale forest green, decorated in roll-down world maps. Old-fashioned globe lights hang from the ceiling.

Nancy stops speaking and waves at me. "Kyra!" She turns to the students. "We have a surprise guest speaker."

"I didn't come here to teach—"

"I don't know how many of you remember Kyra Winthrop from last summer, just before school ended. She got you all excited about marine biology. Let's give her the floor, shall we?"

I shake my head. "Oh, I don't—"

"Come on up." She motions me forward.

Before I know it, I'm standing at the front of the class, facing a sea of eager kids. What am I doing here? I take a deep breath and smile around at the rapt young faces. How do I begin?

"Raise your hand if you think marine biology is all about saving the whales," I say. "Or training marine mammals." My voice comes out rusty, unpracticed.

A few hands shoot up.

"I thought so. I might call myself a marine biologist, but there's really no such thing." I've done this before.

The kids stare at me with puzzled faces. The hands drop.

"You'll specialize!" I say and their eyes light up again. "You might become a marine invertebrate zoologist, or maybe a marine phycologist specializing in algae and seaweed or in conservation of a particular species. Or you might be an ichthyologist. Does anyone know what that is?" *Who is this person, speaking to these children? Who am I? How do I know these things?*

A pretty girl with a blond ponytail raises her hand. "Someone who studies fish."

"Correct," I say.

"I knew it!" She grins, revealing a missing front tooth.

"Did you know the male sea horse carries the eggs in a pouch for ten days before he gives birth to miniature sea horses?"

"Whoa," the kids say.

"A sea cucumber under stress will spew out internal organs—but will eventually grow them again. Not like us!"

Mouths drop open, and the questions come fast and furious. *How do they grow new organs? What does a sea cucumber look like?* I keep the kids enthralled with strange marine facts. The audience of faces begins to shimmer and fade. I'm standing behind a lectern in a large lecture hall with tiered seating. The students saunter in carrying backpacks, college freshmen. I adjust the microphone, straighten my notes on the lectern's sloping surface. My heart hammers. I'll faint before I can even start speaking. Then I see him, standing at the back of the hall. He's in a crew neck sweater and jeans. Aiden Finlay, cheering me on. *You can do it,* he mouths to me.

"Kyra?" Nancy says. She hurries to the front of the room and turns to the students. "All right, everyone, let's give Mrs. Winthrop a huge hand. What do we say?"

"Thank you, Mrs. Winthrop," the kids say in unison, and there's a flurry of movement as they zip backpacks and grab their coats.

"Are you okay?" Nancy says to me.

"I zoned out, I'm sorry."

"You stopped talking and stared at me like I was someone else."

"In my mind, you were."

"Who was I?" she says, searching my face.

"Someone I used to know. A guy who came to watch me teach at the university."

"I look like a guy?"

"No, not at all. It was just being in the classroom . . ."

"Old boyfriend?"

"I'm not sure. Did I ever mention anyone to you?"

"Other than Jacob? Not that I know of. But you remember teaching. That's good."

"I also remembered a hike with you and Van. Out to Windy Reef Park."

"We did go there last August."

"I need to ask you something about that outing." We wait until the students have gathered their coats and backpacks and have left for the day, then I tell her about what I remember, about our discussion of methods of murder, what Jacob said about the way the conversation played out.

"I do remember," she says, nodding. "It was a strange discussion, but he's right. We were joking around."

"That's all?"

"That's it."

"Did we go back to Windy Reef Park again after that?"

"No, you were gone by September. Jake came back this past spring to fix up the house. We didn't see much of him. He was busy getting the place renovated. He said you were moving here."

I flinch at her nickname for Jacob. "I didn't come with him?"

"You were teaching. He was so focused on the remodeling, he wouldn't even come over for dinner. When he sets his mind to something—"

"I know what you mean. He's focused on writing his novel now. But he took time off to show me around today."

"I wish Van would do something so romantic. At least he brings me gifts from his dives." She points to a delicate ceramic vase on her desk. "He got this one from a fourteenth-century shipwreck."

"It's beautiful."

The coins are from a Spanish galleon, Aiden says to me. He's showing me old, rusty coins he retrieved on a dive. *I'm giving one to Jacob for his birthday. Don't tell him.* So Aiden Finlay is a diver. He's standing close to me, *too* close, his arm brushing mine. He's in a turtleneck, and he gives off the faint scents of soap and pine. He hasn't shaved in a couple of days. *You like it?* He scratches his chin. *I'm growing a goatee. Do I look like an outlaw?*

I laugh and say, *Do outlaws have goatees?*

He leans down toward me. *This one does.* He moves in closer. I catch the minty scent of his breath. Anticipation rises in my chest. Where are we? Not here on the island. I hear the distant rush of traffic, or is it the rush of the waves? The background fades into gray, indistinct shapes, but the details of his face come into focus. His bushy brows, the light flecks in his brown eyes, the wavy, deliberately unkempt hair descending into a perpetual five o'clock shadow. His intense gaze makes me feel like I'm his only concern on the planet. And then . . . he steals a kiss. So quickly, I don't have time to pull away.

Am I surprised? Startled? Do I kiss him back? *Did I?* Or did I step away from him, putting distance between us? Maybe I said, *I can't do this, Aiden, I'm a married woman.* Or did I kiss him back, pull him toward me? The truth is, I have no idea what happened next. The moments break apart and fly away in the wind.

CHAPTER ELEVEN

"Earth to Kyra," Nancy says, waving her hand in front of my face.

"Sorry. I was spacing out again."

"More memories of an old boyfriend?"

"No," I lie. "I was thinking I could use a walk. If you have time. I've been spending too much time alone with Jacob."

"I was hoping you would say that."

After she locks up the school, we head down to the beach, a quiet stretch of sand curving along a protected bay.

"Sorry about showing up unannounced like that," I say.

"No apology necessary. I'm glad you stopped by. You're a natural teacher." The wind recedes, allowing us to hear each other talk. The smells of the sea, of salt and kelp, fill the air. We've been here before, walking along the southern shore. *Why don't you stay longer?* Nancy says in my memory. It's an early-September day, the sky bright with a last gasp of summer.

School is starting, and I need to straighten out a few things.

What things? Is this about you and Jake? Are you two in trouble? Do I detect a faint note of hope in her voice? *You can talk to me. I won't say a word to him.*

I don't trust her to keep a secret. Nancy is not like my best friend. While Linny remains steadfastly loyal, Nancy bends in the wind . . .

I've made hasty decisions, I say. *Things are difficult.*

I understand, she says. *I should tell you something about Jake, about the way he is. He needs to have his own way. I've known him since we were kids . . .*

"The kids were a little worried," Nancy says to me now. "When you were zoned out, I mean."

"How long was I in La La Land?" I say, shoving my hands into my coat pockets.

"Only a minute or so. But they're not used to it. They handled it very well, though."

"Are you going to tell them about my situation?"

"If they ask, I'll say you get nervous talking in front of people. They'll be able to relate to that."

"I'm sorry," I say, navigating around a small pile of kelp, like a wig stranded in the sand. "I was remembering teaching in a big lecture hall. And actually, I was nervous. So you're not far off the mark." *Aiden gave me the thumbs-up. He stayed for the full hour. I was aware of him the whole time, as if I were addressing him and not two hundred sleepy students. His presence gave me confidence.* But what about the kiss? Were we at the university? In the lecture hall?

"I felt that way when I first started teaching," Nancy says. "I got my certification at City University in Seattle. But I didn't feel ready at all. I was young. I met Van there, at a party."

"Was he a student, too?" I say.

She gives me a curious look, searching my face. "You really don't remember our conversations, do you?"

"Only bits and pieces." I look down at my damp running shoes. I feel detached from my own body. *I am made of bits and pieces.*

"He was already working for Silver Marine Services in Seattle. He was a commercial diver. He practically lived in the water. Somebody invited him to a party in the dorm, and we binged on Sutter Home Moscato. We got pretty drunk that night . . ."

Aiden's drunk, Jacob said, leading me into Café Presse in Seattle. *I put him to bed.* I see Jacob resting a gentle hand on the small of my back, steering me to a booth, ordering me a cup of tea at nearly midnight. The French ambience wraps around us; the buttery smell of *pommes frites* permeates the room.

Will he be all right? I say, worried.

Not the most mature response to life's challenges, Jacob says.

"We were wild that night," Nancy says, breaking into my reverie.

"Wild," I echo, disoriented. I've forgotten what she was talking about.

"Van and I. At the party. And for a while after that, too. When you're young, you don't think about the consequences. Hormones rule."

"And the consequences were . . ."

She rests her hand on her belly. "A bun in the oven."

"You were pregnant?"

"I was so scared," she says. "I thought I might like to *not* be pregnant. It wasn't in my plans. I almost got rid of the baby. I wasn't sure."

I'm not sure of anything, I say to Jacob in Café Presse. *When I think of being a mother, I can't catch my breath.* I cup my hands around the mug, a life raft. Jacob closes his hands around mine. I take comfort in the warmth of his touch.

It's natural to be scared, he says. *You wouldn't be human if you weren't.*

I'm afraid I won't be a good mother. I'll snap at the kids. I'll expect too much of them.

You'll be perfect, he says, looking deep into my eyes. *I'm certain.*

"Nothing was certain," Nancy is saying. "We were messing around. But Van had a sense of duty. We got married at city hall with only a few witnesses."

"You didn't invite family?" I say. A freighter appears on the horizon, gliding east toward the distant mainland.

"My mom was there, and his parents. And our best friends. We didn't tell anyone else. We got married fast."

Is this too fast, too soon? Jacob says in the dressing room. He slipped in before the wedding. He leans down to look at me in the mirror, so handsome in his tailored tuxedo, and my heart falters. Maybe he's right. Maybe everything is happening too quickly.

You shouldn't be in here, I say to him.

You can talk to me about anything, Kyra, I hope you know that. Are you having second thoughts?

No second thoughts, I say. He backs away into a mist. What happened before that moment? What happened after? There is something wrong about the encounter, the way the details come back to me. It seemed like afternoon, but maybe it was late morning. Maybe I only imagined him coming into the dressing room. Linny rushed in soon afterward, her face flushed. *Everyone's here,* she said. *Are you ready?*

I turned to her and said, *Do you think it's too soon?* Maybe Jacob didn't come into the dressing room at all.

She hugged me. *It's your life. Seize the day.*

I'm impulsive . . . but we're in love. Love is all that matters.
She kissed my cheek. *Then I give you my blessing.*

Nancy zips up her jacket, the sound grating through my memory. "My mom got sick pretty soon after Van and I got married. We came back to the island to take care of her until she passed away."

"I'm sorry," I say.

"She died right after my son was born," she says, her voice breaking. "She got to see him, but he never got to know his grandma."

"So you have a son."

"Tristan, yes. I told you about him. He's in college."

"I'm sorry, I forgot."

"My mom left us the house, so Tristan grew up here."

"Was it what you wanted, to move back here?"

She hunches against the wind, which has changed direction, coming from the north now. "I didn't think about what I wanted. I did what was practical. Times were tough. Van started the salvage business, I stayed home with the baby. I took over teaching at the school, and the rest is history."

"Are you happy now?" I say.

"I'm happy enough." She looks at me. "What's happiness anyway? We make the decisions we have to make, under the circumstances. I had my son. He became my joy."

"But your marriage . . ."

"Would I have married Van if I hadn't been pregnant? I don't ask myself those questions anymore. They can't be answered. The past can't be changed." She sighs, picks up a large white clamshell, chipped at the corner. I step around a stranded, dead crab, turned upside down, the meat picked clean by seagulls.

"You two love each other, though," I say.

"You could call it love." She stops to sit on a dry, weathered log, driftwood long ago washed up to its sandy grave. "What we had grew into love, I suppose."

I sit beside her, the cold breeze in my hair. Frothy waves ripple across the sea. There is nobody else on the beach. The island often feels this way, I realize—devoid of human habitation.

"But you weren't in love when you got married," I say. "It really was only about the baby?"

"We liked each other well enough. Anyway, love is a verb, isn't it? It's the way you treat someone. What we actually feel about people can be . . . complicated. Don't you think? Couples get married for all kinds of reasons. But you and Jake married for love. You're lucky."

Did I marry Jacob for love? I must have. I can't imagine marrying for any other reason.

"You have a son," I say, "and Van seems like a solid, decent man. You're lucky, too."

She rolls up her sleeve to show me a small tattoo near her elbow, resembling a blue knot wound into the shape of a triangle. "A Celtic knot," she says. "Tristan and I got these matching tattoos on the Ave. Spur of the moment."

She told me this before—how she feels about her son. "He's at the University of Washington."

"Finishing his freshman year." She unrolls her sleeve, letting it fall loosely over her wrist.

"He was leaving last summer, when we visited. You were sad."

"I'm getting used to it now," she says. "But I was a little insane after he left. Even with Van around, the house felt empty. I missed Tristan so much, still do. I'm sure Van didn't approve of the number of times I went over to visit. Tristan started getting sick of me, too."

"I'm sure he loves seeing you," I say.

"He's the best son a mother could ever hope for. He was always sensitive, always a reader. He had intelligent questions from the time he could talk. He started speaking in complete sentences at the age of two."

"That's remarkable," I say, a stirring of melancholy inside me.

"You and Jake were trying, you said."

"We were."

"In my case, it was the opposite. Van's sperm barely blew in my direction, and I got pregnant. It was the last thing I wanted."

"Yes, isn't it ironic, the way things work out?" I sense an unseen river flowing beneath the surface of my marriage to Jacob. We were trying to get pregnant, but there was more to our story, just out of reach. I'm surprised to feel a tear sliding down my cheek.

CHAPTER TWELVE

Jacob and I arrive at the Whale Tale at dusk. The restaurant sits on a high bluff overlooking the sea. The dining room is small, only ten tables widely spaced for privacy. Another couple huddles together in a far corner. The sky is brushed with the last rosy shades of an October sunset. Jacob reaches across the table to take my hand. Our wedding rings glint in the candlelight. The flame flickers between us, accentuating the angles and shadows of his face. He's clean-shaven, in a white button-down dress shirt.

"How did it go at the school?" he says.

"It went well. Speaking to the students felt natural. I guess it came back to me."

"That's good, right? You sound thoughtful."

"Nancy and I went for a walk afterwards, too."

"And? Did she ease your mind?"

"More than sufficiently. But . . . she told me other things."

"Uh-oh, what? I told you to be careful of her."

"I didn't realize she and Van were pregnant before they got married. I remembered feeling sad when we were trying, maybe because we couldn't?"

He reaches across the table to rest his comforting hand on mine. "It doesn't mean we won't be able to have children in the future."

I slip my hand out of his, take a drink of water. "I don't know if I want kids. It was just a feeling. Nothing specific came back to me." This is a lie, and I'm not sure why I have this instinct to hold back the truth, but Sylvia said I should trust my instincts. I wish I could talk to her now, but in her answering machine message, she said she's away for a few days. She didn't tell me she would be gone.

"Does this place bring back anything?" Jacob says.

"It is romantic," I say. "But no. Nothing."

"Let me help you along. I could start with the pleasure points."

My blood is rising again. I open the menu in front of my face, and he chuckles.

"What's so funny?" I say.

"You're cute," he says. "Shy."

"For all I know, you say the same thing to all your secret girlfriends."

"Yeah, that's me. I have secret girlfriends stashed all over the world."

"Do you?" I look over the top of the menu.

"Do I what?"

"Have secret girlfriends stashed all over the world." My stomach makes a strange turn.

"Hell yeah," he says, opening his menu.

"Where are they, these girlfriends?"

He keeps looking at the menu. "I can't keep track. France, Iceland, Canada . . ."

"Here on the island, too?"

He gives me a lopsided grin. "She's the only one I care about."

"What's she like?" I'm trying to focus on the appetizers. *Feta cheese wrapped in grape leaves . . . corn masa cake.*

"Wild hair, the kind you can get your fingers tangled in . . . gorgeous eyes." He looks into my eyes, and I feel a stirring inside me.

"She sounds like quite something." I focus on the main menu. *Mediterranean salad. Shredded romaine and Napa cabbage tossed in lemon vinaigrette with fresh mint . . .* "Should I be jealous of her?"

"Not at all."

"Good evening, folks!" The young waitress trots over. Everything about her is bouncy, especially her ponytail. "What can I get for you two?"

I order the East Indian vegetarian platter. *Chard leaves stuffed with a spiced potato–pine nut filling . . . served with red lentil dal . . .* Jacob orders the pan-seared scallops with ginger sake, served with sesame scallion rice cakes and seasonal vegetables.

"Great choices!" The waitress bounces off and returns a moment later with the wine menu.

"No, thanks," I say automatically.

Jacob grabs the menu. "Wait. You love sweet wines."

"But I shouldn't—"

He smiles at the waitress. "The Mystic Vineyards Chardonnay."

"Of course," she says. "Bottle or glass?"

"Glass," I say. "I'll just have a little."

"Two glasses," Jacob says.

"I'll be right back." She hurries away.

"I shouldn't," I say.

"One is okay. You're not an alcoholic."

"You said I stopped the alcohol when we were trying . . ."

"So we'll stop the alcohol again, when we try again." He

pulls his chair around the table, so he's sitting closer to me. "I want to make you happy. Why don't you let me?"

"Jacob . . ."

The waitress brings the wine and then lets us be alone.

Jacob lifts his wineglass. "A toast to us. To starting again."

We clink glasses, and he leans over to kiss my cheek, and I hurtle back to the last time we were here. He leaned over to kiss my lips. *You're not yourself,* he whispered. My heart ached. I took in the curve of his jaw, the soft sunset, his brilliant blue eyes, as if memorizing his face.

"Are you okay?" Jacob says, putting down his glass. His forehead creases with worry. "We can leave."

"No. We're staying." The wine goes down smoothly with a touch of sweetness. I begin to feel warm.

"But you're not happy," he says.

"I'm perfectly fine." Our food comes and I pick up my fork, the flickering candlelight reflected in the metal. "I'm with my handsome, patient husband, eating a delicious meal at a nice restaurant."

"I have reason to hope, then," he says, smiling, and as we eat, I catch him looking at me now and then with an expression of promise, anticipation.

"Dessert?" the waitress says later, when she comes to pick up our plates.

"I'm full," I say. "I can't eat another bite." I'm a little tipsy.

Jacob pays the bill with a credit card and steers me out to the truck. He reaches over from the driver's seat to kiss me. The wine seeps through my body, dulling my judgment.

How many glasses did I have? More than one. Two, three? I can't recall. I kiss him back, the way I know I have before, many times. *His lips taste familiar.* I'm enjoying his touch. I want him. I wanted him before. But something went wrong between us. And I suddenly remember thinking, *What secrets would I hide to save my marriage?*

CHAPTER THIRTEEN

At home, while Jacob makes a fire, I change into comfortable sweats. Will this be the night he joins me in the master bedroom? How will it feel, to be with him again? I'm infused with excitement, trepidation, and fear. I pace in my room, glancing at my gaunt, worried face in the dresser mirror. The dinner at the Whale Tale recedes into a fog. Aiden Finlay's face emerges in my mind. He reaches out to me, then fades. I see Nancy hurrying to the front of the classroom today, while I stare into space, lost in the past.

A few minutes later, there's a tentative knock at my door.

"Come in." My heartbeat kicks up. Jacob's about to cross a boundary. So am I. No, I already have.

He's carrying a shimmering gown on a hanger. The dress I'm wearing in the wedding photograph.

Tears spring to my eyes. "It's so beautiful," I breathe. "We still have it. You still have it."

"I kept it in the back of my closet. Until you were ready. Now seems like the right time to give it back to you."

He lays the dress across the bed next to me.

I touch the silk, soft and familiar against my fingers. "I'm glad you kept this."

"I wouldn't get rid of it. It's Lucia Embroidered Motif." The designer language sounds awkward coming out of his mouth.

"How do you know?"

"You told me. You used to tell me everything."

"I'm sorry." I don't even know why I'm apologizing anymore, but it always feels like I should.

"Things will go back to the way they were. How many couples can say they're starting again with a clean slate?"

"Not many, I'm guessing." I hold up the dress in front of the mirror. "It might still fit . . ." I search the shiny folds, the crystals, the beautiful stitching, for some sign of the past.

Jacob comes up beside me. "You will still look beautiful in that dress. You always did."

I look at him in the mirror. "We got married in Discovery Park."

"Your uncle flew in from Oregon to give you away."

"Uncle Theo." My mother's only brother, fifteen years her senior, kept in touch with me after my parents died, but because of his dementia now he doesn't even remember my name.

"Uncle Theo, yes," Jacob says.

"There's no chapel train on the dress."

"You didn't want to trip."

"I wanted to dance." An image comes to me, of Jacob sweeping me off my feet.

"Do you want to dance again?" he says.

"I'm not sure I remember how."

"Wait here. I'll be right back." He leaves the room and returns with the heavy gold earrings I wore in the wedding photos. And something else. A delicate gold necklace inlaid with emeralds.

"Gorgeous," I say, dazzled.

"It belonged to my mother."

"Did your mother . . . come to our wedding?" I say.

"She passed away before I met you. She had cancer. The one thing I couldn't protect her from."

"You had to protect her?"

"From my father. I told you before."

"Oh, Jacob. That's awful."

A soft look falls into his eyes, fleeting vulnerability. "Sometimes I wish I could forget the past, like you."

"Your father was violent?"

"It was a long time ago."

"But we're shaped by our past. The past makes us who we are."

"It influences us, but it doesn't make us. We can do anything, *be* anyone."

"You've overcome a lot to become who you are today."

"It was all worth it. I got to meet you. May I put the necklace on?"

I nod, my heart in my throat, and as I look in the mirror, he puts on the necklace, his fingers brushing my skin, and a kaleidoscope of butterflies takes flight inside me. He attaches the clasp at the back of my neck, looks in the mirror to adjust the necklace.

"There," he says.

I put on the earrings.

He stares at me in the mirror, stoops with his head next to mine. "This is how it was. But your hair was different."

"I wore it down in the pictures."

"For the ceremony, it was up." He twists my hair into a loose knot at the back of my head. Wavy wisps tumble down onto my cheeks. His eyes light up. "Just like that. Beautiful." He holds my hair with one hand, traces the curve of my jaw with the other. His finger runs down my neck to my collar-bone. His touch is charged, rippling across my skin. Now I remember. He broke the rules when he came to see me before the ceremony. He stood in my dressing room, arms folded over his chest, admiring me.

"We could pretend it's our wedding night," he says. "You could put on the gown."

"What, now? It'll be too loose."

"You'll look beautiful in it, no matter what."

"What about you?"

"I'll wear my tuxedo."

"You brought it with you?"

"I would never give up the clothes I wore when we recited our vows." As he leaves the room, my headache returns, the cotton fuzziness in my brain. My reflection blurs in the mir-ror. The dress, Jacob, the wedding, the weight of the earrings. This has all happened before, in another life, in another place, but something was different. Maybe I wore different lipstick, or a diamond-studded clip in my hair. An indistinct face appears behind me. I turn around, but nobody is there.

CHAPTER FOURTEEN

As I change into the wedding dress, images flit through my mind. A plethora of roses, the three-tiered, ocean-blue cake. Linny hugging me. Moments of laughter. Jacob guiding me onto the floor.

The dress hangs a little loosely on my frame, but it still fits. The Swarovski crystals glint in the light. I find Jacob in the living room in a black wool tuxedo, expertly tailored. The jacket has a single button. He whistles and looks me up and down. "Wow. Just wow. You are the most beautiful woman this side of paradise."

"And you are . . . stunning."

He pulls me into his arms.

I look down at my bare feet. "Do we still have the shoes?"

"I don't know what happened to them, but I don't care."

I'm curiously light-headed. My blood runs hot. He's kissing me again, his lips firm, insistent. He smells familiar, feels familiar. He pulls me close, whispers something against my mouth. My body responds from a primal place.

"Damn," he says, lifting me bodily, carrying me down the hall and across the threshold into my room, the bedroom we once shared. He sets me down gently, turns me around to unzip the gown. It falls to the floor, and I step free, unable to catch my breath. He unclasps my bra, takes it off, and throws it on the chair. I'm in only bikini panties now. *I should wait.* But my thoughts move in slow motion. The wine. I could never handle more than half a glass.

In a moment, Jacob is undressed. How did this happen so quickly? I know his body. I remember what he looks like, his shape.

"This could be our second wedding night," he whispers to me.

My body needs to be touched. It has been so long. How long?

He pushes me back on the bed, bracing himself above me. He kisses my cheeks, my neck, and my collarbone with reverence. The mere touch of his lips sends me into a fever. "I've missed this so much," he says.

We've been here before, in this bed, in summer moonlight. In cool cotton sheets, not winter flannel. He holds my hands and I close my eyes, letting the pleasure seep into me. He always knew how to touch me, how to bring me to him, how to make me lose all reason. I stop thinking, stop worrying, and I give in to pure sensation. Every moment of our union becomes familiar in a way that only the body remembers.

CHAPTER FIFTEEN

In my dream, I'm striding through a sunlit room to a large stained glass window. The ocean glints in the distance, barely visible through the trees. The room is empty, redolent of floor polish, the walls painted soft butter-yellow. On one wall, a painted tree grows a riot of emerald leaves. This house is perfect, old and quaint, quirky and bright. I move through the rooms, comfortable, as if this is already my home. I imagine a child's laughter, dolls and building blocks strewn in a playroom. The smell of garlicky spaghetti on the stove. The heady scents of jasmine and Mexican orange plants in bloom. I'm in the blue dress, glowing in shiny cobalt silk, but when I look down, a dark stain spreads across the fabric, swallowing all the color, seeping out across the room, turning everything black.

I awaken disoriented, unnerved. It takes me a minute to figure out where I am. In the dream, I was somewhere else. But where? And when? The water is running somewhere. A waterfall—no, the shower. I'm beneath the comforter. *I'm not wearing any clothes.* Jacob is whistling in the bathroom. A veil lifts from the sky as the sun rises.

The night climbs back into me. The restaurant, our wedding attire. Jacob carrying me into the bedroom. What we did afterward. My head throbs. Is this a hangover? The last time I drank too much and woke up naked in bed, I was an undergraduate in my dorm room. I think.

Jacob emerges from the bathroom, toweling his hair. "You're up." He looks even more handsome in the morning light, every muscle defined; the small mole where it has always been on his right shoulder.

"Barely. I was having a dream. Not about the dive, though. It was a good dream this time—"

"About us?" He sits on the bed and touches my cheek, leans forward to kiss me gently. He smells of toothpaste.

"I was in a house all painted yellow. In the blue dress, but then the stain ruined everything."

"The tea stain."

"Must be. But the house was beautiful."

"So are you. Especially when you've just woken up."

"I look a mess." I reach up to touch my tangled hair, rub my eyes.

"A beautiful mess. A natural mess."

I pull the covers up to my chest. "Could you pass me my robe? It's in the closet." I'm suddenly self-conscious.

He hands me the robe. "Breakfast?"

"We need to talk about what happened last night."

His mouth tightens. "You regret what we did."

"It's not that. We moved a little fast."

"We're married," he says sharply. "We've made love a thousand times."

"I know it wasn't the first time."

"Did it feel like it was?"

"Not really."

He looks at his hands for a minute, then seems to force a smile. "It was a great night."

"It was," I say. "I'm not saying anything was wrong. It was amazing."

"But fast," he says. "We can go slower next time."

Next time. Something feels . . . off. As if there might have been a time when we thought, when *I* thought, there might not be a next time.

"The house in my dream was so vivid, like we were there. Like we wanted to live there. Or like we *did* live there."

"Dreams can be like that," he says gently. "Maybe you visited a house like that once."

"Maybe," I say.

He kisses my forehead. "I should go into town. We're almost out of coffee. Don't wander off before I get back."

"If I do, I won't go far."

"Good." He goes into his room. He's whistling while he gets dressed. I wonder if he will move back into my room now. Our room.

While he's gone, I slip into the bathroom to take a shower. Beneath the hot water, I work up a lather. The night with Jacob, the romantic dinner, what we did in the bedroom—did it all really happen? What about the house in my dream? The beauty, the comfort, and the hope I felt there—it seemed real, but then, so did recurring dreams I had as a child. I kept returning to the same treehouse made of blankets and pillows, as if that imaginary fort really existed. Could this yellow house be a figment of my imagination, appearing only in dreams? The dark stain spread across the scene almost as an afterthought, suggested by Jacob's explanation of what happened to my blue dress.

I rinse off, pull aside the shower curtain, and grab a towel. There's a dent in the bathroom door—a deep impression that

I didn't notice before. Almost as if something hit the door with great force. Or maybe it's simply a flaw in the wood.

A headache pounds at my temples. I consider taking an aspirin, or an ibuprofen pill, but I discard the thought. I'd rather down a cup of strong coffee and take a long walk. First, I check through the photo albums in the living room again, but I discover no hint of the yellow house. Not that I expected to find one.

In my office, I sign into my email. More ads, news, and a message from Linny.

Dear Kyra,

You didn't tell me about an affair, but I warned you about getting too close to Aiden Finlay. I can't imagine you ever having an affair with him. You're in the perfect marriage to Jacob—the way things are supposed to be. Whatever mistakes you made before, they're in the past. You got a second chance at life—start living in the present!

Love you, gotta go,
Linny

I read her message twice. Her buoyant tone feels unfamiliar. She never valued marriage. When she was young, her parents yelled at each other nearly every day. They separated when she was twelve. Linny doesn't believe in tying the knot. Or at least, she didn't four years ago.

What changed her mind? She's always wanted the best for me, and even I could see that Jacob had more faith in me than I might have deserved. *People change in four years. People change in one year. People can change in only one month.* I sit back, the dizziness setting in again.

I send a quick message. *I'll try, Linny. But first I need to clear up some things in my past. Did Jacob and I ever argue? Was I ever unsure of our relationship? Thank you, miss you, I'll be in touch soon,* and I sign off, wondering why I've asked her these questions. No, I know why. I go back to the bathroom, run my fingers along the indentation in the door, right beneath the chrome towel rack. I didn't see the dent before, because the towels were in the way. Nothing comes back to me, no suggestion of how the dent was made.

I head down to the beach, walking south this time on a new path, to shake off the headache. Maybe today, the Tompkins anemone will magically appear. But the creature has other plans. I'm beginning to wonder if it even exists. Red sea cucumbers, barnacles, mussels, and sponges cling to rocks. Occasionally, a spate of purple jellyfish washes up on the sand, their sails no match for the wind.

A Dungeness crab watches me from a rock. It doesn't move as I approach. I lift the crab and the shell of its back splits apart to reveal nothing inside—only a complex of empty chambers. The crab has been molting, shedding its shell. The real crab is long gone.

The wind calms as I round a bend to a protected beach. This is the way to Windswept Bluff, where the old man might live—the man who thought he recognized me. Far ahead, a boat is anchored to a dock. Makeshift wooden steps lead up the cliff into the woods. Someone's standing at the top of the steps, a dark silhouette of a man. He descends toward me, moving stiffly in a black, hooded raincoat. I wave at him, and he waves back. As he reaches the bottom step, I see that he *is* the man from town, the man who approached me at Mystic Thyme.

"Hello!" I say. "Remember me?"

"I've been watching you walk down this way," he says.

"You could see me from around the bend?"

"I watched from up there." He points up the steep, rickety wooden steps to the top of the cliff.

"You do live close to us," I say.

"Windswept Bluff is up there, dirt driveway, only one house. Mine." He marches toward me, bent forward as if his back hurts. "Who are you? Where do you live?"

"A bit north of here."

He's close now, giving off a strong scent of wood smoke. He peers closely at my face, a sudden spark of recognition returning to his eyes. "You left him, then?"

"Left whom? My husband? No, I didn't leave him." The tide laps at my shoes. The earth tilts, then rights itself. I can't get dizzy now, not when I have to walk all the way back along the beach.

"You should leave him," the man says. "Go, right now."

The wind ripples across the ocean, shivering through me. "You're saying I should leave Jacob? I don't understand."

His expression shifts to a startled frown. He blinks, rubs his eyes, and looks at me again. The wind roars in my ears. "Hell, I'm sorry. I . . . I must be dreaming. I need to go." He starts to move past me toward the dock.

I follow him. "Hey, don't go. Not again. You said I should leave him. What did you mean?"

"You look like someone else, that's all. I get mixed up these days."

"Who? Tell me what you know about me."

He looks at me, and I can see he's embarrassed, as if he was caught with his pants down. "I'm sorry, my memory is faulty sometimes."

"So is mine," I say with urgency, feeling a strange affinity with this man. I point to the scar on my forehead. "I forget things. Sometimes I don't remember what someone told me a week ago. I hit my head."

"I'm sorry to hear that," he says. "I wish I'd hit my head, but I'm just old." He strides out onto the swaying dock. I'm not sure I want to brave it.

"I'm Kyra!" I call after him. "Could we talk?"

"Doug. And sure, yeah, we can talk." He looks at me again. His eyes are haunted. "You remind me of someone from a long time ago, that's all. Years and years have gone by."

"The memory makes you sad."

"It does, I'm afraid." Now I see he's fighting tears. He doesn't want me to see him cry. He unhooks his boat from the dock and jumps onto the deck.

I venture out after him. The dock moves to and fro beneath me. "I look like someone you had feelings for. Who was she?"

"Let's talk when I get back. I gotta sell some fish." He points down to a cooler on the deck, then toward the steep wooden steps. "I live up there, but don't take the steps like I did. Those stairs are rotting. Take the driveway."

"When?" I say. "When should I visit you?"

"When I get back," he says.

"When will that be?"

"Couple of days."

The engine roars to life as he steers away from the shore.

"You're always leaving!" I yell.

The boat takes off into the distance, bobbing on the waves. Only when he has disappeared around the curve of the bluff do I realize I've been making fists, my fingernails digging into the palms of my hands.

CHAPTER SIXTEEN

By the time I get back to the house, my feet are soaked, and my teeth are chattering. Jacob is reading on the couch, mug in hand.

"Did they have coffee at the mercantile?" I say.

"New shipment," he says. "What took you so long?"

I peel off my wet boots and socks and stand with my back to the woodstove, absorbing the warmth of the fire. "I met a man on the beach, a couple of miles down."

"What man?" He looks over his reading glasses at me.

"He said his name was Doug."

"Don't know him."

"He was strange."

"The island attracts recluses. Don't walk down that far without me."

"He mistook me for someone else."

Jacob looks at me intently now, suddenly interested. "Did he say who it was? Who is this guy?"

"I have no idea. He took off in his boat. I saw him in town, too. Same deal."

Jacob puts on his reading glasses again, turns the page in his book. "He's probably bonkers. Quite a few like him around here. Who knows what he could do?"

I turn to warm my hands over the stove. The man's words

echo in my mind. *You should leave him. Go, right now.* But I don't know him, and when he took a closer look, he claimed not to know me, either. Yet I can't help but feel a connection to him, an echo as if we knew each other before. Perhaps we did, and neither of us remembers.

"I'm going to ride into town," I say. If I hurry, I might catch Doug's boat coming around to dock in the harbor. I'm not exactly sure why I want to catch up with him—whether it's more about his mysterious history, or to find out if he's connected to mine.

"I'll drive you," Jacob says.

"No, no, enjoy your book. I'll take my bike again."

All the way into town, the old man's voice plays through my head. *You should leave him. Go, right now.* To whom did he think he was speaking? The landscape unrolls ahead of me, the air moist with salt and the sea. I pedal past the library, the post office, and the mercantile. At the dock, the mossy sign reads, *Mystic Island Ferry, No Service Sunday and Monday.* There's a list of low-tide cancellations, and a note, *subject to change based on weather conditions.* I take off the helmet and walk my bike around the landing. Doug and his boat do not appear. But he was heading this way. He must've turned out to sea.

"Ferry's late today," a soft voice says behind me. The smell of cigarette smoke wafts through the air. I turn to see a young woman in a heavy white sweater, standing nearby in threadbare running shoes and jeans. She smokes, one hand across her waist, tucked beneath her right elbow. She holds the cigarette away from her to flick off the ash.

"How do you know?" I say.

She taps her cigarette, then crushes the ash into the dirt

with the heel of her worn shoe. "Radio. I'm guessing low tide. Engine breakdown. Or somebody jumped." She blows a plume of smoke behind her.

"I hope nobody jumped."

"Happens more often than you would think." She takes another puff. "People disappear around here. Might as well jump from somewhere. People jump from cliffs here sometimes, too."

"Like the one out at Windy Reef Park?"

"But you don't wanna jump or nothin'. You're not, like, *depressed*?"

"Me? No. But I appreciate your concern."

"Hey, I had to ask. 'Cause, like, you weren't so happy before. You feeling better?"

"I'm feeling a lot better, yes." My fingers tighten on the handlebars. "Do I know you?" I don't recall anything about her. Her memory of me feels creepy, as if she has been watching me through one-way glass.

She gives me a curious look, her nose wrinkling. "Yeah, you know me. Rachel Spignola. And you're Kyra Winthrop. But . . . Oh yeah!" She snaps her fingers. "You forget stuff. My mom told me what happened to you."

"Word gets around fast."

"I know, right? I moved away for a while, came back six months ago, and everyone knew in, like, two seconds. I'm staying with my mom. She owns the mercantile. I'm helping her out. Me and my boyfriend were living in Friday Harbor but we broke up."

My boyfriend and I, I think, but I don't correct her. "I'm sorry to hear that," I say, glancing toward the mercantile. The dark windows gaze back at me, reflecting the cloudy sky.

"Don't be sorry. I came home to get back on my feet." She blows smoke from the corner of her mouth. She finishes her cigarette, stamps out the stub, and then picks it up. "Come in?" She turns and heads back up the hill to the mercantile.

I follow her inside, and I'm hit by a wave of familiarity, in the smells of coffee and apples, tea and bread, in the creak of my shoes on the old wood floor.

"Anything I can help you find?" She walks around opening curtains, straightening shelves. The slanted sunlight reflects off dust particles in the air.

"What was I looking for when I came in before, when I wasn't feeling so well?"

"You wanted tea to help you sleep. Herbal stuff made from a stinky root. I can't remember the name."

"Valerian root," I say.

"Yeah, that's the one. We only have, like, chamomile."

Valerian root and skullcap will prevent the tossing and turning, Eliza Penny said to me in Mystic Thyme. I can't remember when. *Helps when you have a troubled mind.*

"Did I have insomnia?"

"Not this last time," she says.

"Last time?" The edges of the room grow fuzzy.

"You stopped in last Thursday."

A cloak of fear wraps around me. "Did I ride my bike into town?"

"You were in with your husband. You don't remember?"

"Jacob drove us down here."

"Yeah," she says, giving me a curious look. "I was waiting for you to remember."

"You didn't tell me, just now, when I thought I was meeting you again for the first time in at least a year."

"Sorry," she says, looking sheepish. "I didn't want to freak you out."

"Too late. I'm freaked out." A puzzle piece falls into place. As if from a dream, the memory returns, of the drive down here for groceries last week. The mercantile was closed. A sign on the door read, *Back at 2pm.* Jacob cursed, and we got out of the truck and strolled around town until Rachel showed up again. "He said he came down here to buy coffee this morning, too."

A beat of time passes, then she says, "Yeah, he was in a rush."

"Did he say why?"

"No," she says.

"The last time we were here together. I don't remember what we bought." *The shelves were half bare.*

"We were out of a lot of things," she says.

"I know," I say.

"You got dizzy, waited in the truck. Your husband bought some stuff . . . And, um . . ." She looks out the window, bites her lip.

"And?"

"Nancy stopped by, too . . . had a chat with him. They were talking about old times."

"What do you mean, old times?"

She drums her fingernails on the countertop, shifting from foot to foot, clearly uncomfortable. "I thought it was weird. She said, *I'm so glad you're back for good.* I didn't mean to eavesdrop, but it's kind of hard *not* to in here."

"And how did he respond?" I say, picking up a box of Lipton tea. I try to sound casual, but my voice comes out slightly tremulous.

"He said, *Yeah, for good.* She said, *Was this the right thing for you?*"

I put the box of Lipton tea back on the shelf. "What did he say to that?"

She reaches into her back pocket, places her slightly squished carton of Marlboro Lights on the counter next to the register. "I didn't totally hear that part. Someone came in. I *thought* he said, *That's not your business.*"

I lean against the counter, surprised at how relieved I feel. "And . . . ?"

"She nodded and . . . she left."

"I see. Anything else?"

She looks out the window, then at me. "She seemed, like, mad at him for something."

"For what?"

"Beats me. She slammed her stuff down on the counter and stormed out."

"Maybe she was upset about something else," I say.

"Can't say. Seemed like they knew each other pretty well."

"They grew up here together. On holidays."

"Yeah, and so did me and my mom. She grew up here. I grew up here. Once you live here, you never leave. Except I did. When I can get my act together, I'm leaving again."

"You don't want to stay in the long run," I say.

"Hell no," she says. "You know what the problem is with living on a small island? Nothing to do. For me, anyway."

"I can see that," I say. "But for me, it's a treasure trove of marine life. You can find things to do if you put your mind to it."

"If you like that kind of thing. Living in the middle of nowhere. But for me, no way. And you know what else? Everybody's in your business. You can't get no privacy."

You can't get *any* privacy, I want to say, but again I refrain from correcting her grammar. I'll only insult and annoy her. In fact, I have a feeling I've done so before.

"I can see the drawbacks of living in a small community," I say diplomatically.

"I can't get an acting job, for one thing. If I can get back to Friday Harbor, I could audition for Island Stage Left. I'm pretty good at Shakespeare."

"Well, that sounds lovely," I say, smiling.

"I could even play a guy. All you need to do is dress me up, add a white beard. I could be Sir John Falstaff, knight of the realm in King Henry the Fourth!"

"Speaking of beards," I say. "I was wondering about a man with a beard. Kind of eccentric. He ties his boat to the dock. He lives up our way. He said his name was Doug."

"You mean Doug Ingram? He's a fisherman, built his log house all by himself."

"Yes, I think that's him."

"He's handsome for an old guy. Sorry. You know."

"He is good-looking," I say.

"In a gnarled sort of way, right? Keeps to himself. Total hermit," she says, examining her fingernails. "But he's a good artist. You can see his paintings on display in the library."

My excitement must be obvious. Rachel gestures to the door. "You'd better hurry if you want to go see them. Sometimes they close for lunch."

CHAPTER SEVENTEEN

As I park my bike outside the library, I recall rolling my suitcase down the cracked sidewalk, briskly, toward the ferry landing. Where was I going, walking so fast? The clang of metal against the dock, the abrasive call of seagulls—it all echoes in the wind. I take a deep breath and climb the steps. The sign on the window reads, *Mystic Community Library*. The heavy wooden door squeaks as I push it open.

Inside, the library smells of old books and wood floors, pine cleaner and dust. Two large rooms, on either side of a narrow central hallway and staircase, are lined with shelves of books. To my left, a woman sits behind a desk marked *Checkout/Information*. Trim and elegant, her cinnamon-colored hair tied back, she sports a soft gray sweater, jeans, and rimless oval glasses. The library is quiet, except for the occasional swish of paper.

She looks up briefly and smiles at me, and I slip down an aisle. I'm in the mystery section. Two other patrons peruse the shelves, and a woman in a knit cap and sweater sits in a study carrel, reading.

I wander around and spot a series of vibrant watercolors along the back wall, and all down the hall leading to the restrooms. The signature at the bottom right of the paintings is barely legible: *D. Ingram*. The man with the wild white beard and crazy eyes captures whimsical images of Mystic Island—the desolate, starkly beautiful beaches strewn with driftwood and kelp; crabs scuttling across the sand; cormorants floating on a log on the sea; a breaching orca in the distance, against a backdrop of gray mist. Ingram understands the shades of gray of the northwest winter, but when I look closely, the layers of yellow and blue appear, brushstrokes of green, an underlying brightness.

The landscapes of dense fir forests and the stark seascapes give way to close-up studies of conch shells, volcanic rock, an outcropping along a sheltered cove. I recognize Doug Ingram's dock in one painting, and his boat bobbing on the waves. Another image suggests his view of the ocean from high on the bluff. And then, he painted a person, a woman walking away from him on the beach. Barely a black silhouette with her hair flying, her summer dress flapping in a splash of red against the dark hues of a Northwest autumn evening. Something about the painting evokes a sense of deep melancholy, regret—the past walking away. The woman's beauty is conveyed in her shape, in her gait, in the way the sky lights up around her, like a faint halo.

In the next painting, he moves closer to her, and now the pattern of roses on her dress comes into focus. In the next image, he leaves the beach and offers a view of the woman through a café window, as if he is glancing in at her as he passes on the sidewalk. I recognize the Moonside Café down the road. The ocean is faintly reflected in the glass, her profile in shadow inside. Strong jaw, full lips, high cheekbones. Wild, dark hair. She looks like me, but not enough to give me pause. Not enough to make me believe she's a doppelgänger. The paintings end here.

Who is she? Why does she haunt Douglas Ingram? It can't be a coincidence that he mistook me for her on an island I've visited before. I can't help but believe he holds a key—to what, I don't yet know.

I go back to the front desk. The librarian smiles up at me. Her nametag reads *Frances*. At close range, she appears older than before, white hair mixed in with the cinnamon, tiny creases next to her eyes, giving her a perpetual smile. "How may I help you?"

"The painting in the hall," I whisper, although there is nobody around to hear.

"Yes, isn't he gifted?" She clasps her hands on the desk.

"Do you know any of the history behind the paintings?"

Her brows rise, and her smile widens. "Are you thinking of purchasing one? He'll be thrilled. He may not *show* that he's thrilled, but he will be."

"I'm interested in the one with the woman in the café. Do you know anything more about that one?"

Her nose wrinkles, and she looks perplexed. "Let me see which one you're talking about."

I lead her down the back hall to the painting. Her rubber-soled shoes squeak on the floor. She gives off a faint scent of gardenia. When we reach the painting, she draws in a breath, tapping her chin with her index finger. "Gorgeous, isn't it? I do know she was a real person. The café is fairly new in the picture, as you can see. Could be his wife, but she left the island some time ago. She didn't want to live out here, or so the story goes. Nobody knows his background, so people gossip. He's a bit reclusive."

"But the paintings show how sensitive he is. He has an eye."

"People aren't always the way they seem to be, are they? We all have secrets. Rumors were that he was quite a handsome guy when he was young. He's still handsome, but he's gotten so . . . eccentric. One of the older librarians suggested that the woman in the painting was another island resident. A married woman. But that may have been idle gossip."

"I'm curious about his relationship with her," I say. "He mistook me for her. But if she's still around, she must be much older than me."

She looks from the painting to me and back again. "I see the similarity. He must still miss her after all these years. Maybe she's your long-lost mother."

I laugh. "Definitely not. I'm fairly sure my mother never came out to these islands. She passed away many years ago."

"Oh, I'm sorry, dear." Her eyes register sympathy, but to her credit, not pity.

"Thank you. I do wonder about this woman and who she was to him."

"Did you ask him?" she says.

"I tried to—but he wouldn't say more, and I didn't want to pry."

"I don't know for sure, but word is, after his wife left, he stayed on for a reason. He might've fallen in love with this . . . femme fatale. But it didn't work out. Sad story. Maybe that was why he kept to himself."

"I would love to know more about his background and the mysterious other woman."

"I could talk to the librarian who used to work here. She retired, but she knows a lot about the history of the island."

"If you don't mind," I say.

"It's no trouble at all. I'll let you know what I find out."

CHAPTER EIGHTEEN

The current swirls around us, the water aglow in emerald light. We're diving along a sea wall teeming with life—swaying yellow urchins and orange-tufted anemones. I'm pushed along faster than I expected. A tiny crab snaps at me, then withdraws its pincers. Striped fish dart in and out of the rock crevices. Lingcod, cutthroat trout. The variety of life forms clinging to the vertical rock face steals my breath away. Where are we diving? Strange, multicolored fish swim by in schools—they're not like any real fish I've ever seen. *Dream fish.*

I wake in the dimness of dawn. Where am I? *When?* In the cottage, in the room I share with Jacob now. A half moon shines in through the window, casting a meager light on the bedspread. The clock on the nightstand reads 6:31 a.m. Nearly dawn. A soft wind slinks in from the sea. Jacob is snoring softly next to me, one arm flung over his forehead.

I turn on my side, facing away from him, away from the window. I close my eyes, but sleep eludes me. Jacob rolls over, rests his arm on my waist, and pulls me back toward him. "You okay?"

"Fine," I whisper, settling against him.

"Diving dream?" he whispers in my ear.

"Everything was vivid this time."

"How so?"

"I could see everything. We dove along this . . . solid, steep rock wall. There were so many anemones. White ones, lavender, orange. Tinted green from zoochlorellae—"

"Zoo what?"

"Zoochlorellae. Commensal algae. The word just came to me."

"What the hell is that?"

"It grows inside the anemone. It's a complicated symbiotic relationship."

"I like the sound of that."

"There was so much to see . . ."

His arm relaxes on my waist. He has drifted off. His breathing takes on a steady rhythm. I lie awake, playing back the dream, a calm precursor to something much darker and unremembered. My mind drifts back to yesterday, when I asked Jacob about our trip to the mercantile last week. We rode our bicycles and found the store closed, the downtown road deserted. Later, we returned to the store in the truck. He remembered Nancy stopping in, but he didn't remember Douglas Ingram. *Vaguely, maybe,* he says. *But we were young. We didn't pay attention to the old survivalists who hid out in the woods. He was probably one of them.*

I slip out of bed, pull on layers of clothing for the cold. The sun is just rising as I reach the beach, but the tide is high. The waves crash against the cliffside where the shore juts into the sea, making the route impassable to Douglas Ingram's secluded beach.

To avoid wading in ice-cold water, I have to hike back home through the grassy dunes. The terrain looks different here, littered with driftwood. I come across the skeletal remains of a fort built of weathered limbs coughed up by the sea. *I've been here before, inside this makeshift teepee,* with Jacob, only the day was warm, the ocean calm. It was summertime. I wore a sleeveless silk shirt, shorts, and flip-flops. I took off the flip-flops, dug my toes into the warm sand to feel the cool, damp underlying layer. Jacob pulled his shirt up over his head. He was utterly appealing. He took me in his arms. *Nobody can see us here,* he said, kissing my neck, my shoulders. We made love right here, on this deserted beach on a beautiful summer afternoon, when the sun shimmered on the water, the salty smell of the sea wrapped around us. Sand got into our clothes and all over our skin. Every sensation was heightened by the heat, intensified by the recklessness of our lovemaking. I felt daring, exposed, but we were alone.

No, not alone.

Someone was watching us. Nancy had come down the steps from the garden that afternoon. We didn't notice. She approached in stealth. Maybe she saw Jacob's shirt draped over the side of the fort, like a flag. I looked up and caught her watching us, a stunned look on her face.

Nancy! I scrambled out from under Jacob, grabbed for my clothes. Jacob laughed and said, *Oh, shit.* He was not embarrassed. He seemed to take her voyeurism in stride. We were covered in sand, our faces flushed.

Orcas, a whole pod breaching, she said, looking at Jacob. *Dozens of them. They're in the cove in Mystic Bay. Someone said there's a new baby . . . See you there.*

She turned and walked away, as if she had not seen anything.

"Kyra!" someone calls from the top of the steps. I look up at the figure of a burly man. He's waving at me.

"I'm down here!" I yell, waving back. From this distance, the man looks a lot like Van Phelps. I race back along the beach, away from the fort, and up the steps to greet him.

CHAPTER NINETEEN

"I was about to give up," he says when I reach the garden. He hands me a carton of eggs. He's in cargo pants, rain boots, and a hooded windbreaker. The familiarity returns—we've conversed before, and I remembered what I thought of him, a solid, earthy fix-it man, a fearless diver. He seems uncomplicated. But then, looks can be deceiving.

"Thank you," I say. "Jacob's not around?" How long was I walking on the beach? I've lost track of time. I can still see Nancy's face, the surprise in her eyes, and a touch of jealousy.

"He's not here, and he's not in the cottage."

"I don't know where he went, but I'm sorry to keep you waiting. Would you like to come in?"

"I could use a cup of coffee." He follows me inside, into the warmth. Jacob has made coffee, as usual. The pot is full, the fire crackling pleasantly in the woodstove. Maybe he drove back into town, or he went for a jog on the beach, heading north.

"How's Nancy?" I say brightly.

"Same as ever."

"Meaning she's well?" I say.

"Meaning she's Nancy."

I reach up into the cabinet to bring down two coffee mugs, and when I turn around, Van looms over me.

He steps back. "I was going to reach those for you." *Let me reach that for you,* he says in my mind.

"Thanks, I can reach on tiptoe."

"I see that." He pours us both coffee, hands me my mug. His gaze shifts to Jacob's latest to-do list on the counter.

Sweep deck, check gutters, weeding.
Buy salt, olive oil.

"Milk?" I say, opening the fridge. He's still too close.

"I take my coffee black." He makes no move to go and sit down.

I put the carton of eggs in the fridge.

He leans back against the countertop, points with the mug to the scar on my forehead. "Does it still hurt? Looks like a pretty bad scar."

"I don't feel it anymore. Only its aftereffects."

"Aftereffects." He turns the word over on his tongue, as if he's tasting a bouquet of wine. "What does that mean? You feel phantom pain or something?"

"My vision blurs now and then, dizziness. Gaps in my memory. It's annoying."

"It would annoy the hell out of me, not remembering."

"Funny, though, certain things are coming back to me. Something about you."

His brows rise. "What about me? You remember coming to the boat?"

I nearly drop my mug. My knees go weak. "We've been on your boat?"

"You weren't with Jacob." His eyes darken, creases forming on his forehead.

"I went alone. Why didn't you tell me this before?"

"Jacob told me not to tell."

"He knows. Why would he want you to keep information from me?"

"He said not to bring up the past with you, to let you figure it out on your own."

"What if I never figure it out? Without help? He's the one who said I would never remember."

"Maybe that's what he wants." He looks closely at me, taking in all my features, my skin flushed by the cold, my hair mussed from the wind and sand. It's as though he can see my memory of Nancy catching Jacob and me in flagrante delicto in the driftwood fort. If Van had seen the jealousy in Nancy's eyes, the complicated regret, what would he have done?

"You're suggesting he doesn't want me to remember," I say. A cactus of prickles covers my skin. "That's . . . silly."

"He said you would get all riled up. But to tell you the truth, I was hoping to find you here alone."

"Why?" Maybe I should not have invited him in. I'm aware now of his size, his imposing presence, the way he disturbs the air like an unstable weather system.

His voice tightens. "It's been bugging me. I thought you should know. You came to me for help."

For help? "What kind of help? To fix something?"

He laughs softly. "Hell no. This was not a solar panel situation."

"Then what was it? When was this?"

He rubs his upper lip, then runs his fingers through his hair. "Last September. You came to the boat to ask for my help."

"What was going on?"

He gulps his coffee, taps the mug. "I promised Jacob I wouldn't mess things up for you two."

"Wouldn't mess *what* up?"

He makes a motion with his hand. "You two are trying to patch things up. I can't stand in the way."

"Are you saying you and I were involved? You were in the way?"

"Not in so many words."

"Then in how many words?"

"We weren't involved, okay?" He goes to the window, looks out to sea. "Promise me you won't tell Jacob I'm telling you this, since you two are back together."

"We weren't together last September?" I press my hand on the countertop, bracing myself. I might faint.

"You were, but you wanted to leave without him. Ferry broke down. You asked me to take you to the mainland, only I couldn't. Nancy was having a meltdown."

"Why would I ask you to take me away from the island?"

He gulps the rest of his coffee, comes back to the kitchen, and plunks the mug in the sink. "You didn't tell me why, but you were upset. I hated that I couldn't leave. Nancy was angry with me at the time. She says I go away too much. I'm only trying to give her what she wants. The *life* she wants."

He's heading off on a tangent, but I can't follow right now. "Jacob knew about my plan to leave?"

"He knew you came to the boat, not because I told him. He followed you down there and picked you up."

"So I came back here with him."

"Yep, you did. The next day, the ferry was running again, and you left."

"On my own, with luggage," I say. *I strolled past the library, rolling my suitcase . . .*

"Obviously, you two worked out your differences. You're here with him again."

"Obviously," I say, the room closing in on me.

"I hope you know what you're doing. You were so ready to get the hell out of here."

"Well," I say, "I'm not now."

"I can see that." He taps his fingers on the counter.

"I have to tell him, you know. About this conversation."

"Yeah, I figured," he says. "I'll take the heat."

"You can't take heat for something that's not your fault. Jacob should have told me we fought. I didn't say why I wanted to leave. Are you sure?"

"You were pretty cagey, about a lot of things. When you and Jacob met us the first time, I thought you were a woman with secrets. You brought them with you from the city."

"What secrets? What would make you say that?"

"Whenever Jacob would start talking about you, how you first met or your wedding, you would get quiet. Sometimes you'd tell him not to bother us with the details. Or you'd get up and walk away. It seemed like it embarrassed you." He looks out the kitchen window and frowns. "Speak of the devil. There he is. Look, forget I said anything. You guys seem to be fine now. Thanks for coffee." He leaves the house, taking the porch steps down two at a time.

"Wait!" I call after him, but he's already getting into his truck as Jacob pulls into the driveway.

CHAPTER TWENTY

I'm in Sylvia's office, ripping a tissue into threads in my lap. I've just told her about Van's visit to the house.

"What happened when Jacob came home and saw Van leaving?" she says. She's in jeans, a long, loosely knit pullover, and black shoes.

"He asked what Van was doing there."

"And what did you tell him?"

"The truth. Van's story."

"How did he react?"

"He was angry. He agreed that we fought last summer. But he said we were okay after that."

"Did he say what you fought about?"

"He couldn't remember. I don't know whom to trust, Jacob or Van. Or myself. Except I can't contribute anything to their stories."

"Sounds like you're still feeling confused."

"I can't trust my own brain." I clasp my hands together in my lap. My knuckles are white. "If I went to Van for help, I must've trusted him, or I was desperate. But why would I have been desperate to leave Jacob?"

"You don't have any idea?"

"Not really," I say.

"Were you desperate to leave, or desperate to go somewhere?"

"What do you mean?"

"I mean, maybe it wasn't leaving Jacob that concerned you, but going toward something or someone else."

"You mean there was something important back on the mainland."

"Perhaps," she says.

"I remember the intensity of us . . . of Jacob and me together, but I know I was being pulled away from him, too. In the Whale Tale, I was certain I was about to leave him for good. I *felt* the sadness, like something was ending. But then it wasn't. Van told me I went to him for help. Did I? Jacob and I might've been in trouble, but he tells me our marriage was perfect. I don't know what's real."

"It's not going to make sense all at once."

But even the immutable aspects of reality—the rise and fall of the sun, the phases of the moon—seem suspect to me now. "Did you ever see the movie *The Truman Show*? A guy discovers his entire life is a TV show. Nothing is real. His wife is an actor, his town is a movie set. Everyone's in on the joke, but he's not. He believes everything is real."

"Do you feel that way now?"

"What if I never escape from the show? What if I never remember everything? What if I never get to the truth?"

"You will. We're making progress."

"What if my marriage was truly over?" I say, rubbing my upper arms. "What if Jacob's only telling me it wasn't?"

"What would his motivation be for lying?"

"He didn't want our marriage to end?"

She nods thoughtfully. "Sounds like you think that might be the case."

"I thought that if I started remembering things again, I would remember falling in love with him. Instead, I'm getting a confusing jumble. I'm kissing Aiden. I'm in the shower with Jacob. Then I'm falling into Aiden's arms on a hiking trail— something isn't coming to me yet. Something important."

"Maybe you're not quite ready to remember the missing pieces."

"Not ready? If my marriage was ending, should I leave Jacob now?"

"Do you want to leave him?"

"Apparently we patched things up. It seems somehow we did."

"I wouldn't make any hasty decisions," she says. "You need time to sort through your memories and emotions."

My days in rehab, a blur, darken the edge of my memory. "I do get impatient sometimes."

"This doesn't have to be all or nothing, black or white. You could've had problems, true. But you'll know when and if you're ready to leave, or whether you want to stay."

"Thank you, I know you're right." As I leave her office, I should feel calmer, less confused, and better equipped to face the mystery of my past. I do, in a way. But I also feel as though my memories stop short, before the storm, at the edge of a precipice leading down into an abyss.

CHAPTER TWENTY-ONE

I'm standing in a square of warm sunlight, in my dream house. It's exactly the way it was before. Only now I realize the house is modest, giving the illusion of space in its open rooms and large windows. I love the saffron-colored walls, the skylights. Sunlight shines through the rustling fir trees. A beautiful summer ocean winks at me from a distance.

This time, I leave the room, the *nursery*, and I go down the hall to the open kitchen. The living room is all windows facing the sea. My heart fills with warmth. Jacob stands in the kitchen, talking to a young woman in a blue pantsuit and matching pumps. *Other offers? . . . Love the place,* he's saying. I walk up to him, but I'm confused. We're supposed to be in the house on Mystic Island. This is all wrong. He looks up and smiles, and Aiden Finlay comes in through the sliding doors, into the living room, the sun at his back. The wind rustles his dark hair. He gazes at me. A dark cloud passes over Jacob's face. Aiden doesn't seem to notice. *Hey, you two,* he says, *you should see the Jacuzzi tub.*

In a slow transformation, possible only in dreams, Aiden becomes Douglas Ingram. *You look like someone I used to know . . .* The sunlight fades into the gray, oppressive clouds over Mystic Island. I'm under the comforter next to Jacob. He's snoring softly. The dream is gone.

I slip outside into the cool, crisp air. The dawn feels scrubbed clean. I imagine this kind of autumn day is why I wanted to move here. The tide peels back from the beach to reveal a whole new world of stranded shells and crabs. As I head south toward Doug Ingram's dock, my legs grow tired. But this time, I make it all the way to the secluded cove, only to find his boat gone.

Overcome with a deep sense of disappointment, I sit on a rock to catch my breath. The tide pools are teeming with a rich array of marine life, including a lined chiton, an otherworldly little marine mollusk clinging to a rock, feeding on algae.

What is that little alien? Aiden says, crouching beside me. I see him as if he's here with me now, examining the chiton, which resembles an armor-plated, oversized caterpillar. I hear his breathing, smell his scents of soap and pine. He's looking at the chiton with a focused sense of wonder.

Tonicella lineata, I say. *A subtidal mollusk.*

Could you say that in English?

It has eight overlapping plates or dorsals, you see? They're bilaterally symmetrical.

Like humans.

Only the chiton sticks to rocks with a suction cup foot. And they're herbivores. Animalia: Mollusca: Polyplacophora.

Poly what?

Sorry, I say.

Don't be sorry. You're amazing. He's looking at me with admiration.

You're not bored out of your mind?

Are you kidding? I'm fascinated. We should go diving. I bet you would see a whole lot more. He takes my hand and we clamber across the rocks into another cove, where we find more tide pools. We're not on Mystic Island. But we're close, maybe on a nearby island. We're careful not to step on the numerous fragile anemones. I recite the scientific names for the species we see. He tries to pronounce the words. We come upon a jellyfish in the sand, a flat puddle of amber.

Strange to see jellyfish motionless, I say. *They move twenty-four hours a day in the sea.*

He kneels next to me, looking at me, not the jellyfish. *You're sad,* he says.

No I'm not, I say, but I am. *Washing ashore is a natural part of the jellyfish life cycle.*

Can we put it back in the water?

I smile at him. *You're so sweet, but the tide will only bring it right back again.*

Then what can we do? His dark eyes register concern— for me, for the jellyfish, for everything I have ever worried about. He wants to protect me from pain, from grief, but it is too late for that. There are some things in this world from which we can't be protected.

Nothing, I say. *There's nothing we can do.*

Hell, if we can't save the damned jellyfish, let's have a funeral.

A funeral? I say, in disbelief.

Memorial service, whatever. To honor the life of the jellyfish.

I laugh as we arrange seashells around the jellyfish. *I used to do stuff like this when I was a kid. But it's been a long time.*

Never give up being a kid, he says. *I'll give the eulogy. 'All good jellyfish go to the great Sea in the Sky.'*

Even bad ones get to go there, I say. I feel as though I'm a child again, doing childish things, but happiness is suffusing me like filtered sunlight.

"Kyra!" Jacob calls to me from far away. I'm no longer in my memory of Aiden. The jellyfish is gone. I'm crouching in the cold water, my pants wet to the knees; my feet soaked in my running shoes. Jacob's rounding the bend in his Spandex jogging pants, windbreaker, and fluorescent green running shoes.

"I'm here!" I wade out of the icy water onto dry sand.

"What are you doing way the hell down here?"

"I found a lined chiton. They're abundant up the coast, or at least they were four years ago. But this is the first time I've seen one here. They—"

"You're shivering. Come on, let's get you home."

"I'm fine." But my teeth are chattering now, and my toes are going numb.

"The telephone woke me up, and I saw you weren't there." He takes my arm and steers me back toward the house.

"Who called?" I say. Aiden's smile stays in my mind. His dark eyes, so sincere, so *interested*.

"It was Nancy, reminding us about dinner Saturday night. We should make something to bring with us."

"Okay, you're the cook," I say. I want to go back to that protected cove. How many more moments did Aiden and I share, peering into tide pools on that rocky shore, holding solemn funerals for the dead creatures coughed up by the sea?

CHAPTER TWENTY-TWO

We're in the pass again—the dream takes me back to the rock wall, to the anemones swaying gently in the current. Another diver hovers a few yards off, filming a congregation of urchins. The current is too strong—stronger than it should be. Is it possible we didn't time the dive correctly? Could we have made a mistake? A wave of anxiety washes through me. I begin to hyperventilate. I count, *One, breathe in, two. Breathe out. Three.* Why am I here? I'm not ready to dive here. The waters are too rough. Where are we? In Deception Pass? Somewhere else?

You'll be fine, Jacob told me. *I'll be there. I'll take care of you.* But there is no true slack current here. The current pushes one way, stops for a minute, then changes direction. My mask grows tighter, my suit heavy. I'm cold, too cold. I can't draw a deep breath. *We are not alone.* A third diver swims up behind us. Another man? Is there a fourth diver behind him? Two other divers? Or only one? The water is murky now, silty. Full of shadows.

In an instant, the current whips us away. The undertow churns up the sea bottom. A cloud passes over the sun, and my view plunges into darkness. Where am I? At what depth? Forty feet? Sixty? The loud rush of my breathing fills my ears. I have a strong urge to rip off my mask, race for the surface, and gulp a deep breath of fresh air. *Don't panic. Panic is what kills most divers.* If I ascend too quickly, I'll get the bends, deadly nitrogen bubbles in my bloodstream. But I'm running out of air. Another diver swims up below me. His eyes widen with confusion, or fear, or both. I have to help him, but I can't fight the undertow. The sea yanks him away. I awaken gasping for breath, my heartbeat pulsing in my ears.

I sit up, rub my forehead, trying to clear my mind. The clock on the nightstand reads eight o'clock. I slept later than usual. Jacob is already humming in the kitchen.

I pull on a robe and slippers over my pajamas and go down the hall to my office computer. In Google, I type in "Kyra Winthrop," "diving accident," and "Deception Pass" again, and I click on results in only the *News* category. The same stories appear—two divers rescued from the pass, both miraculously alive, except for my head injury. What did I expect to find? A fresh article, sprouting from my dream, reading, *Correction: our previous piece erroneously reported only two divers nearly swept to their deaths in Deception Pass. In reality, a couple of ghost divers survived the treacherous currents . . . courtesy of Kyra Winthrop's warped imagination.*

So much for the revelatory power of dreams.

In my email inbox, I find a message from Linny.

Kyra,

Did something happen? Did you and Jacob get into a fight? Why are you asking me if you argued? Tell me what's going on!

He was always careful and gentle with you. I'm sure he gets pissed off sometimes. We all do.

Xoxo,
Linny

Well, that's a relief.

I sign off and go back down the hall to the kitchen. Jacob is seated at the dining table, reading glasses propped on his nose, jotting a list on a lined notepad.

I peer over his shoulder at his cramped handwriting:

SWEET POTATOES, MAPLE SYRUP, CINNAMON, BUTTERNUT SQUASH, PECANS...

"A recipe?" I say.

"Butternut squash pecan casserole," he says.

"I'm not fond of the word *casserole*," I say, pouring a mug of coffee. "It's what my dad made when he wanted to disguise leftovers."

Jacob takes off his glasses and smiles. "At least your dad cooked. My dad didn't know the difference between a colander and a cooking pot."

"We weren't a conventional family," I say. "Except for the casseroles. For some unknown reason, my dad considered himself the male Betty Crocker."

"This isn't a conventional casserole," Jacob says. "Vegan, crunchy, and sweet, just like you."

"A sweet casserole?" I say. "Yuck."

"Trust me. It's good."

"If you say so." I yawn.

"You didn't sleep well," he says, a note of concern in his voice.

"I had the dream again." I sit at the table with him, holding the warm cup in both hands. "Only it got scary. The current shifted and pushed us—"

"Wait, you think this recurring dream is a real memory?"

"I'm not sure, but this time there was someone else, at least one other diver."

His brows rise, his expression puzzled. "Another diver? Who?"

"I don't know. Did we dive alone?"

"Yeah, just the two of us," he says, frowning. "Why would you dream of someone else?"

"Could other people have been diving with us?"

"Not with us, but when the conditions are optimal in the pass, there might be other divers."

"Did we see anyone else?" I say.

"We might have. Wait. We did. Now I remember. One experienced diver with a less experienced diver trailing him. But we didn't dive with them. We nodded hello. That's all. We were diving along the wall, and we passed them."

"Going in the same direction?" I say.

"We had to have been," he says. "They're not going to swim against the current. You drift with the current one way, then you let it carry you back the other way."

I peer into my cup. I've finished my coffee, without even noticing. "This dream didn't have much of the usual strangeness—you know, when the impossible happens. It felt real."

"It could've been from another time."

"It seemed like the pass."

"We dove in other places."

"But the dream."

He looks up at me. "You had a dream of other divers before, and you've asked me this question before. My answer has always been the same."

I step back, stunned. "I don't—"

"You don't remember, I know." He tears off the sheet from the notepad. "I need to gather these ingredients for the dinner. I'm going into town." As he shrugs on his coat, I pour a second mug of coffee to kick-start my fuzzy brain. I wish I could replay the dream like a movie, know for certain what I saw.

CHAPTER TWENTY-THREE

"I'm recording light on silver atoms," Jacob says, snapping a picture of me in the kitchen.

"You're what?" I pat down my hair. I'm not prepared for another session for the scrapbook.

"You know, imprinting your beautiful face on photographic paper."

"Lined with silver," I say.

"Absolutely. That's how real photographs are made. Not the digital ones."

"Please don't take any more pictures of me cooking." I push my hand over the camera lens. "I can't even boil an egg. I turn everything I touch into stone—or ash."

"The Medusa Touch," he says. "With the Medusa hair."

"Stop," I say, yanking the camera out of his hand.

"Too late. Your beautiful image has been committed to film."

"Then uncommit it."

He kisses my cheek. "Not a chance. Come on. I'll show you how to cut the sweet potatoes. But first we have to clean them." We wash all six small sweet potatoes in cold water.

"Show me your magic," I say.

"Glad to oblige." He wraps his arms around my waist and lifts me bodily, heading for the bedroom.

"That's not what I meant!" I laugh, squirming out of his arms. "I meant your magic cooking techniques."

"Oh, *that*." He feigns a look of disappointment. "Fine. The recipe calls for the sweet potatoes halved with the skin still on." He hands me the gleaming, serrated knife. "Don't cut yourself. I'll cube the squash."

On the countertop, the pear-shaped squash leans to one side, misshapen and bulbous. *We could plant our own vegetables in my mother's old garden,* Jacob whispered long ago. *We would never have to leave the island.*

How lovely that would be, I said. A gorgeous burgundy sunset spilled across the sky. As that summer day left us, I felt my hopes and dreams taking leave, too. How could I possibly stay in this magical world of forests and birds, sunsets and beaches? The island felt *uncomplicated* in comparison to my life in the city. How I loved the rosy twilight reflecting off the sea, the unhurried days exploring the tide pools and quiet trails. But I had to go back to my obligations, clogged highways, and the frenetic pace of life. In Seattle, I sense that every hour was spoken for. I had no time to plant anything at all.

"Where was your mother's old garden?" I say.

"What?" The knife slips from his hand, hitting the counter with a clang.

"The last time we were here, you mentioned your mother's garden."

He picks up the knife. "Over there." He points to the south side of the house, toward the cottage. "I'll show you when we have time. Tomorrow?"

"Tomorrow would be great," I say.

Look at all these weeds, he said. He kneeled in the soil to yank out dandelions, almost angrily, as if they had invaded his mother's neglected garden on purpose.

I place a sweet potato on the cutting board, slice down the center, splitting the potato in half. On another cutting board, Jacob slices the squash, revealing a core full of seeds.

"Did we make food together a lot, like this?" I say, slicing the rest of the sweet potatoes.

"Sometimes. I cooked, you helped." As he chops the squash, he drops the cubes into a measuring cup. The countertop shimmers and changes color from pale granite to cerulean blue. The kitchen cabinets elongate. They were different, a lighter oak color. I'm seeing our old kitchen on the mainland. The sink had a two-handled faucet, unlike this one with a single handle. The house felt large, empty. I'd left the lasagna to cook too long. The top had burned and dried up. I was in a panic.

Jacob strode in. He took one look at my stricken expression and rolled up his sleeves . . . *I'll fix this,* he said.

It's ruined, I said. *I can't do this. I never should have tried.*

Allow me. An incredible feeling of relief washed through me.

The kitchen morphs back into the cottage kitchen. I wrap my arms around his waist, pull him close.

"What's this?" he says.

"I'm just appreciating you."

"I'll take a few orders of appreciation to go," he says.

"I was remembering something. Did our old house have light oak cabinets and a blue countertop?"

He gives me a look of shock, which quickly melts into a grin. "You're close. The countertops weren't blue. They were leaning more toward green."

"Funny, I remember them as blue," I say.

"In what context?" He turns on the oven to preheat to 400 degrees, pulls two large baking sheets from a high cabinet.

"You were cooking . . . and I was upset. In anguish about having burned lasagna. Someone important must've been coming over . . . and I wanted to impress."

He frowns. "Burned lasagna, let me think. That must've been the night Professor Brimley was coming over for dinner." He's arranging the squash and sweet potatoes on the baking sheets. He drizzles them with coconut oil and slides the baking sheets into the oven.

Something more happened that evening. Aiden walked in while Jacob was cooking. I see Jacob wearing an apron, holding a spatula. He turned to face Aiden. *Hey, buddy,* he said.

My heart leaped at the sight of Aiden with his tie askew, his hair a mess. He must've been coming from work. But I hid what I felt. Why? Had he come over expecting to find me alone? Was Jacob supposed to be away?

I'm interrupting something, Aiden said, looking uncomfortable. The air was charged with tension.

You're not, Jacob says. *Drink? Something you need to discuss?*

No, it can wait, Aiden said. He placed a Tupperware container on the table. *I was in the area, thought I would bring this back.* He turned to leave. I wanted to run after him, but I stood rooted to the spot. The memory recedes into shadows, large pieces missing.

"Fifteen minutes for the squash," Jacob says, setting the timer on the stove. "The sweet potatoes will take longer." He empties the bag of pecans onto the cutting board and begins chopping them into smaller pieces.

"Aiden's a good friend of yours, right?" I say, watching him work.

"Yeah, why?"

"You haven't talked to him since we've been here."

"I called him yesterday while you were walking on the beach."

I nod, leaning back against the counter. "Should we invite him to visit? I mean, we liked doing stuff with him, right?"

He looks thoughtful, his eyes distant. Then he smiles. "Yeah, we could. I have to go back to the city next week, to check on things, remember? I'll talk to him then."

"Did you tell me you had to go back?" The familiar prickle of anxiety sneaks under my skin.

"You don't remember." The pinch of irritation returns to his voice. "I'll have to go back now and then to keep an eye on the company. Shareholders' meetings, board meetings."

"Aiden didn't work with you? He worked at your company, right?"

"He's a manager in IT," Jacob says. "Engineer. I gave him a job. We didn't see each other every day."

I'll always be grateful to Jacob, Aiden told me. *I have to be careful. I don't want to alienate the guy.* Alienate him how? And when?

"You were friends before that, right? In college?"

"Yeah, he was a brilliant scientist. Good programmer, too. We both love the outdoors."

"We hiked together a lot. Did we dive together?"

"A couple of times."

"In the pass?" I say.

"No, we dove in the pass only that one time." He gives me a curious look. "Why all the questions about Aiden?"

"I remember him stopping by unannounced, that's all."

Jacob nods slowly. We're quiet for a moment.

"What's next in the recipe?" I say, taking a deep breath.

"Heat the pecans and add the magic ingredients. Coconut sugar, maple syrup, cinnamon, salt."

"I'll help. Should I—?"

"You go on." He gives me his *I've-got-this* expression. "I'll take it from here."

CHAPTER TWENTY-FOUR

"Move over, Angelina Jolie," Jacob says, looking at me as he drives up to the Phelpses' farm on Dream's End Lane. "Kyra Winthrop's in the house."

"But where is Brad?" I say, grinning.

His face falls. "Damn. We're history."

"Anyway, you're way better-looking than Brad Pitt."

He smiles. "My name is better, too."

Twilight spreads across the horizon in a strip of bright orange. I'm in jeans, black boots, a soft beige knit sweater, and simple silver earrings. When I emerged from the shower, Jacob had laid out these clothes on the bed for me. I'm holding the casserole in a glass baking dish warming my lap.

"Seriously, am I fancy enough?" I say. "I mean, I love the sweater you chose for me, but . . ."

"You're perfect. What about me?" He's a step up from casual in gray flannel trousers, black turtleneck sweater, and black shoes.

"Perfect," I say. "Better than Brad, like I said."

As he drives up to the garage, the sweet smell of freshly cut grass fills me with a deep ache of nostalgia. I've been here before, smelling the grass, gazing through the trees at the welcoming lights of the farmhouse.

As Jacob parks beside Van's truck, Nancy comes out onto

the porch, waves at us, and descends the steps, holding her fuzzy white sweater close around her. Van strides out after her in a black T-shirt and jeans, surrounded by two leaping black Labrador retrievers.

Jacob lifts my hand to his lips and kisses my wedding ring. He squeezes my hand, the way he squeezed my hand on the deck of the ferry as the island came into view. I remember now. There was no wind in the harbor. It was early summer. He took my hand and slipped a wedding band on my finger, made of hammered gold.

What's this? I gasped in delight and bewilderment.

To replace the one you lost.

Jacob . . . Tears of joy and confusion blurred my vision. The ring was gorgeous but a little loose.

You used to be a six, he said.

Only a half size off. I turned my new gold wedding band around and around on my finger. I was brimming with hope, worry, and trepidation. I thought our wild trip to the island might be the biggest mistake of my life.

"Kyra, come on." Jacob is standing next to the truck at the Phelpses' house, waiting for me to get out. Nancy rushes down the porch steps, and the next few minutes pass in a haze of hugs, greetings, and the dogs weaving around our legs, their tails wagging. Nancy introduces them as Salt and Pepper.

In the house, the dogs flop on the rug in front of the woodstove in the corner, their tails thumping.

In the spacious living room, Van's tending the fire. He smiles at me, his expression betraying nothing of what we discussed when he visited. Nancy disappears into the kitchen and returns with a plate of deviled eggs and raw veggies. "Appetizers. Help yourselves."

"Wine?" Van says, putting a bottle of white on the table and popping the cork. *Wine? Red or white?* He asked me here, in his house. Nancy and Jacob were standing outside on a warm summer evening, admiring the ocean view. I said, *White,* and he poured me a glass. *This is the first time I've had any alcohol in months,* I said to him. *Feels warm going down.* We both looked out the window at Jacob and Nancy, chatting about some childhood secret, no doubt.

Cheers, then, he said, and we touched our glasses together. *Here's to good friends.*

Good friends, I said. *Should we let them in on the toast?*

Nah, leave them to themselves.

I felt it then, the twisting corkscrew of jealousy beneath my ribs. I knew Van felt it, too. *No, let's go out there and talk to them.* I went outside onto the porch. Jacob and Nancy sat in wicker bucket chairs. The evening sunlight glinted off Jacob's glass of beer. Nancy's wineglass was empty. Jacob was nearly doubled over with laughter, Nancy giggling uncontrollably. Jacob summoned me to sit in his lap. I obliged, the setting sun in my eyes. *Let's get out of here,* he whispered to me, holding me close. Nancy gave us a look. Then she got up, staggered over to Van, and fell into his arms.

"Wine?" Van says to me now, uncorking a bottle of white. Jacob has gone into the kitchen to get a cold beer from Nancy.

"You remembered I like white," I say.

His left eyebrow rises. "Halfway, like before?"

"Halfway," I say. "I figured out I get tipsy easily. Depends on the type of wine."

"Mystic Vineyards Chardonnay," he says. "We get a limited selection here."

I pick up the bottle and read the hand-painted watercolor label. Organic, no sulfites, made by Eliza Penny of Mystic Thyme.

"Not the caliber you're used to, I bet," he says.

"Caliber?"

He nods toward the kitchen. "I can't compete with that guy. I'm guessing you two drink some pretty good wines." Do I detect a slight note of envy in his voice?

"We're not that sophisticated," I say, sipping the wine. "This is pretty good. Smooth and slightly sweet. Undertones of apple and berries."

"You've got a sensitive palate. We should all go wine tasting."

"I'm surprised there's even a vineyard here."

"We like to support local businesses. My buddy made this, too." He points down at his T-shirt. The faded picture on the front shows an old-fashioned diving helmet and the words *The Original Heavy Metal.*

"Clever," I say. "Maybe he could make me one."

"I've got a better one. It says, *Scuba Diver Evolution: Air, Nitrox, Trimix.*"

"What does that mean?" I say.

"Nitrox is a breathing mixture made of nitrogen and oxygen," Van says. "But with less nitrogen and more oxygen than air. You don't need to worry about it. Nitrox is hardly ever used for recreational diving. You could get oxygen toxicity. Extra nitrogen could give you the bends, but too much oxygen isn't so great, either."

"And trimix," I say, feeling suddenly a little woozy. The concentration of sugar in the wine seems to increase with each sip.

"You add helium to the mix. But trimix is only for the deepest dives, like over four hundred feet."

"We wouldn't have been diving so deep in the pass."

He laughs. "Hell no. You're at maybe forty feet in the pass."

"Ready to eat?" Jacob carries a plate of asparagus and potatoes in one hand, his beer bottle in the other. "Nancy says we have to eat now or the food will get cold."

"If Nancy says so," Van says.

"I hate to rush us," Nancy says, carrying out a plate of wild rice pilaf.

"It all looks wonderful," I say as we sit at the large oak dining table. "You went to so much trouble."

"It's no trouble," Nancy says. "Harvest season always gets me in a cooking mood."

"Nancy started cooking way back when with her Easy-Bake Oven," Jacob says.

She laughs. "You *remember* that thing? I was, like, ten years old."

"Who could forget?" Jacob says. "It was the ugliest thing on the planet."

"It was Dual-Temp!" she says. "My best toy ever."

"I didn't play with ovens," I say. "I was too busy doing ocean puzzles."

"I played with guns," Van says. "Toy ones."

"Right," Nancy says. "And he married a pacifist."

"Opposites attract." Van pulls back the foil cover on our casserole dish. "What did you bring?"

Nancy peers over his shoulder at the casserole. "Oh, I love pecans, Jake!"

"You always did," Jacob says, taking a swig of his beer. It occurs to me that he may have chosen this particular casserole for Nancy's benefit. I have a sudden urge to upend the dish and dump its contents.

"It's a bit sweet," I say. "It's made with sweet potatoes."

"I don't eat sweets," Van says, sitting at the head of the table. "But Nancy will have no problem eating it all."

"Oh, Van," Nancy says. "Don't be a party pooper."

"Is that what this is?" Van says. "A party?"

She swats his arm affectionately. Is she already a little tipsy? "We're having a dinner celebration."

"What are we celebrating?" Van says.

"Old friends," she says, lifting her wineglass. Jacob raises his beer bottle in a toast. Irritated bees swarm through my insides. What's going on between them?

"I wouldn't call us *old* friends," Van says. "But friends, yes."

"Oh, I forgot something." Nancy jumps to her feet again, goes to the kitchen, and brings back a bowl of dinner rolls. "Homemade," she says. "I love baking bread."

"You've gone to so much trouble," I say again, feeling suddenly inadequate. I learned to boil an egg for the first time in college, and even then, I wasn't good at it.

"Did you make the casserole?" she says to me. She must know I didn't.

"Jacob's the cook in our family," I say.

"Must be because I taught him," she says.

"Oh?" I say. "What else did you teach him?"

She looks down at her plate, and an awkward silence follows.

"Sorry," I say, although I don't believe I should be the one apologizing.

"Me, too," Nancy says.

"Let's all enjoy our dinner," Van says.

The room tilts, and I feel my breathing quicken. I get up abruptly, scraping back my chair. "Bathroom," I say.

"End of the hall," Van says, pointing through the arched doorway.

"Right." I escape down the narrow hallway, taking deep breaths. Jacob's voice drifts down the hall. "How's the solar panel repair coming along?"

". . . have it ready for you in a couple of days," Van says.

In the small bathroom, decorated in a beach theme, I take deep breaths, absorbing the solitude. I examine my gaunt, pale reflection in the mirror. *Nitrox, trimix.* The words sounded familiar. *We're using nitrox this time,* Jacob said. We were on a beach, testing our scuba tanks. I turned the valve halfway, and Jacob told me to sniff the air coming out of the tank. *It should be odorless,* he said. Was it?

I flush the toilet, wash my hands, and slip back down the hall. I peer into a study with a desk, walls of books, and photographs. Murmured conversation wafts toward me from the dining room. I make a detour into the office. On the desk is a photograph of Nancy, Van, and a teenage boy who must be their son. He looks like a blond version of Van—built strong but with Nancy's coloring and her narrower nose. I pick up the picture and peer closely at it, trying to detect some evidence of marital discord. The boy appears to be the glue holding the three of them together, his arms around his parents' shoulders. If he lets go, they will fly apart.

"He just turned nineteen," Van says behind me.

I whip around, my face burning. I put the picture back on the desk. "I'm so sorry. I shouldn't be in here. I walked by and saw the picture—"

"We're hoping he'll come home for Thanksgiving," Van says. "We thought he'd be back for the summer, but he picked up a job in the city. Nancy was devastated, but there's nothing here for the kid to do."

"It does seem like a difficult place for a teenager," I say.

"He's a good kid, a hard worker. He would find something to do wherever he is. I'm glad he came into this world."

"Even if . . ." I stop myself before the words come out.

Van cocks his head and gives me a wry look. "Nancy's been busy bringing you up to speed on our life story?"

"She may have mentioned that a child wasn't necessarily part of your original plan."

Van laughs. "Is anything ever planned? It doesn't matter in the long run. We fell in love."

You fell in love, I'm thinking. Nancy's laughter drifts out from the dining room. She's a flirt. Maybe she doesn't even know what she's doing. "She does love you," I say.

"Yeah, I know. Maybe more when your husband isn't around." He steps closer to me, pain and confusion in his eyes. Longing. He touches my cheek, and I flinch.

"Van," I say.

"Sorry." He withdraws his hand.

"This isn't about you and me. This is about you and Nancy. You need to talk to her."

"I know I do." He has to deal with her complexities, her crush on Jacob.

Do you think? Van asked me, a long time ago. *If circumstances were different?*

They're not, I told him, backing away. *You're only upset about Nancy.* The edges of our tangled relationships begin to blur, the blacks and whites fading to gray.

"We need to get back," I say. "I shouldn't be in here with you."

"Right," he says, taking a deep breath. "You're a beautiful woman, Kyra. Jacob is lucky."

"Nancy is lucky, too," I say. "I hope she knows that."

He gives me a half smile of resignation, of acceptance of a path not traveled. "My turn to hit the head," he says, going down the hall to the bathroom.

Back in the dining room, Nancy and Jacob are in deep conversation. Nancy is completely focused on Jacob, clearly taking delight in his presence, while Jacob taps his fork on the tablecloth, looking distracted. He looks relieved when he sees me, but he gives me a questioning look.

"Are you going to make a go of it on your own?" Nancy is saying. "Raise poultry or livestock?"

I sit next to Jacob. "Um, no," I say. "We're going to plant a garden."

"Oh?" Her brows rise. She stabs a potato with her fork. "Where will you get your meat? Fishing?"

"I'm a vegetarian," I say.

"We'll figure it out," Jacob says.

"You're a gardener, then?" Nancy says, pressing on.

"Not exactly," I say. "But I'll give it a try."

"She's an excellent gardener," Jacob says. He rests an arm around my shoulders. "You don't remember—you took up container gardening and developed an interest over the last couple of years."

"I did? Well." I laugh, a little nervously. "I guess I did."

"Do you grow starters in a greenhouse?" she asks.

"Greenhouse?" I say. "We don't have a greenhouse."

The toilet flushes down the hall. I hear the water running.

"We're going to pick up some plants from the nursery and start that way," Jacob says. "In the old garden."

"The old garden!" Nancy says, chewing her potatoes. "I remember that garden. We had a lot of fun there." She gives Jacob a knowing grin.

Van comes back in and sits down, making a sour face.

"We did have fun," Jacob says.

"Oh, what did you two do . . . in the garden?" I say.

"We stole carrots," Jacob says, downing a gulp of his beer.

"And put them back in the soil," Nancy says. "Half eaten."

"We pulled all the rhubarb and ate it with sugar—"

"And the berries, lots of berries," she says.

"Those were the days, huh?" Van says in a flat voice.

Nancy's smiling at Jacob, smiling at the past. An invisible wall goes up between Van and Jacob, a palpable tension in the air.

"His mom chased us out of the garden more than once," she says. "We thought we were sneaking but somehow she knew."

"My mom had a sixth sense," Jacob says. "We must've aggravated her no end."

Nancy sips her wine. "She was always laughing. Your mom had a beautiful laugh."

"She did," Jacob says. "So does Kyra."

Van's lips are turned down at the corners, and he's picking at his food.

Nancy seems to stare into the past. "We did have a good time back then. You know that old, beat-up Ford we used to hang out in? It's gone. Someone must've hauled it out of the woods and used it for something."

"Oh?" I say, looking at Jacob. "What beat-up Ford is this?"

Van clears his throat. "It was some old rusted heap of metal someone illegally dumped in the woods here. How they got it out there, nobody knows."

"We used to pretend it was a spaceship," Nancy says. "Jacob was the captain. He was always the captain, no matter who played with us."

"I'm not surprised," I say.

Nancy reaches for a plate of wild rice pilaf. "He was so good at creating this whole universe out in space."

"And who were you?" Van says.

"I was his first officer," she says. "But come to think of it, why didn't I ever get to be captain?"

"I was better-trained," Jacob says smoothly.

"No, it was because you always insisted on having your way," she says.

"It worked out," he says.

"Well, you can't have a ship here," Van says. "You would need communications. We're off the grid."

"We didn't need the grid back then," Nancy says. "But I wouldn't mind being a little more connected now."

"We do fine," Van says. "We're not the only island off the grid. Look at Lasqueti. Ninety miles from Vancouver with no connection to BC hydro. Solar panels for heat, fireplaces, water from a stream."

"We choose the life we want," Jacob says. "We make our own world here."

"You're an expert at that, aren't you?" Nancy says. "Weren't you a hacker? It makes total sense that you would become one."

Jacob's face flushes. "Not a hacker."

"Computer whiz, then. Creating worlds for video games."

"I started with video games a long time ago. And then—"

"You were a hacker?" I say, elbowing him.

"I was employed by a security company to *prevent* hacking. There's a difference. I helped protect consumers. I built a business on protection."

"But aren't identity thieves getting more innovative?" Nancy says. "The only way to protect ourselves is to stay offline."

"You've got a point," Jacob says.

I stuff a forkful of casserole into my mouth.

"Life is simple off the grid," Van says. "I do my work, go on my dives. Stay offline."

"Life is a little *too* simple," Nancy says. "Maybe a little *too* relaxed."

Van frowns at her.

"But it's better now that you're back," she says. She's looking at Jacob again. Van reaches out to take her hand, and she shifts her gaze to him and smiles.

Jacob fills my glass with water from the carafe on the table. Conversation motors up again. Nancy gets up to bring dessert from the kitchen. "Homemade cheesecake with blueberries from our garden."

Everyone *oooh*s and *ahhh*s. Van coughs. Once, twice, three times.

"You okay?" Nancy says.

His face reddens. He gasps for breath.

"Drink water, honey." She tries to hand him a glass. He shakes his head. She puts the glass on the table.

He's wheezing loudly now, his eyes widening.

Nancy leaps to her feet. "What did you eat?"

Van shakes his head, as if to say he doesn't know. He's wheezing.

"There's no shellfish here!" Nancy says, looking confused. "What was it?" She looks at his plate in shock.

"Do you have an EpiPen?" Jacob says.

Nancy looks around, flustered, blinking. "In the bathroom. Under the sink." She rushes down the hall.

"Where's the phone?" Jacob says.

Van coughs and sputters, pointing behind him.

Jacob goes into the kitchen. "We're on Dream's End Lane," he says to someone on the phone. "You need to get here right away." He comes back into the dining room. "They're on the way."

Van coughs and wheezes, gasping for breath.

Jacob pats him on the back. "Easy, buddy."

I'm frozen in place, the scene surreal, time slowing.

"Where is it?" Nancy yells from the bathroom. "Where's the EpiPen?"

Van slumps over in his chair. Red welts form around his mouth. His lips are swollen.

"Hey, buddy," Jacob says. "Deep breaths."

"What can I do to help?" I say.

"Help her look for the EpiPen," Jacob says.

I rush to the bathroom, find Nancy sitting on the floor, toiletries strewn around her. "It was here. It's not here!"

I kneel beside her. "Where else could it be? Think."

"I don't know! Bedroom."

"Go and look in there. I'll keep searching in here."

"There's nothing here," Nancy says. "We have an EpiPen. But it's not here!"

"Everything is going to be okay," I say, although I'm not sure this is true. "The medics are on their way."

"It'll be too late!" Nancy says, but she goes out to the bedroom.

As I search the bathroom, I try to ignore the horrifying sounds coming from Van—choking and gasping. There's nothing here. No EpiPen. But I find a bottle of pink liquid in a drawer. Benadryl. Better than nothing. I race back to the dining room, open the top, and offer the bottle to Van. He can't even swallow. He chokes, and the liquid spills down his chin.

"How long is it going to take the medics?" I say, putting the bottle on the table.

Van's barely breathing as the sirens approach, bright lights flashing. A red firetruck parks right in front of the house, and two men rush in with a stretcher. They're in yellow suits, one man gray-haired, the younger one with jet-black hair.

"Oh, Earl, thank goodness," Nancy says, rushing in from the bedroom.

"What happened?" the older man, Earl, says.

"No EpiPen! I don't know where it is! Honey, breathe!" She whacks Van on the back. He keeps choking.

"Nan, out of the way," Earl says in a calm voice. "We'll take it from here." He and the younger man put down the stretcher and motion to everyone to move back. Earl plunges a syringe directly into Van's thigh, right through his jeans.

Van cries out. The younger man wraps a blood pressure cuff around his arm. We all stand back, watching the men work.

"Van, you hear me?" Earl says, shining a penlight in each eye.

Van's gasping for breath.

Earl takes Van's pulse, and then the two men maneuver Van onto the stretcher while the younger firefighter talks into a radio. "We need an airlift at Helipad 1 on Mystic . . ."

Van is lying on the stretcher, an oxygen mask over his face. We all stand back, Nancy crying. I wrap an arm around her shoulders.

The men hoist the stretcher and carry Van to the front door.

"I'm going with you," Nancy says, grabbing her coat from a hook by the door.

"We'll take care of things here," I say. "Don't worry."

"Thank you." She grabs her purse and whips past me. The dogs try to run after her, but Jacob grabs their collars. My breath is trapped in my throat. Jacob holds the front door open with one hand, for the medics. As they pass, Van looks at me, his eyes wide with terror. *The diver rises below me in the churning water, his eyes wide with terror. He's gasping for breath. I swim toward him, fighting the current. Another diver comes up behind me. The third diver, the diver below us, points back over his shoulder to his compression line. He's not getting any air. He's drowning, drifting away, and I can't reach him.*

CHAPTER TWENTY-FIVE

"He'll be okay," Jacob says on the drive home. We cleaned up the dishes and fed the dogs before we left.

He reaches across the seat to hold my hand. "They gave him the Epi shot in time."

"I can't get his face out of my mind," I say. I feel mildly nauseated.

"It was a freak accident . . . something he ate."

A freak accident, like me hitting my head.

"We didn't have any shellfish at the table," I say.

"It was something else. He must have developed an allergy to milk or peanuts."

"So late in life?"

"He's not that old, and yeah, it's been known to happen."

"Poor Van. Poor Nancy."

"This will bring them closer together."

"It shouldn't take a medical emergency," I say.

He squeezes my hand. "I'm sorry about all this. You don't need any more trauma." His eyes are soft, caring.

"It did bring back a strange image of another diver. It looked like he was drowning."

He lets go of my hand. "You saw someone drown?"

"Gasping for air, or . . . I don't know. Yes, drowning. I don't know when or where. But we were diving."

"You never went diving without me. We never saw anyone drown."

"Someone was running out of oxygen. Another diver."

"Nobody was running out of oxygen."

"I thought I saw . . ."

"Your mind must've been playing tricks when you saw Van wearing the oxygen mask."

"Must've been." We're quiet the rest of the way back, watching the dark fields flit by. The island takes on a new, mysterious personality at night. Forms that were once easily identifiable as animals or trees become unrecognizable shape-shifters.

At home, he makes a fire, pours himself a stiff glass of whiskey. "What a damned night." He collapses on the couch.

The sky is clear, moonlight casting an eerie glow through the window. "What if they don't get him to the hospital in time?" I say.

"Like I said, they got the shot into him." He swirls the whiskey in his glass. "You should get some rest."

"I'm not sure I can get any sleep tonight." The synapses in my brain are firing.

"You could take one of your sleeping pills," Jacob says, downing the rest of his drink.

"I'm not taking any more drugs. I'm going for a walk."

"Now?" He sounds incredulous.

Let's take a midnight walk, Aiden says, holding my hand.

"The moon is full. I'll take a flashlight."

"It's not safe," Jacob says.

"There aren't any predators on the islands. No mountain lions or bears."

"But there's the guy down the beach."

"He's harmless." I dress for the cold. Out in the icy air, I feel free, relieved to be alone. I need to talk to Sylvia. I can't fit all the puzzle pieces together. Van's frightened eyes haunt me, the eyes of the phantom diver.

I walk to the water's edge. The shoreline looks different in darkness, the driftwood like bodies stranded in the sand. On a rocky stretch of beach, I sit on a boulder and watch the lights of distant freighters on the horizon. Far from the city, the stars jostle for space in the night sky. I've been here before, in the dark, my mind rife with regrets and worries. I always loved the beach at night, even when I was very young. I sneaked out my window to be alone with the sea. The moonlight on the waves calmed me. I catch an image from long ago, of Jacob walking toward me on a night like this one, on a beach with a view across the Puget Sound. We were waiting for Aiden to arrive. He was late—we were all going somewhere together. Jacob kept checking his watch, sighing with exasperation. I said maybe we shouldn't go. I didn't feel well. Jacob said we could go without Aiden. *The guy doesn't like the symphony anyway.* Ah, so that's what it was. The symphony. But it was my stomach, roiling and heaving, that kept us from going, in the end. Right there, I threw up in the sand, sat down to catch my breath. I apologized to Jacob, but he said not to worry. He brought me a glass of water and stayed with me until I felt better.

I'm lying on my side at the edge of the bed, facing the bathroom door. Moonlight casts mottled patterns on the wall. I follow the movement of shadows. Jacob's tucked his knees against the backs of my legs, his arm heavy on my waist. His familiar smell envelops me. But it's not his voice I hear in my ear. It's Aiden's. *I've missed hanging out with you,* he says in my memory. I've missed him, too. But we're not here—we're somewhere else. I know the shapes of the furniture—a tall antique dresser, a window much like this one. I can't hold on to the place or the time. But Jacob's arm becomes Aiden's arm around my waist. *You came back. I was worried you wouldn't.*

How could I not come back?

We have so much to talk about, he said.

Jacob pulls me close. I wait until he snores, and then I slide out of his arms. I can't sleep at all. I go into the garage and pull my scuba suit off the wall. Our tanks and equipment gather dust on a shelf. What happened on the dive?

I put on the scuba mask, listen to my own loud breathing. *Attach the cylinder to the BCD,* Jacob says in my mind.

I'm trying, I say.

Attach the regulator to the cylinder valve. Then open the cylinder valve. He's patient, but I'm frustrated. I can't do this so quickly and easily. Diving is new to me. But not for him. He's experienced. He's logged thousands of hours in training.

So why did we put ourselves at risk diving in the pass? He told me to stay close, not to stray. I would be okay if I just stayed behind him. Did I? Or did I break the rules?

Jacob picks up a pot of beet plants to put in our shopping basket. He has driven me east across the island to Mystic Nursery, hidden on an acre of lush forest.

"I'm not a big fan of beets," I say, eyeing the plant in the basket.

"I love them," Jacob says. "But get what you want."

Carrots, parsnips, globe onions, cauliflower. I choose a variety of root crops and leaf crops to plant in the fall. They'll mature in the spring. Jacob chooses his own plants, and when we get back to the house, we cart them all out to his mother's old garden. This corner of the property feels haunted, as if his mother still wanders through her overgrown series of weedy, raised beds, the stone borders thick with moss. "How long has it been?" I say, pulling up my hood in the spitting rain.

Jacob looks around the garden and smiles. "After I stopped coming out to the island, long after my dad died, she still came out to tend the garden now and then. Before she got sick. She was here maybe . . . fifteen years ago? She died twelve years ago."

"I'm so sorry. This garden must have been special to her."

"It was the only place my dad wouldn't follow her," he says. "He was allergic to lavender." He points to the thick lavender bushes still thriving in two of the raised beds.

"So the garden was her sanctuary," I say.

Jacob nods sadly. In the few images of her in his photo albums, she's at the water's edge, wearing a headscarf and waving from a distance, or seated at a restaurant across from Jacob, wearing huge sunglasses.

He brought his camera out to the garden, and he snaps a photograph of me digging a spade into the ground, turning over the damp soil.

"Hey, come on," I say. "I'm a mess."

"A beautiful mess." He snaps another shot.

"I'm not a gardener."

"You started digging here last summer. But we didn't have time to plant anything. We were on vacation."

It's therapeutic to get down on my hands and knees, digging in the soil, making room for new life. We work in tandem, digging holes, dropping the plants inside, and adding new, organic soil. I uncover a faded, handwritten plant marker that reads, *Thymus citriodorus "Aureus."* I hand the marker to Jacob. "Is this your mother's writing?"

"Yeah," he says, sitting back on his heels. His eyes cloud over with sadness. "This was her favorite plant ever."

"Thymus citriodorus?" I say.

"Lemon thyme. I looked everywhere at the nursery, but I couldn't find any. She loved lemon thyme lotion, the smell of lemon. Everything had to be lemon thyme with her. I wish I could've found some in her honor." He presses the marker into the soil behind the plant.

"We can keep looking," I say. A few minutes later, I find another marker. *Allium schoenoprasum. Chives.*

"Wow, I can't believe I missed these," he says.

I find no more markers. We plant such a variety of herbs and vegetables, tilling up the soil as we go, that the raised beds look transformed when we've finished. The garden takes on a cheery, hopeful demeanor, waiting for the sunshine and rains of spring.

"Do you think the plants will survive?" I say.

"My mother knew where to put them," he says, as we head back through the yard. I'm pleasantly tired. When we reach the house, I remember a flash from last summer. *That's your mother's old garden?* I said. *So many raised beds.*

She spent a lot of time out there, Jacob said to me. *She had a green thumb. Sometimes I feel her here, like she's watching me.*

Like a ghost? I said.

Not exactly, he said with his signature touch of suppressed irritation. *Like a mother watching over her son.*

CHAPTER TWENTY-SIX

I'm riding my bicycle down to see Van on his boat. He came home from the hospital this morning and went straight back to work. He's anchored a mile south of the harbor in a secluded bay. I follow a narrow dirt road down to the water's edge. The fields and forests race by, autumn clouds tumbling across the sky. Driftwood litters the beach, and tethered to a weathered dock, Van's boat gently bobs on the waves—a large dive and salvage vessel painted in red and gray. There are no other boats, no houses anywhere in sight, nobody on the narrow beach.

Van emerges from the cabin in a striped sweater, knit cap, jeans, and boots, squinting although the sky is not bright. "Kyra!"

"Van." I'm gripping the handlebars so tightly, my fingers hurt. I loosen my grip and walk my bike the rest of the way on the dock.

"Come aboard."

I put down the bike, and he takes my hand, helps me onto the boat. I've stood here before, on this faded deck with its faint smell of salty sea and new paint.

"I'm glad you're okay," I say.

"It was not my idea of a trip to Disneyland."

"How did it happen? Do you know what you ate?"

"Complete mystery, but I'm a changed man. Every time we dive into a wreck, I put my life on the line. But this time, I stared death in the face over dinner."

"Don't joke. You never know what's going to happen. Life can change in an instant."

"You know that as well as I do." Van leads me into the cabin. Laid out on tabletops are the rusty remains from sunken ships—old shoes, wine bottles, and ceramics. The room is also packed with equipment—metal tools and cameras, dive gear, scuba suits hanging on the walls. Life jackets, ropes, a dinghy. "How can I help you?" he says.

"What do you know about the diving accident?"

"Only what Jacob told us."

"I feel as though someone else was there. Was it you?"

"Me!" He looks startled. Then his face closes, concealing . . . what? "What makes you say that?"

"Someone else was there."

He frowns at me. "It wasn't me."

"I wonder who it was."

"How do you know someone else was there? Did Jacob tell you that?"

"He said nobody else was there. But I'm seeing images of a third diver. I'm certain the third diver struggled for air. What could cause someone to run out of air while diving? The nitrox you told me about, could that do it?"

"You could get oxygen toxicity. If you don't keep an eye on your gauge."

"But you could survive, get rescued."

"I suppose. It's possible, yes."

"What else could go wrong?"

"Lots of things. You could lose your tank if you don't

secure it to your BC—your vest. The strap expands in the water. If the strap slips, you're in trouble. Or the regulator could malfunction. Happened to me once."

"Was it accidental?"

"Yeah. Why are you asking me this? You and Jacob survived. He's an advanced diver. He had to go through rebreather training."

The word *rebreather* echoes distantly. "What about someone on a scientific dive? Documenting sea life?"

"Depends. Inexperienced diver, out of shape, overexerts himself and uses up his air. He panics and rises to the surface too quickly. Fatal air embolism. Nitrogen bubbles in the blood."

"But what if a diver is healthy and experienced and isn't ascending too quickly?"

"Doesn't happen to experienced divers. They check their equipment before they dive. It's more common for a diver to misjudge, panic. If you've had a cold or allergies, you could still be congested. You're not thinking straight, you use up your gas—oxygen, as you say. You breathe deeply but you feel like you're not getting air. Your body gets stressed."

"Jacob is a master diver. He taught me to dive. And yet—"

"Divers panic in the rough waters. About one in ten diving deaths is due to rough seas, strong currents. Diver can't deal with it."

"One in ten. That's a lot."

"It was probably the current. You fought it and got to safety."

"You're right . . . but there's something nagging at me. Something I need to remember."

"If you need any other help, I'm here until tomorrow.

Then I leave for Colombia, got a job there off the coast. I'll be back in about a month."

"You're fast back to work after almost dying."

"Yeah, I gotta make ends meet," he says, taking a deep breath. "For Nancy. She wants to do more things together, go to romantic places. Last romantic thing we did together was a night down at the B and B."

A thought comes to me. I turn to him. "The same one we stayed in when we first got here last summer?"

"Yeah, out on the north side of town. There's only one. You want to go back there?"

"Just to see if I get anything . . . a memory."

"You'd better hurry over there. They might be closing for the season."

CHAPTER TWENTY-SEVEN

The Mystic Cove Bed & Breakfast Manor is a large Victorian mansion nestled in the woods, with a grand view of the sea. The wraparound porch has been restored, and the gardens and gazebos are impeccably maintained. I ring the bell at the front counter. The air smells of wood polish. A portly, dark-haired woman emerges from the back room, her ruddy face beaming. She's wearing a flowing, colorfully patterned dress, a long wool sweater over the top. "Ah, Mrs. Winthrop, how lovely to see you again!"

"Call me Kyra."

"And you must call me Waverly."

"I'm relieved to find you still open."

"We close for the winter season in November. I wish we could stay open year-round. Maybe next year."

"Lovely place you have here."

"Thank you. Let me give you a hug." She comes around from behind the counter to envelop me in a comforting embrace, then she steps back and touches her soft hand to my cheek. "My husband, Bert, passed away six months ago. He would have loved to see you again."

"I'm so sorry," I say, hugging her again.

This time, when she pulls away, her eyes are wet with tears. "Thirty-five years we were married, and we loved every minute of it. I hope you and your husband are as happy as we were."

"Did we seem happy?" I say.

"You sure did. Is something wrong?" She searches my face.

"No, not exactly. I was interested in the place we stayed last time we were here together."

"Gargoyle Cottage. Lovely cottage for honeymooners. You two arrived early summer of last year, I believe it was."

"I'd like to see the cottage again if it's okay with you."

"Serendipity! Gargoyle Cottage is empty. We're slow this time of year." She grabs a key from the hook on the wall, pulls on a long coat, and leads me out the front door and along a path through the woods. The day is growing cold, a hint of winter wafting in. She leads me several yards away from the main house, to a secluded Victorian cottage on the bluff. "This may have been the servants' quarters," Waverly says, out of breath. "Originally." The cottage is painted in solid blue and gold, with a double staircase climbing to a wraparound porch. Inside, the air smells fresh, the rooms furnished in ornate antiques, a four-poster bed from the 1800s taking up most of the bedroom.

"This is amazing," I say.

"We take pride in our accommodations. I'll leave you to look around. Just give me a holler if you want to book the room again."

"Thank you. I will."

She shuffles back along the path. As I stand in the center of the living room, I see Jacob on the couch, beckoning me. I curl up in his lap. He takes my hand in his, turns the wedding ring around on my finger. *We're finally here,* he says. *Do you know how long I've wanted to do this?*

I didn't realize you were so romantic, I said. *Why did we wait so long to come here?*

Good question. I always wanted to. He touched my mouth with his thumb, parted my lips, ever so gently. A promise, a question, an invitation.

I drew a breath. He lifted me bodily, carried me across the threshold into the bedroom. We were unfettered here, free of obligations.

I shift my gaze away from the bedroom, and I see us in the afterglow, sharing pastries and coffee in the morning. Summer sunlight slants in from the east, a million sparkles on the ocean. That first morning here, life was perfect. But underneath my skin, a vague uneasiness grew. This would not last forever.

Your family house—does it have a view like this one? I said, parting the lace curtains.

Better, he said, coming up behind me. *The view will take your breath away. As soon as the renters leave, and the cleaners get the place in shape, we'll head up there, okay?*

Renters. Now I remember. His family home on the bluff became an occasional vacation rental during the summer months, after his mother died. How many cold winter nights had the house stood empty, waiting to become a home again?

On the living room bookshelves, I find mostly classics, some mysteries, and a few romance novels left behind by previous guests. On a middle shelf, I find a row of printed cloth journals. Some are much older than others, with yellowed pages, loose binding in the spines. The journals are arranged in chronological order, in which guests praise Waverly's hospitality, the tranquility, the ambience. *We saw a pod of orcas passing Mystic Bay,* one guest wrote. *Two bald eagles circled overhead this morning. They landed on the fir tree at the bottom of the path.* Another guest wrote, *Try the Whale Tale restaurant.* Yet another guest wrote, *We were lucky the cottage wasn't booked for the week. The ferry broke down. We were stuck here four extra days. Four perfect days.*

I flip through the entries from last June, my heart rate increasing. What if I didn't write in the journal at all? What if I left no record? But there it is. I recognize my confident handwriting, the cursive slanting to the right.

Our stay here has been idyllic. I can pretend my complicated city life doesn't exist. Since we've been here, I've been able to focus on gratitude. I'm thankful for the wilderness, for the view, for my friends. I'm grateful for those who comfort me, for wonderful souls in my life. I'm grateful for the Gargoyle Cottage and Waverly's hospitality. Thank you for having us.

Kyra

I don't find another entry. What did I mean by "my complicated life"? My entry is maddeningly vague, but I wouldn't have revealed secrets here, on paper, for the world to see. I try to read between the lines, but no magical, invisible ink comes to light.

Back at the front desk, I ring the bell, and Waverly huffs in from the back room. "How did you like it?"

"Brought back fond memories," I say, only partly a lie.

She hands me a small white paper bag. "I almost forgot. It's been so long. You left this in the room. Must've fallen between the cushions on the couch."

I open the bag, which contains a small box of prescription pills—ibuprofen mixed with famotidine. Half the label has been ripped off the flat box, but my name, *Kyra*, remains, and the name of the physician, *Dr. Louise Gateman*. The reason for the prescription, dated last April, eludes me. Yet my heart sinks, and an unbearable sadness darkens my soul.

"Are you okay?" Waverly says. "I'm sorry I couldn't reach you earlier. Things get thrown into our lost and found—"

"I'm fine," I say, flustered. "Um, but I wonder . . . could I use your phone? We don't have long distance."

She motions me into a tiny office cluttered with files and papers and collectible lunch boxes. Batman, Disney, and every theme under the sun, crowded onto shelves and any other available surface. She points toward a cordless phone on the desk. "I'll leave you to it, then." The bell rings at the front desk. She rushes out, closing the door after her.

I call Dr. Gateman's office in Seattle.

"Obstetrics and Gynecology," a perky female voice says at the other end of the line. Time slows. My heart stops beating, then everything starts again at a frenetic pace.

"This is Dr. Gateman's office?" I say in a shaky voice. The line begins to crackle and hum. *Please, please keep the connection.*

"Yes, ma'am. How may I help you?" Phones are ringing in the background, the murmur of voices drifting through the line.

"I believe I was a patient there some time ago, maybe a year or two ago?"

"Would you like to make an appointment? Dr. Gateman is scheduling about three months out now." Static on the line. Her voice echoes.

"I just want some information. I've lost my memory . . . I was in an accident, and I need to piece together some things from my past."

"Oh, I'm so sorry! I'll leave a message for Dr. Gateman. I'm sure she will want to get back to you. She's on vacation right now."

"Is there anyone else I could speak to?"

"I'll see if I can get the nurse for you."

"Thank you." Relief rushes through me. She puts me on hold, and instrumental elevator music wafts into my ears. After about twenty seconds, the music stops, and a throaty voice comes on the line. "This is the nurse."

"I'm Kyra Winthrop . . . I was there a while ago to see Dr. Gateman. Do you remember me? I need my records. Quickly."

In the background, more telephones are ringing. The clock ticks on the wall. "I would have to pull up your file."

I let out a shaky breath. "That would be wonderful," I say, nearly fainting with relief.

"I need to verify that you are who you say you are."

"Kyra Winthrop," I say, my heart tapping in my ears.

"Hmmm. I don't have you in here."

No, no. A dead end. I spell out my name for her.

"That's how I spelled it. You're not in here."

"Was I there too long ago? Maybe I'm not in the computer?"

"We moved to an electronic system five years ago. If you came in since then, you would be in here."

"But then . . . I have to be."

"You're not. Anything else I can help you with?"

"Wait! The records could be under my maiden name, Munin. Kyra Munin."

More typing. "I do have you in here under Munin. Kyra?"

"Yes, that's me." I'm suddenly light-headed. I give her my Social Security number and my mother's maiden name.

"Are you still on Cedar Court?"

An image of a house flashes into my mind—a cedar A-frame with a metal roof and big windows. Then it's gone. "Cedar Court, no . . . I'm on Mystic Island now. Twelve Ocean View Lane."

"Okay, I'm pulling up your file . . . You were a patient for quite a while."

"I was married, right? But I used my maiden name?"

"Your status was married, yes. When you got pregnant."

When I got pregnant. I nearly drop the phone. The room vibrates around me. "Pregnant. I was pregnant."

"The first time was in April, two and a half years ago."

"The first time." Bile rises in my throat.

"You had a miscarriage in late June . . . You were about twelve weeks along."

I can't catch my breath. "A miscarriage?"

"Yes, I'm very sorry."

"Did I go into the hospital or . . . ?"

"Normally we don't hospitalize for an early miscarriage. The doctor might prescribe ibuprofen."

"I have a prescription with famotidine."

"To protect your stomach lining."

"And I didn't . . . go into the hospital or anything."

"No, you didn't. At least, we don't have a record of it."

"I see . . . And the next time . . ."

"Looks like early April of last year . . ."

"Another miscarriage?" My hands tremble. I can barely hold the phone.

"You were a little further along, but similar situation."

I gasp. Another one?

"Don't worry—there are many reasons why women miscarry. There's nothing necessarily wrong with *you.*"

"Nothing wrong with me. Clearly, there is something wrong with me."

I hear papers flipping. "You didn't have any infection or blood clotting abnormalities or a weak or tilted or septate uterus."

"What's a septate uterus?"

"A septate uterus means a uterus divided into almost two chambers by tissue. You don't have that. No fibroids or adhesions or diabetes or polycystic ovary syndrome."

"That's all good, right?" My voice is barely a thread.

"Are you all right? I'm throwing a lot of information at you."

"It's okay. I needed to know. What else is there? In my file?"

"That's all I have. So you were in some kind of accident?"

"Head injury," I say.

"I'm so sorry. I'll be sure to pass this along to Dr. Gateman. If there's anything we can do—"

"No, thank you. This is all I need for now. I appreciate your help."

"There's always hope, you know."

"Thank you." I hang up and bend over in the chair, holding my middle. My muscles seize up, and my hands go numb. The massage oil for spiritual healing. Our long summer trip to the island, to get away. The decision to escape, to leave the city. *You feeling better?* Rachel said at the mercantile. Jacob kept my medical history from me—what else is he holding back?

CHAPTER TWENTY-EIGHT

I knock on Sylvia's office door. No answer. The lights are off. I slip a note under the door, *I need to talk to you. It's urgent.* On the ride home, I pedal hard against the wind. Jacob greets me in the foyer. "Where have you been?"

"Why didn't you tell me?" I say as I hang up my coat.

"Whoa, you look upset. What's going on?" He tries to wrap his arms around me, but I stiffen and pull away.

"The miscarriages. Why didn't you tell me?"

All the blood drains from his face. "What are you talking about?"

"You knew about them."

He strides past me and sinks into the couch, rubbing his forehead with his fingertips. "How did this come up? How did you find out?"

"I shouldn't have had to *find out.*"

"You remembered."

"Not exactly. But I know about what happened. I called the doctor."

"Which doctor? Why? How . . . ?"

"It doesn't matter. The point is, you didn't tell me."

His shoulders slump. "I'm sorry. I didn't think it would come up. I thought it was behind us."

"*Everything* is behind us."

"I'll tell you everything you want to know."

"If I didn't know I had miscarriages, how could I ask you about them?"

"Believe me, my decision did not come easily."

"A lie of omission is still a lie. Did it happen here? The most recent miscarriage?"

He looks uncomfortable. "The fire's out. You need to get warm." He gets up abruptly and starts arranging logs in the woodstove.

"I need an answer. That's what I need." I'm shaky, a headache piercing my skull.

"What did the doctor tell you?"

"I spoke to the nurse. I had two miscarriages, but I might still be able to have children." I try to keep my voice steady. It's all I can do not to scream.

"How have you been making long-distance calls?"

"We don't have long distance here, so I called from the bed-and-breakfast."

"I'll add long distance to our line. It was an oversight. The technician has to come out from San Juan Island."

I nod, but it's the last thing I'm worried about right now. "What if I hadn't found out on my own?"

"There are reasons I didn't tell you."

"I hope they're good."

"Wait here. I'll be right back." He goes to his room. The hall clock ticks interminably, while acidic emotions eat through my stomach. Sadness, anxiety, and anger at Jacob. He returns a few minutes later carrying a small wooden box the size of a large hardcover book. The latch is made of polished brass. He places the box on the coffee table and sits on the couch, clasping his hands together on his lap, elbows on his thighs.

"What is this?" I say, touched by dread.

"Pandora's box. The reason for everything."

"What do you mean, everything?"

"The reason you got depressed."

"I was depressed."

"It was the reason we left Seattle and came here last summer. You wanted to be away from everything. So I brought you here. To get better."

"From the miscarriage? Why didn't you show this to me before?"

"I was going to show you, when you were ready."

"When did you think I would be ready?" I open the box, and the smell of scented powder wafts out. *Baby powder.* With trembling fingers, I pull out a tiny white jumper for a newborn. Pale purple leggings and a matching knit sweater. White booties. A rolled up, lavender-scented blanket, as soft as a puff of air.

Despite the roaring fire in the woodstove, the room is suddenly too cold. "What is this, Jacob? Why did you keep this from me?"

"You asked me not to show it to you."

"That's impossible."

"You wanted to forget. It was too painful for you. I thought, if you started to remember, then I would tell you. I'm sorry I didn't."

"I'm confused. I don't know what to think." I wipe tears from my eyes. He's right. This *is* painful. Even without my memory of the miscarriages. "What if I never started to remember on my own? Would you have eventually told me?"

"I don't know. Look, it's not just the baby clothing. You

need to see something else." He reaches into the bottom of the box, hands me a folded sheet of pale blue stationery. "I swear you didn't want me to say anything. This is *why* I didn't tell you." The letter reads, in my distinctive, bold handwriting from before the accident:

> *Dear Jacob,*
>
> *You have been here for me through all of the pain—a steady presence, the only person I can count on. I want more than anything to escape with you to Mystic Island. I want to forget everything. I'll go with you, to be away. Don't even mention the past. Don't even mention the way my body has betrayed me. Don't mention what is lost, ever again. Promise me. Cross your heart. I want to move forward from here.*
>
> *Love,*
> *Kyra*

I drop the letter on the coffee table. My words slant across the page, clear and direct. He was only following my wishes. "I'm sorry," I say. "I should've trusted you. It's just . . . this is so hard. Seeing these little outfits . . ."

"Maybe I shouldn't have brought out the box after all."

"I'm glad you did." I get up and go to the window. I need distance from the evidence, from the letter. The memory rises inside me. I wanted a girl. I wanted to show her the shells on the beach, sea stars, sea snails, bald eagles. Orcas, porpoises, migrating humpback whales. I wanted to be the tooth fairy, Santa, the Easter Bunny. Every rite of passage would fill me with wonder—her first words, first steps, first laugh, and her first gold star in the first grade.

I turn around to face him. "You said there were reasons

you didn't tell me. More than one, then. More than the letter?"

He exhales, rubs his temples. "The dive. I didn't tell you everything about the dive."

"What about the dive?" My feet grow heavy, immovable, as if they're cemented to the floor. "There *was* someone else drowning."

"No, it was you."

A beat of time passes, stretching into an eternity. "But you told me what happened. We were saved . . ."

"Did you ever think maybe you didn't want to be saved?"

"What? That's not even possible."

When he looks at me, his eyes are tortured. "You swam away from me. You swam into the strongest current."

"You're saying I wanted to drown? That's impossible. I'm not suicidal!" But in the fabric of my self-assurance, a tiny hole has been torn. Is there a version of me that wanted to die, under certain circumstances? Or at least to become oblivious?

"At first, I thought you had seen something spectacular. But you wanted to just take off and swim away . . . I went after you. I tried to save you. To get you to come back."

"You're saying I put you at risk. I put both of us at risk." My heartbeat thrums louder and louder in my head.

"You didn't intend to. But it happened. I went after you and you . . . ended up hitting your head. I managed to get us up onto the beach. If I hadn't acted quickly . . . We both would have died."

I want to say, *You're lying. It didn't happen that way. I could not have put both of us at risk.*

But I can't say another word. My voice dies in my throat, and my body has turned to stone.

CHAPTER TWENTY-NINE

"He should've told you about the miscarriages," Sylvia says. She has met me for an emergency session early in the morning. Her hair looks hastily combed, and she's in jeans and a sweater and sneakers. Without makeup, her features look more angular, but her expression is soft and kind—and genuinely worried.

I was up most of the night. Jacob slept alone in his room, to give us each some space and time to think. "Even with my note and what he says happened on the dive?"

She taps her pencil on her notebook. "He kept something very important, very emotional, from you."

"He was trying to protect me. I'm angry at him. At myself. For not trusting him, for writing that note in the first place. For pushing him too hard. But maybe he should've ignored my letter and shown me the baby clothes. Everything in that box. Maybe he should've had faith that I could handle the truth."

"Kyra, a thought just occurred to me. I hate to play devil's advocate, but are you sure he didn't show you the box before?"

Her suggestion stuns me, and for a moment, I can't speak. "I don't think so," I say finally. "If he had, he would've told me."

"But he didn't tell you about what really happened on the

dive—at least, not until you confronted him about the miscarriages."

The room feels suddenly cold. A thread is beginning to unravel in the cuff of my sweater sleeve. "That's true. Now he's saying I swam into the strongest current on purpose. But I can't imagine that I did. I don't get a sense that I was depressed . . . I'm guessing the miscarriages would've made me feel sad and hopeless, but . . ."

"But?"

"Still not enough to want to kill myself. I know people get that depressed, but . . . I can't imagine ever wanting to do away with myself. Life feels far too precious. But I don't know who I was a few months ago, or last year."

"Have you ever been deeply depressed?" she says, uncrossing her legs and recrossing them in the other direction. She looks at me directly.

"You mean before, in the years I remember?"

She nods, looking at me intently.

"No, never," I say without hesitation. "I've been sad, sure, but never sad enough to want to end it all. At least, I don't think so . . ."

"What do you mean, you don't think so?"

I take a deep breath. "In high school, I was pretty down and out. I was never in the popular group of kids. I wasn't a cheerleader type. I went to a large high school with lots of cliquish groups."

"Did you have any close friends?"

"A couple, but I made my closest friends in college. Anyway, I never wanted to hurt myself. I certainly wouldn't do it on a dive. I would take pills or something, just fall asleep and not wake up. Hypothetically speaking."

"Have you thought of doing that? Taking pills and not waking up?"

"No," I say. "Never!"

"I didn't think so."

My head is throbbing; the dizziness has returned. "Maybe Jacob doesn't want me to know the truth."

"What truth do you think that might be?" She sits very still, her pencil unmoving, the eraser end resting on her notebook.

"He's only ever lied to me to protect me. What if I might have done something terrible?"

"Like what?"

"Hurt someone, or . . ."

"Do *you* think you hurt someone?"

"It doesn't seem like me." I look out the window, at the changing clouds, the sky transforming itself from solid blue to an angry gray. *Drowning would work better.* The room moves in circles, the shadows whipping around and around, as if in a blender at slow speed. "I have to go. I need to think." I get up and make my way to the door.

"Are you all right?" Her voice is full of worry.

I turn to her and say, "Honestly, I don't know."

CHAPTER THIRTY

The air hangs heavy in the house, thick with unspoken secrets. *Unknown* secrets. This afternoon, Jacob and I have
barely spoken to each other. He's making pasta for dinner.
Now and then, I cast a sidelong glance in his direction. In
my office, I find no new messages from Linny. Maybe she's
out on a research vessel without access to email. Sometimes
she goes a couple of days without replying. I need to write
her a real letter, send it to Russia by snail mail. I check back
through our messages for her contact information, and I
search my computer files but I find only a defunct address
in Seattle.

I sign out of email and search Google again for information about the dive, but there is no mention of what might
have caused our accident aside from the treacherous currents. I turn off the computer and search through my files.
I do not find a journal or any notes I wrote that might give
me a clue.

In my room, I look through my books, my papers, my
belongings. The only subtle indication of my recent state of
depression: the clothes in muted, somber colors. Grays and
browns, blacks and dark blues. It was as if I wanted to blend
in and disappear.

In the bottom drawer of my dresser, beneath a gray

sweater, I find a pair of form-fitting exercise pants I haven't worn since we arrived. Did I ever wear pants so tight? Maybe I wore them for yoga or Pilates. I'm not a jogger. I pull out the leggings and a fragment of red fabric drops to the floor. I pick up the scrap of material, which must've clung to my pants in a dryer cycle. But it's not a scrap at all—it's a silk G-string with a narrow lace border. Underwear featuring a tiny triangle in the front, nothing but a string in the back.

I see my hand reaching out to take the G-string off a hanger in a lingerie shop. Silk teddies shine in a rainbow of colors on hangers. *Maybe a charmeuse,* I thought, looking at a loose satin sleeveless top. *Or a lace corset.*

Why not? He came up behind me. *I would love to unlace you.*

I blushed. *Corsets are too retro.*

No garters, either. I hate unfastening those things.

I turned to him. I touched his five-o'clock shadow. *So you've had experience unfastening those things?*

No, I'm imagining they would be hard to undo.

Uh-huh. Right. I gave him a look.

Seriously. I've never undone a garter, and corsets don't turn me on. They look uncomfortable. I can't believe women had to wear them for so damned long.

This is why I love you, I said, smiling up at him. *You want me to be comfortable.*

It's my mission in life.

I pulled a black transparent lace suit off a hanger. *How about a body stocking?*

Looks sexy, but way too much trouble to take off.

I showed him the G-string, and his eyes lit up. *That's what I'm talking about.*

I snap back to the present, collapsing on the bed, gripping

the G-string so tightly my fingernails dig into the palm of my hand. *I put on the G-string for him, somewhere else, not here. I wore nothing else.* He lay in bed, patted the mattress. *Come here, right now.*

A cloud passes over the sun. I can hear Jacob calling for me, telling me dinner is ready. I'm trembling all over. The memory sharpens. The bed, the light, the curves of his muscles. Were we in a hotel? A bed-and-breakfast? The location, the time, and what came before and after—the context eludes me. But I know for sure what we did that night, what we did for many nights. *Shhhhh, don't make a sound,* Aiden said, pressing his hand over my mouth. *Someone will hear.*

CHAPTER THIRTY-ONE

Jacob lit candles for dinner. They waver softly in the center of the table, sending a glow over our plates. He set two woven place mats close to each other, at right angles on the table. Cloth napkins, silver cutlery, two glasses of white wine.

"You went all out again," I say. "A bottle of wine, too?"

"From Van's collection," he says.

"This is lovely, but I'm not all that hungry." In truth, I'm not sure I could keep any food down.

"Here, sit." He pulls back my chair, and I sit.

"You're good at feeding me," I say, looking at the colorful salad tossed in a bowl on the table. He brings out ravioli and a bowl of tomato sauce.

"Homemade sauce," he says. "My own special recipe. No sugar. Most tomato sauce recipes include sugar."

"You're the healthiest man I've ever known."

"Only a touch of red pepper." He plunges the corkscrew into the wine bottle. "You don't like your food too spicy, but a little red pepper is good for you."

"Thank you," I say.

The popping sound makes me jump. Jacob holds up the corkscrew with the cork attached to the end. "First time I did this without losing the damned cork in the bottle."

"Good going," I say.

He pours me a half glass of wine and gives me a concerned look. "Are you okay?"

"I'm fine," I say, as casually as I can. The arms of the chair feel like the walls of a prison cell.

Jacob pours his own glass, sits in his chair. He gives me another peculiar look. "There's something wrong. You're still angry at me."

"Why would I be angry at you?" I'm sure I don't sound convincing.

His face falls, the corners of his lips turning down. "You have to believe I did what I thought you wanted." He gives me a pleading look. I've never seen such a vulnerable expression on his face.

"I believe you," I say.

He lifts his glass. "A toast to starting again, to trusting each other." He looks into my eyes.

"To starting again," I say halfheartedly, clinking my glass against his.

He opens the cloth napkin on his lap, and I mirror his actions. He grabs the salad tongs and places a generous portion on my plate. "When the vegetables mature in Mom's garden—I mean *our* garden—we can have our very own salad."

"That will be nice." I pick up my fork, put it down. "You went all out to make this a romantic dinner. Thank you."

"It's not working, is it?" he says, searching my eyes.

I touch his cheek. "It's not you, it's me."

"That's what people say when they're breaking up. Are you breaking up with me?" He doesn't really think this. His slight smile says that he's trying to be charming.

"No, I'm not. I'm telling you I'm flawed. I know I'm not

perfect. I never was, was I? Even though you keep telling me I was."

He looks at me. "But you are perfect to me." His words are laden with a different truth, running beneath them, unspoken. Did he know about Aiden? Is this why he hardly ever talks to him anymore?

I spoon a few squares of ravioli onto my plate. I barely taste the meal, although I smile and tell Jacob how good the food is, what a great job he did in the kitchen, as usual.

After dinner, we share fruit salad, and we load the dishwasher together. *This is the part I hate, having to be domestic,* Aiden said next to me that night, after I bought the G-string. *Let's leave all this. Life is too short.* He tugged me back toward the bedroom. He didn't mind the piles of unwashed dishes in the sink.

Jacob makes sure the plates and bowls are loaded neatly, then he uses the kitchen sponge to scrub the sink. "Stainless steel is not really stainless," he says.

Later, after I've changed into my pajamas, he stands in the doorway. "Good night, Kyra." He hesitates.

"Good night," I say, looking up at him. I'm brushing my hair on the bed.

"Will you tell me when you're ready for me to move back in here with you?"

"I will," I say, and I let him go.

I hardly sleep at all, and when I do, shadowy nightmares plague me. I wake with an acute uneasiness, but no specific images in my mind. In the morning, I make a pot of coffee and peanut butter toast for breakfast before Jacob is even up.

As I wash my face in the master bathroom, the scar on my thumb seems to pulse. I see it now, in a flash, Jacob throwing the soap, then hurling the soap dish, making a dent in the door. *What do you mean, you're not sure?* he shouts at me. I was picking up a shard of glass. The sharp edge cut my thumb. The blood seeped out of the wound and dripped on the floor. Why did Jacob tell me I cut my thumb on a dive? Did he want to pretend we never fought, that he never got angry?

After a quiet breakfast of coffee and cereal, he drives into town. The house, which once felt so airy and spacious, closes in on me, every shadow full of secrets. I flip through the photo albums. I'm in a kayak, on the beach, sipping morning coffee, eating a hard-boiled egg. Digging in the garden. In every picture, we seemed so happy together. Did Jacob carve out all evidence of problems between us? Hide it away?

I slip into his bedroom. The fragrance of laundry detergent and his familiar, spicy scent waft into my nose. He made his full-sized bed without a lump or a crease. In his closet, he folded pants and jeans over wooden hangers, arranged by color and style. Same goes for the shirts, sweaters, shoes. His dresser drawers offer up the same methodical arrangement of clothing. White undershirts folded just so. He even folds his briefs, trifolds his socks.

There are no photographs on the walls, no coins scattered on the dresser. His books on the nightstand are arranged from large to small, bottom to top, like an Egyptian pyramid of books. The top three paperbacks are thrillers. The hardcover on the bottom is *Atlas of Remote Islands.* I open the atlas, page through drawings of islands off the grid. Tromelin, in the Scattered Islands of France, is barely a strip of sand with a couple of palm trees. Ascension Island in the Atlantic Ocean, boasting 1,100 residents, is a wasteland of cooled lava. In the Arctic Ocean, only nine residents populate Norway's Bear Island.

Mystic Island is not in the book. Perhaps we're so remote we don't even make it into any books. A note slips out from between the pages, one of his lists. But this one strikes me as more cryptic than the others:

Photoshop
Update keywords: Kyra, Aiden, me
Linny email

Update keywords? What on earth does that mean? *Linny email.*

Why did Jacob write the note? Why did he include Aiden's name? I sit on the edge of the bed, staring at the list, trying to make sense of the words. My heart is racing. Is he trading emails with Linny? Or is he somehow reading my messages?

I can feel panic exploding to the edges of my body and I wrap my arms around myself, breathing deeply and rocking back and forth. After five minutes, maybe ten, I get up, fold the note into my pocket and put the book back in its place. The wind is rising outside. All I can think is, *I need to know the truth.*

I go to my office, sign into my email, and change my password. I start typing a message to Linny. *Are you talking to Jacob? Has anyone hacked into your account? Is anything strange going on?* No, I have to start again. If he's seeing the messages first, he could possibly alter the text. He would know I'm suspicious.

What am I doing? I start again.

> *Dear Linny,*
>   *Jacob might be reading these messages. If he is*

If he is . . . I start again.

> *Dear Linny,*
>   *Thank you for always being such a dear friend. I don't know what I would do without you. Memories have been coming back to me in pieces. I'm hopeful, now, that I might recapture the lost years of our friendship. If not everything, then at least the key moments. The carved giraffe you gave me, the one your mom brought back from Kenya, I can't find it. I've looked everywhere. That giraffe was one of my favorite, most cherished gifts from you. Do you think your mom would consider bringing back another one on her next trip? Xo, Kyra*

I turn off the computer, bundle up, and ride my bicycle into town through the cold wind. Nothing on the route suggests I ever came to the island with Aiden, but I slept with him many times. I feel him in my bones—his scent etched into my skin. Our affair was not a one-night stand. My relationship with him meant something to me. Where is he now? What is he doing?

In the protected bay, Van's boat is gone. He's on his way to Colombia. I ride back along the harbor, past the fishing vessels gently bobbing on the water. I don't see Jacob's truck anywhere. The mercantile is closed. The modest strip of downtown shops is all dark and silent, with an air of abandonment. The island feels desolate, uninhabited.

I stop in front of the library and gaze toward the ferry landing, and I see myself as I was that day, rolling my suitcase toward the waiting boat. Jacob strode after me. *Don't go, don't leave. This isn't right.*

I can't stay, I said, turning toward him. He looked bereft, his hair lit by the midday sun. I planned to take the last ferry. Was I planning to leave him for Aiden? *I'm sorry, Jacob.* Part of me didn't want to leave. A ghost of me stayed behind. The decision to leave was not easy, the truth was not clear. I hesitated. I almost turned back. The summer waned around us. The days were still warm, but the nights were growing cool. Our idyllic summer of rediscovery on the island—it hadn't worked. The wounds had not healed.

I hoped if I brought you here . . . , he said.

I hoped so, too, I said.

You shouldn't leave. You're making a mistake. It's not what you want, to go back to him. We can have a family, you and I . . . I know that we can.

My hands tighten on the handlebars. What happened between us? If Jacob is reading my email, perhaps censoring what I see, is he trying to protect me from the truth? Does Linny know what really happened?

The door to the library swings open. "Kyra!" the librarian, Frances, says. "You're down here early. I've been meaning to contact you, but I got busy with orders for the school. You're going to want to see what I found. Took me a while. I had to do some digging."

I park my bike and take the stairs up two at a time. In the warmth of the library, I follow her to her desk. The smells of old wood and dust waft up to me. She rummages through the drawers. "I knew I had it here. I had to talk to the old librarian. Something nagged at me about the paintings. Here it is!" She opens a manila file folder and shows me a photocopy of an old newspaper clipping.

"What is it?" I say, my heart thumping.

"It's from 1977. The *Bugle of the San Juan Islands*." She points at a man and woman. The man, dressed in a T-shirt and coveralls, is helping a woman step from a yacht onto the dock. In contrast to his rough appearance, she's a breath of brightness in a floral summer dress, her dark hair fashionably tousled by the wind. The caption at the bottom reads, *Tourist Season Heats Up on Mystic Island.*

"That's Douglas Ingram," I say. "And the woman . . ."

"Yes, the woman," she says. "Shocked me, too. There was no story to go with the picture. Just the caption."

There is something terribly familiar about her, in the shape of her face, the arch of her eyebrows, her cheekbones. The eyes, too—the pensive, guarded expression. Her wild, dark hair tumbles past her shoulders. She's smiling, her face turned up to the sun.

"She's the woman from the painting," I say.

Frances nods.

"She definitely looks like me." The resemblance is not exact. But the similarities between this woman and me are so striking; I could be looking at a version of myself. She appears to be in her early twenties.

"She does look a lot like you," the librarian says. "You must be related to her."

"But I'm not. Who was she?"

"I wasn't here back then, but you might want to ask Doug."

I fold the photograph into my pocket and ride my bicycle up the main road, eventually turning left at the gnarled Western red cedar. A soft rain has begun to fall. The bumpy, overgrown driveway gently slopes downhill, winding through a meadow and a copse of trees. A log house appears in a clearing, a plume of smoke rising from the chimney. I park my bike and take the stone footpath to the front porch. I climb the steps with a pounding heart. Before I raise my hand to knock, the door swings open. Doug Ingram peers at me through sleepy eyes. He's wearing a loose-knit sweater, jeans, and slippers. His white hair flies wild, as if he last brushed it a decade ago.

"I thought I was dreaming," he says. "But I wasn't, was I? You look so much like Malinda."

CHAPTER THIRTY-TWO

"I'm Kyra Winthrop. Remember?"

He looks confused. "What are you doing here?"

I show him the picture. "The librarian found this in the archives."

His gnarled fingers tremble, and his eyes soften with sadness. He looks up at me. "Why don't you come in?"

I enter a bright room full of rustic wood furniture, the walls adorned with watercolor paintings of the island—the ocean views through the mist, the cedar forest, deer, and seashells. The smell of pine. The coffee table, made of a sliced stump, is neatly stacked with magazines. A fire crackles in a woodstove in the corner.

"I'll put the kettle on," he says, shuffling to his left, through an open doorway to a small kitchen. I hear pots and pans clanking, and he comes back out looking at me and shaking his head. "Remarkable."

"When did you know her? Malinda? This photo was taken nearly forty years ago."

"Was it, now? Time flies. I've been here a lot longer than that." He points to a faded photograph of men squinting in the sun in green army fatigues, sweating, with their caps pulled down over their faces. One shirtless man has a cigarette hanging out of his mouth. The man kneeling at the far right in the front row looks familiar.

"That's you," I say, pointing at the man. He's young, handsome, and clean-cut. The man in the photograph from the library. "When was this taken?"

"Circa 1964. I was barely out of high school."

"You were in Vietnam. How did you end up here?"

"Had to come up this way for alternative service. Heard about the islands. Lasqueti, Waldron, the likes. I settled on Lasqueti first. After the war, I came down here."

"Those were your army buddies? In the picture?"

"Lost three over there. Two more to Agent Orange. Only one still alive, last I heard."

"I'm sorry about your friends."

The kettle whistles, and he disappears again, returning with a tray holding a white teapot and two matching teacups on saucers. He pours two cups and hands me one. The liquid smells smoky.

"Lapsang souchong," he says. "My daughter's favorite."

"You have a daughter?"

"Out near Bellevue. Works for Microsoft."

"How often do you see her?"

"It's been years." He sips the tea, returns the cup to the saucer, his fingers trembling. "She writes to me, wants me to visit. I know what she's got up her sleeve. She wants to put me in one of those old folks' homes."

"Did she say that?"

"Not in so many words."

"Maybe she just wants to see you. You're her dad."

"I was a bad father, left when she was little. She can't believe I've been thinking of her all these years. But I have."

"You could visit her. She can't force you into a retirement home. It's your choice."

"Not much is our choice in this life," he says, looking into his teacup. He puts the picture of him and the woman on the coffee table between us.

"Who was she?" I say. "Malinda?"

"Her full name was Malinda Winthrop."

Winthrop. Malinda Winthrop. My mind does a flip. The liquid thickens in my cup. I can't get my bearings. *Winthrop, Malinda Winthrop.* "Are you sure? Winthrop?"

"Winthrop. Her married name. It's been so long. You're related to her?"

"I only look like her. Coincidence."

"Well, I'll be damned," he says.

"This means I'm married to her son, Jacob Winthrop. Doesn't it?"

"Ahhh. Yes." His eyes narrow. "She did have a son. It's been so long."

"We're living in the house on the bluff, the one they used to stay in."

He nods, his eyes sad. He seems suddenly much older and frailer than he was only a minute ago.

"If you don't mind my asking, what was your relationship with her?"

"My memory isn't so good anymore. I don't remember dates or when exactly she left for good, but I remember *her*. Like it was yesterday. Her voice, her hair. Her perfume."

"You painted such a beautiful likeness."

"It was love at first sight. For me, anyway."

"You fell in love with a married woman."

"Everyone fell in love with Malinda. Couldn't help it. She was an angel."

"How did you meet her?"

"I was a commercial fisherman in those days. Met her in the harbor. She didn't have a son yet. But she was married. It was her husband's yacht. Big-time businessman. All pompous and whatnot."

"Did you two become involved at that time? You and Malinda?"

"No, we weren't involved yet. Her husband was a bloody bastard, but she stuck by him."

"How do you mean?"

"It was a long time ago now . . . He treated her like dirt. Beautiful, kind woman like that . . . He hit her. She tried to cover it up but it was obvious to everyone around her."

"He must have charmed her in the beginning. Before his true personality emerged?"

He touches the picture gently, as if he's touching Malinda herself. "I thought for sure she would leave him. I told her I would always be here for her. She knew where to find me."

"But she didn't leave him."

"They had the son, and . . ." He puts his cup and saucer on the coffee table, gets up, and goes to the window. "The day we started . . . it was a sunny summer afternoon. She came up those stairs, just like you did. By herself. She must've told her husband she was taking a walk. She must've decided she was ready."

"Ready for what? To leave him?"

"She wanted to leave but she couldn't."

"You had an affair with her."

He scratches a bald spot on the top of his head. "Wasn't an affair. I was in love, like I said."

"Was she in love with you?"

"I thought she was."

I look down into my tea. "What happened? Your love affair ended?"

"We were together as much as we could be for a time. But she was devoted to her boy."

"She couldn't leave her son," I say.

"I was supposing so. I never met the kid. But she talked about him a lot."

"Why didn't she bring him to you? If she loved you?"

"She said if she left her husband, he would come after her. He would have her committed. He would make out that she was crazy and take the kid. She couldn't let him take the boy."

"Did he find out about you and Malinda?"

"All I know is, she showed up one day and said it was over. She never came back to me. They kept visiting the island for years, on and off, but she kept her distance."

"That must've been hard. To see her but not be with her."

He looks down at his gnarled, trembling fingers. "It's hard even now. I pleaded with her, tried to get her to see reason, but she wouldn't budge. That man had some kind of hold over her. It was hell for a while but time heals . . . or so they say."

"You lost touch with her."

"When I saw you, it was like I went right back to that time."

I pick up the picture. "Thank you for talking to me." My mind is turning in frantic circles. "Would you be willing to talk to me again?"

"Come back anytime. I don't get many visitors around here."

CHAPTER THIRTY-THREE

As I ride my bicycle home, my panic level rises. Every man marries his mother, right? There's nothing wrong with this picture. Nothing untoward. It shouldn't matter that I look so much like Jacob's mother. But it does. During the four years I've lost, did I know about my resemblance to her? If so, did I find the likeness strange, troubling?

When I reach the house, Jacob's not home, but he came back while I was away. He left a mug on the counter. I traipse outside through the wind to the garden. The white stakes, labeling the plants, have multiplied. In addition to the labels I found, Jacob has added new ones to mark beets, chives, garlic, and a myriad of other herbs and vegetables. But the labels are old, all of them printed in his mother's handwriting. Every single one of them.

I turn and run back to the house. Whitecaps roar in across the sea, portending a storm.

In my office, I boot up my computer with trembling fingers. I enter "Malinda Winthrop" in the Google search box. Only a few hits appear, referring to other Malinda Winthrops. No information about Jacob's mother. Nothing at all.

In the living room, I flip through the photo albums again. Photos of Malinda were taken from a distance. This I already knew. I search in vain for a single close-up. She's on the yacht in a wide headband, bell-bottom jeans, and sunglasses, dangling her legs over the side. Young Jacob points out to sea. His father looks very much the way Jacob looks now—tall, handsome, with a quirky nose and a slightly lopsided grin. But Malinda is always far away. There are no photographs of Jacob as a teenager or adult before I met him.

I page through the pictures of Jacob and me, on the beach, taking a selfie, dancing at the wedding. Out to dinner with friends. The photograph of Aiden on the bluff brings back the memory of falling into his arms. Only this time, I see him hiking ahead. He turned to summon us. *Come on, you two. You're always lagging.* I ran after him, but Jacob hung back, determined not to hike any faster. I caught up to Aiden, and he winked at me. We shared a secret. The photograph is printed from Jacob's computer. The red ink was running low—Aiden's hair shows a subtle blue tint, from the blue ink. *Blue ink.*

Jacob, so careful to straighten edges, to make his bed to perfection. Jacob, married to a woman who looks uncannily like his mother.

Blue-tinted photographs. *Photoshop, Linny email.*

On my office computer, I check my email and find a reply from Linny.

Dear Kyra,

Sorry I took so long to get back to you. I was out on a research run. What an amazing place this is. But I miss you. As for the giraffe, too bad you can't find the carving! I'll ask my mom about getting you another one, but I can't guarantee a replacement. She may not go back

*to Kenya—she's got a few other countries on her radar.
But I'll check with her. Don't worry, we'll have many
new gifts for you. Xo,*

Linny

I push my chair back, her words pulsating across the
screen. *No, it can't be.* A man so careful, so meticulous. He
has no idea. How else could he reply? He couldn't possibly
know the truth. He swallowed the bait, *hook, line, and sinker.*
Masquerading as Linny, he couldn't reply the way Linny
would reply. I could've done a better job of impersonating
her. I know her so much better than he ever did. I know the
secret she kept about her mother. Pretending to be Linny, I
might've replied:

Dear Kyra,

*What are you talking about? You must've forgotten.
Growing up, I decided the minute I could leave home,
I would fly and fly and fly. So I did. I made a point of
flying as often as I could, as far as I could. I did not
want to be trapped at home like my mom was, stuck
in her small world. They say when you get on a plane,
60% of the people around you—six in ten, that is—
are afraid of flying. They worry the plane will crash.
They're afraid of turbulence. The fear comes from your
utter lack of control. You're hurtling through the air at
four hundred miles per hour, thirty thousand feet above
earth. If there's an accident, it's catastrophic. In a plane,
there is no such thing as a fender bender. You're going to
die a sudden, horrible, fiery death.*

My mother could never live with that. So she never

flew. You know that better than anyone. You had to overcome your fear of flying, too . . . So I'm sorry to tell you, my mom never went to Kenya. She never brought you a carving of a giraffe. She never brought you a carving of anything. Check your memory banks, and you'll know this is true.

Xo,
Your best friend,
Linny

CHAPTER THIRTY-FOUR

I pace in my office, my breathing fast and shallow. Not only has Jacob been reading my messages to Linny, intercepting her messages to me—he's been *writing* her responses. I can't trust anything she wrote to me. I click back through her previous messages. Were any of them actually from her? At what point did Jacob start to intercept them? He may have impersonated me, too.

I look out the window at the woodpile, at the split logs carefully organized in the bin. Jacob wants to bring order to our lives, to our surroundings. Perhaps our marriage had spun away into chaos, and he's trying to shield me from yet another truth, something worse than two miscarriages. He could be trying to protect me. Why does he not want me to contact Linny? Maybe something has happened to her.

Horrible possibilities race through my mind. Linny was on the dive with us. She died. She ran out of air. But this can't be true. The news articles reported only two people on the dive. I have to believe Linny's okay. Maybe she knows something, a secret Jacob doesn't want me to discover. If I planned to leave him for Aiden, I might have told her. She might know I was ready to divorce Jacob.

I take Jacob's latest list from my pocket, the one I found in *Atlas of Remote Islands*.

Pʜᴏᴛᴏsʜᴏᴘ
Uᴘᴅᴀᴛᴇ Kᴇʏᴡᴏʀᴅs: Kʏʀᴀ, Aɪᴅᴇɴ, ᴍᴇ
Lɪɴɴʏ ᴇᴍᴀɪʟ

Photoshop.
Blue-tinted photographs.
In the living room, I search through the photo albums yet again. Some pictures are clearly originals, while others are printed from digital versions. The wedding photographs are all printed. Blue-tinted pictures. The color always looked off to me, but now, even more so. *What is wrong?*
Photoshop.
Update Keywords.
You were a hacker, weren't you?
An ethical hacker.
We make our own world.
Back at my computer, I open Google and type "definition of keyword." *Keywords are words or phrases that describe content . . . Whenever you search . . . you type keywords that tell the search engine what to search for.*
What would Jacob be updating?
I enter a benign term, "rose garden," in Google. Instantly, a number of hits pop up for the Rose Quarter in Portland, Oregon; the White House Rose Garden; and others. For "broccoli salad," images of broccoli salads pop up, an Allrecipes recipe, a *New York Times* recipe, and other variations. I type in "solar system" and the Wikipedia entry appears

above NASA's Solar System Exploration page, *National Geographic*, and "Solar System Facts" on Space.com.

On his list, he wrote, *Update Keywords: Kyra, Aiden, me.* I type "Jacob Winthrop" in the Google search box, and I'm thrown offline. *You're not connected to the Internet.* My heart knocks against my ribs. I reboot the computer, but I can't get online.

Did this happen every time I logged on? The Internet allowed my benign keyword searches but not the personal ones? I try to think back through my previous Google searches, but they blend together. I didn't consider any connection between the keywords I entered and the Internet cutting out. I thought it was an intermittent faulty satellite connection on a remote island. But what if it wasn't?

Did he set up my Internet connection to crash when I entered certain keywords? Invariably, the Internet would work again after a few hours or the next day. Giving him time to do what? Alter the search results? The idea is far-fetched. But the dominos fall into each other, collapsing one after the other.

Photoshop.

I check the landline. Still no dial tone. I don't even get static, nothing. I yank on my sneakers and rush out into the driving wind and rain. I'm soaked when I reach the cottage. The door is unlocked. His office is neat, tidy, cedar-scented. The woodstove is loaded with logs in a careful, symmetrical arrangement. The plush armchair invites me to sink into its cushions. Beside the burnished oak desk, the standing lamp casts its warm glow across the room. The framed photograph on the desk shows the two of us dancing at the wedding reception. In the room to my left, the weight bench and exercise equipment give up no secrets. In the supply room to the right, everything is neatly organized—paper on shelves, boxes of envelopes, his printer, boxes of ink. Extra pens.

In his office, I sit in the chair at his desk. A screen saver shows a school of bright orange fish swimming across his computer monitor. He could be hiding secrets on his hard drive. I move the mouse, and the screen saver disappears, revealing the login window reading, *Enter Password*. I try my name, his name, the name of our street, the island, the telephone number, my Social Security number. Nothing works. Then I try his mother's name, Malinda. This has to work.

But it doesn't. My husband is not stupid. That much I know. He could have hidden a hint to his password somewhere in this room. In the center drawer of his desk I find pens, envelopes, rubber bands, paper clips—the usual office supplies. In the top right drawer, bills to be paid—electricity, telephone. A paper calendar with nothing written on it.

I'm shaking, my damp clothes clammy against my skin. Outside, the crashing of waves mingles with the roar of the storm. I peer out the window. No sign of his truck on the road, but he could return at any moment. I need to log into his computer. The answers must lie here. He probably chose a complicated password. That would be the smart thing to do. Jacob is smart.

But what is his weakness? His obsession?

On a hunch, I type in "lemon thyme," his mother's favorite plant. Nothing.

What was the scientific term? If nothing else, my background in marine biology taught me to remember complicated words. I type in *thymuscitriodorus*, running the two words together, *Thymus* and *citriodorus*. I'm surprised I remembered them. The screen turns blue for a moment, and then the word plays across the screen, reading, *Welcome,* and I'm in. An icon on the task bar indicates the computer is connected to the Internet.

With trembling fingers, I enter "Kyra Winthrop" in the Google search box. The Internet does not crash. Instead, numerous links pop up. The first page shows a few other Kyras. I scroll through the hits, but I can't find anything recent. Nothing about the accident, the dive. Nothing about me. The results don't match the hits that popped up on my computer when I searched the Internet. The question is, why? An idea comes to me.

I peer behind his computer. A gray cable extends from the back of the chassis to the satellite Internet router on a shelf beneath the desk. Could he be routing the Internet through his computer first, before any information reaches my computer? The idea seems improbable, and yet. His words echo in my mind, from our dinner with Nancy and Van. *I'm the boss. I can make anything possible.*

I enter "Kyra Munin" next, and a photo album from a wedding photographer's website pops up: *Kyra's Wedding.* I'm in a familiar, shimmering dress. We're sitting on a stone wall in a tight embrace, cheek to cheek. I blink, look at the photograph again, and rub my eyes. Aiden is wearing a dashing tuxedo. I click back to the main page, *Aiden and Kyra, August 20. Friday Harbor. Our Wedding Day.*

CHAPTER THIRTY-FIVE

In the photographs, late-afternoon sunlight casts faint halos around Aiden and me. Of course we were married three years ago. I've always known. The truth waited patiently in the shadows, hoping to be found. Aiden and I fell deeply, fiercely in love. We planned to be together for the rest of our lives. Here we are, sitting on the stone wall holding hands, gazing into each other's eyes.

The wedding photographer left no setting unexplored. We're running together at the beach, in the forest, hand in hand. Locked in a passionate embrace, kissing. Framed by the sunset. We're standing close to each other, facing each other, with a blur of greenery in the background. Aiden lifts my hand to his lips. I'm smiling up at him. I'm a few pounds heavier, with thick lashes, pink cheeks.

In another artsy shot, a dried sea star rests on a table-cloth, holding a wedding ring on each of its arms. The rings are engraved with iconic Northwest Native depictions of the orca. I remember now. We chose the rings together. We wrote our own vows. We never wanted to be conventional. Aiden gazed down at me, the afternoon sunlight on his hair. His fingers trembled as he held my hands. I hoped nobody could see how nervous I was. The day was pleasantly warm. I could feel our friends watching from their seats, surprised by our hasty decision to marry, but delighted for us all the same. The officiant, a balding man in thick glasses, nodded gently to Aiden, urging him to begin. Aiden cleared his throat and said, *I'm glad to be on this planet, hurtling through space with you, celebrating each moment of our love. I can't wait to find out what tomorrow will bring. I get to spend the rest of my life with you* . . .

The script of our ceremony appears on the screen, but the words blur through my tears. How could I have forgotten? I floated through the wedding on a cloud. I thought, *I will never be happier than I am today.*

Beneath my joy ran a current of melancholy. My parents would never share in my happiness. My father could not give me away. My mother could not help me choose my gown. But I felt their presence in the ocean air wafting over us, clean and salty, in the waves whispering our names. My heart was full of adoration, full of love.

The next dreamy photographs show Aiden and me exchanging rings. I said, *I will always be kind to you, and faithful, and forgiving* . . . Aiden said, *These are only rings, two chunks of metal. What I give you is my complete devotion, my undying love.*

I replied, *Our love cannot be lost, exchanged, or stolen. Unlike these rings, we cannot remove our devotion to each other, now or ever.*

As I said, *now or ever,* I spotted Jacob sitting in the front row of the audience, looking in my direction, his gaze focused, riveted on me. The other guests were smiling, and Linny wiped a tear from her cheek. But Jacob's face was tight, his lips set in a line. He didn't look happy for us, not even a bit. And when the guests threw lavender buds as a send-off, he stood motionless on the curb. Aiden drove us away in his convertible, and I looked back over my shoulder to wave at our friends. Jacob was the only one who didn't wave back. He dropped his cone of lavender buds on the sidewalk, then he turned and walked away.

CHAPTER THIRTY-SIX

The sunshine of that August day disappears. The pounding rain intrudes on my memory. A raging wind rattles the windows. I push Jacob's chair back from his desk, my mind spinning. A more complete picture begins to take shape. I'm falling into Aiden's arms on the trail, showing him the chiton on the beach, buying a silk G-string. I did all these things . . . *with my husband.*

Look at this ring, I said to Aiden. I was excited by the intricate carving, lit from above in the display case. Cars rumbled by; voices drifted around us in Pike Place Market. The fish stands smelled dank, of the sea, the sour odors mixing with the sweet, heady floral scents, the lavender lotions. The crowds jostled past us. Aiden came up next to me. He had to bend down to see inside the case.

Nice, he said.

They're hand-carved by a local artist, I said.

Let's get them.

But you don't even know the price.

You can't put a price on love.

We could look at other options.

What other options? We could look forever. Let's get these.

That's another thing I love about you, I said.

My inability to manage money?

No, your decisiveness.

It never does any good to waffle, he says. *Your first instinct was good. You love orca carvings. We buy the orca rings. While we're on the subject, why wait? Let's get married, right now. Right here.*

I laugh. *Now? But I'm in jeans. We don't have anyone to perform the ceremony. It's too fast! I want our friends to be there. I need to plan, send out invitations.*

Okay, compromise. We'll plan a little. Tell them it's a special event . . . We'll surprise them. They won't know why they're dressing up.

Let's think about this, I say.

There's nothing to think about. You think too much. Tell them you're celebrating a special birthday in Friday Harbor . . . We'll shock them with a wedding. Last minute. I don't want to be without you . . .

You're not without me.

I want to tie the knot with you. As soon as possible.

All right, I say, giggling. *This is crazy, but okay.*

A week or so later, or was it two? When the guests arrived in Friday Harbor, they knew they were attending a special event, but they didn't know what to expect. Jacob didn't know. When he found out, he burst into the powder room at the Victorian Valley Chapel, out of breath. *What are you doing? You're rushing into this. You've known Aiden only a few weeks.*

A few months, I say.

Hardly any time at all. Almost as long as you've known me. How much time do we need?

More time than this.

You shouldn't be in here.

Yes I should. Kyra, are you sure this isn't too fast, too soon? He was not the groom checking on the bride. He was the best man, trying to convince me to postpone the ceremony. To cancel the wedding altogether.

With each click of the mouse, more breath is knocked from my lungs. In another photo, Linny helps me to do my hair. *Wow, you threw us all for a loop!* Several black-and-white still shots show Aiden and me on the dock in Friday Harbor, against a backdrop of old buildings, at the wedding with a small group of friends, including Jacob. The best man. Smiling, like he didn't care. But now I detect the tightness in his lips, the way his smile did not reach his eyes.

What happened after my wedding to Aiden? *Breathe, in and out, keep your cool. Don't panic.* Slow on the exhale. The moments swirl in eddies and currents. *What is going on here? What happened on the dive?*

I click back to Google and read through the news. We were rescued, Jacob and I, but there was a third person diving with us. The shadowy diver. Aiden. He was there all along. Jacob must've altered the news, controlling what I saw on my computer. It seems too fantastic, unreal. And yet entirely possible, especially for a former programmer and hacker.

The news articles, the *real news*, reveal the truth.

Aiden Finlay was swept away by the currents in Deception Pass, but he was picked up by a coast guard boat, unconscious. He fell into a coma.

He was on the dive with us.

He was picked up.

My heart gallops; I can't catch my breath. Where is he now? What led to the three of us diving together? Why did Jacob lie to me? What am I doing here? I'm blinded by intense loathing for Jacob, a wild rage, and . . . an overwhelming sense of relief. Aiden was on the dive, and he's still alive.

Aiden Finlay's friend, Jacob Winthrop, who was also on the dive, and Aiden Finlay's wife, Kyra Munin-Finlay, who suffered a traumatic head injury, made it to a secluded beach. Munin-Finlay was airlifted to Harborview Medical Center in Seattle for treatment. *I am Kyra Munin-Finlay.* I'm still Aiden's wife.

What life have I been living here? The office, Jacob's computer—everything in here. It's all unreal. *What happened? How did I end up here?*

I remember sleeping with Jacob before. I know I did. But when? Did I leave him to marry Aiden? Or was I never married to Jacob? None of this makes any sense. My breathing comes fast and shallow.

Jacob is not my husband. *He is not my husband.* My heart hammers. My hands are tingling. *Breathe, in and out, focus. Keep yourself together.*

I was married to Aiden. I *am* married to Aiden. *He's still alive.* Jacob, Aiden's friend—how did he manage to take me away, to bring me to the island? Who else knows I'm here? *Does anyone know?*

Why didn't I notice? There is no picture of Jacob and me reciting our vows. No image of the exchange of rings. In the blue-tinted pictures in the living room, we're posing with friends, or dancing, or eating wedding cake. The pictures were printed from his computer. He was at the wedding.

There is Jacob, standing to the left of the wedding cake, walking toward me, while I stood to the right. Aiden was out of the picture. Jacob kissing my cheek. Jacob swinging me on the dance floor . . . *May I dance with the bride?*

Was this Jacob's plan all along, to take away my memory? But it couldn't have been. He could not have known I would hit my head on the dive. Did he try to kill me? Or Aiden? Or both of us?

CHAPTER THIRTY-SEVEN

I'm shaking all over, my heart beating so fast I'm afraid I might pass out. Jacob will find me on the floor of his office, and what will he do? On his desktop, he has arranged several folders in alphabetical order. Many of them are work-related document folders, but a familiar name catches my eye. I click on the folder marked *Linny*. A series of message files pops up—containing her emails to me.

> *Kyra, did you get my message yesterday? Something is wrong with my email.*
> *. . . I'm trying your old email address . . .*
> *. . . I've been trying to email you for two weeks, no reply. I'm worried about you . . .*
> *. . . called the hospital. The doctors won't tell me what's going on, only that you checked out of rehab last week . . .*
> *Making plans to come back, can't reach you. Aiden says you left him.*

How could Jacob do this? How could he intercept her messages and keep them from me? Why? In another sub-folder, he included my messages to her, the ones that never reached her. He read the messages and sent me fake replies. *You're in the perfect marriage to Jacob . . . Don't mess this one up*. No wonder I thought Linny had changed so much in four years. She wasn't Linny at all.

A little further down on the desktop, I find a folder marked *Aiden*. I wipe tears from my eyes, take a deep breath. The first message reads,

> *Dear Kyra,*
>
> *When I woke in the hospital, you weren't here. Why didn't you come to see me? The doctors told me you'd been rescued, but you had head injuries and for a while, memory gaps. Even after you recovered, it's hard for me to believe that you remember everything, otherwise, how could you leave me—us—so abruptly?*
>
> *Jacob tells me that you were never quite the same after your injuries. That the Kyra we both knew had become cold, distant—and that you kept saying that you'd made a mistake in coming back to me. I didn't believe him—until he brought me your letter. Why didn't you bring it yourself? Were you afraid if you faced me, you wouldn't be able to go through with it? At first, seeing your familiar handwriting filled me with hope. Until I kept reading.*
>
> *We need to meet. I have to talk to you in person. I love you.*
>
> *Aiden*

Did I meet him in person? What happened after he wrote this first message? I click on the next one.

> *Dear Kyra,*
>
> *I can't believe you stood me up. If you weren't ready, as you say, you should have let me know. I waited and*

waited for you. If you really believe the things you wrote, I have to let you go. But we could have at least met to talk. I should never have walked out on you, I realize that now, but I deserve to hear that face to face.

I want more than anything for you to be happy. If this accident has taught me anything, it's that we have to try for what we want in life.

Aiden

What happened? The moments, the days, come back to me now, a tidal wave of remembered hours with Aiden, flooding my mind. Aiden and I, when our marriage began to crack, before I ever came to the island with Jacob.

CHAPTER THIRTY-EIGHT

Before

I can't wait to get home to Aiden. But it's a long haul from Alki Beach. Traffic slows through downtown, then thins out toward North Seattle. When I finally walk in the front door, he kisses my cheek. "You taste like salt. How was your day at the beach?"

My lower back aches, and I feel as though I could sleep for a year. "We were studying marine invertebrates. I expected to see more shield limpets but I saw only one."

"Shield limpet. Another fascinating species I've never heard of."

"The shell is striped. They live on rocks, and they can actually create a depression in the stone. It allows them to hold on in rough weather."

"Maybe we could learn from them," he says, taking my coat. It is now that I notice the dabs of paint on his clothes.

"You ruined those sexy jeans," I say.

"These? They're old," he says, taking my hand. "I want to show you what I did today, while you were out being a mermaid." He leads me back down the hall, which feels like a long way. My legs are leaden, the dull ache in my back more insistent.

Just outside the nursery door, he stops and turns to face me. "Blindfold."

I place my hands over my eyes, playing the game, knowing he needs me to be enthusiastic. But what I really want to do is lie down. He leads me into the room.

"Ta-da!" he says.

I open my eyes and draw in a sharp breath. "You did all of this yourself?"

"More or less." Along one wall, he's installed white shelves filled with picture books. He's added a crib, chest of drawers, and a Winnie-the-Pooh lamp. He's painted the walls in a soft shade of blue, but I'm drawn to the tree, its lush foliage taking up an entire wall, an owl peering out—and birds in the sky. A soft breeze ruffles feather-light curtains. "It's perfect," I say, tears in my eyes.

He wraps his arms around my waist, kisses the top of my head. "I had the weirdest dream last night," he says. "Our daughter was already four."

"Daughter," I say. "How do you know it's a girl?"

"I have a feeling."

"We decided we don't want to know," I say.

"I dreamed we were in the playground in the backyard, which means I have to build one. It was so damned clear. She wanted to ride the horsey . . ."

"What was she like?"

"She had long dark hair, wavy like yours, but she had my double-jointed thumb. She pouted the way you pout, very effective with the bottom lip."

"She's not even born yet."

"I know, but the dream was so vivid."

A sliver of uneasiness works its way under my skin. The backache, my deadening fatigue. I know, even now, I already know. It's happening again. A sudden, sharp pain doubles me over, and he lets go of me. "What's wrong?" I hear him say from a distance. I run to the bathroom. He's at the door, asking questions, but I keep saying I'm okay, I'll be out in a minute. But he can tell that I'm not okay. He knows the vision of his daughter is already a pipe dream.

At night in bed, Aiden pulls me into his arms.

"I'm sorry," I say.

"It's not your fault," he says, stroking my hair. "It wasn't meant to be." I don't know if he means the little girl, this pregnancy, or our marriage.

"Maybe not," I say.

"We'll try again." But his voice sounds deflated, hopeless.

"What if we can't?"

"Didn't Dr. Gateman say we could?"

"What if she missed something? This is the second time."

A deep silence follows. "Maybe it's stress," he says finally. "We could move away from here. Go to San Juan Island. I'll start my own company." He sounds desperate, as if he's casting around for a solution.

"If it's what you want," I say.

"It's what we need. A change of pace."

"Just like that. You want to move."

"Why not?"

"Maybe we shouldn't make any hasty decisions this time."

He takes a deep breath. "Yeah, you're probably right."

In the morning, something has changed, as if the world of our marriage has tilted on its axis. Aiden seems pensive, distant. He kisses my forehead before he goes to work. No kiss on the lips, no smile of hope and promise. There is a wedge of loss between us. In the nursery, the leaves on the trees seem to be falling.

In the afternoon, a text comes in from Jacob. *Aiden shared the news. I'm so sorry.*

Thank you, I type with a twinge of annoyance. Why did Aiden share this private loss with Jacob? *Our* private loss. *My* private loss. But Aiden and Jacob are friends. Aiden needed to tell his boss what was going on, especially if he's distracted at work. He needs someone to talk to.

I don't mean to pry, Jacob texts. *But he shared on his own.*

Of course, I text back. *I appreciate your concern.*

If there's anything I can do . . .

Thank you, I say again, but what can he do? What's done is done.

The next two evenings are quiet, and Aiden and I tiptoe around each other, speaking little, focusing on inconsequential subjects. Neither one of us can bear to go into the nursery. We've closed the door. We walk past the room, giving it a wide berth, as if we might step on the sharp glass of our shattered dreams. We plan to see a movie Friday evening, to distract ourselves from grief. He hasn't repeated the idea of moving away.

But Friday afternoon, he calls to say he's going out with Jacob and a few other colleagues after work. He sounds strange, his voice hollow. I sit at the kitchen table, listening to the dishwasher churn, and I burst into tears. He should be here with me.

In bed, I lie awake, and at eleven o'clock, I hit speed-dial for his cell. The phone rings and rings, then the call drops into voice mail. "You've reached Aiden Finlay. You know what the hell to do."

"Where are you and what are you doing?" I say, and hang up. Fine, let him stay away forever. I hope he never comes home.

I'm just drifting off when the call comes through. I jolt upright and grab the phone without looking at the screen.

"Where are you?" I say sleepily. "Why aren't you home?"

"Because I'm at *my* home?" a deep voice says. "Is that the right answer?"

"Oh, I'm sorry, Jacob," I say, sitting up. "What's going on? It's late."

"Uh, it's just . . . Aiden had a little too much to drink."

"He *what*?"

"He can't drive. I put him to bed in my loft."

"In your *loft*."

"I keep a loft downtown," Jacob says smoothly. "For situations like this. He'll be okay here. He's safe. I'm sorry I woke you."

"Wait," I say. "Don't hang up." Questions tumble through my mind. Where is this loft?

"He's dealing with some heavy emotions," Jacob says.

"Not very well," I say.

"Yeah," Jacob says, and sighs. "Listen, I'm sorry I upset you, but I thought you should know, so you don't worry."

"I'm worried."

A beat of silence follows, then he says, "Come down and I'll buy you a cup at Café Presse. I'll pay for the cab."

I blink, look at the clock, processing his invitation. "Right now?"

"It's only eleven thirty," he says.

Only? Does this man stay up all night? "I'm usually asleep by ten," I say.

"I'll get you some tea, and drive you home."

The café is oddly comforting, with its soft classical music and dim lighting. Jacob steers me to a table in the shadows. Why did I put on a touch of lipstick and eyeliner in the middle of the night? Comb my hair and wash up? Why did I try on three sweaters before settling on a soft black turtleneck? There is something about Jacob—the smooth, deep voice, his self-assurance, his command of a room. The way conversation stops as he passes and he doesn't seem to notice. His eyes are on me. He gives me the mug of tea.

"You say this will put me to sleep?" I say.

"It'll knock you out," he says.

"But not knock me up." I can't help the bitterness in my voice.

The smile drops from his face. His eyes are so blue, so clear. So different from Aiden's eyes. "I'm sorry about what happened." Somehow, his hand is over mine. Comforting, but I am wide awake now.

"I can't believe Aiden got drunk."

"Aiden's a great guy, but in many ways he's still that perpetual college kid. We were talking, and he was drinking, and talking . . . and . . ."

"And?"

He looks out the window, then at me. "And, I'm not sure if I should tell you."

"Tell me what? You have to tell me now."

"He's not certain," he says.

"Certain of what?" But already I know. I push the cup away.

"You two had a whirlwind courtship . . . You broke the news to all of us at the last minute, about your wedding."

"It was quick," I say.

"He said it might've been too quick."

"He said our marriage was a mistake? He really said that?"

"What matters is what you do from here. What you decide."

"Did Aiden decide something?" I say.

"He thought you two had been hasty about everything, that's all. And now with this horrible news. I think he just feels . . . unprepared to handle it. To help you."

I can't stop the tears, the upwelling of emotion, of betrayal, even though Aiden has not slept with another woman. I grip Jacob's hand so tightly I could break his fingers. He grips me back, providing a lifeline.

"I know it's hard," he says softly. "You deserve to have someone you can lean on, especially right now."

"I'm starting to think maybe I don't know Aiden at all. Now I'm not sure about us, either."

"Are we ever sure of anything?" He's looking at my lips, or maybe it's just a trick of the light.

"Maybe he's right," I say. "Maybe we should have thought it all out."

"Nothing should ever be rushed," Jacob says, looking into my eyes. "I'm never hasty, when I'm focused, when I'm certain. I do everything in my power to get what I want. And I always get it."

I didn't understand then what he meant. I thought he was telling me that I needed to focus on my marriage. But it wasn't about that at all. Jacob did not rush his plan to be with me, but he stuck to a definite goal. He was telling me that he was the grown-up, that he could be the one who was steadfast. He must have pushed Aiden away from me. I can see it now, Jacob plying Aiden with alcohol, suggesting that our marriage was shaky. The truth, with a flourish, an embellishment or two.

In the morning, when Aiden staggered home with a hangover, we argued, and over the next several days, he often worked late. We spoke less and less. We avoided the nursery. Sometimes we avoided each other. We made love infrequently, and when we did we were tentative. I could get pregnant again, and we might have to grieve yet a third miscarriage. The anxiety darkened our lives. But Jacob was always there for us, providing his loft couch for Aiden, taking me out for tea.

Gradually, inexorably, Aiden and I drifted apart, until I could no longer stand to watch the bedside clock on a Friday night, wondering if he would even come home. One evening, while he was still at the office, Jacob came to the house. He sat on the porch with me, watching the stars. I pictured my husband hunched over his desk, oblivious to my pain. Leaving me to suffer and grieve alone.

But I wasn't alone. Jacob's presence had become a familiar comfort. He did not make a move, did not expect anything from me. He simply offered his ear, his presence, his soothing support. "I understand how you feel. The loneliness, the frustration, the dashed hopes and dreams. I have felt the same way before. But time passed and I came to realize I needed a new plan for my life."

I was the one who suggested a trial separation. The qualities that had drawn me to Aiden—his spontaneity and exuberance—now seemed like impulsiveness. But still, when he reluctantly agreed to move out, I cried all night. He stayed in a nearby hotel. Soon after that, he took leave to visit his ailing father in New York. How had our marriage come to this?

"You have every reason to resent him," Jacob said. "How could he walk away during your hour of deepest suffering?"

"He didn't walk away," I said. But the more Jacob suggested that Aiden had abandoned me, the more I believed it.

"He can't come back and expect everything to be okay," Jacob said. "He can't expect you to forgive him."

Jacob sensed my anger and grief, and he swooped in. He had been waiting. He changed lightbulbs for me, made me dinner. He took care of me, listened to my woes. I was vulnerable.

"I know a great place," he said. "My family's vacation home from a long time ago. Mystic Island will heal you."

I agreed to come here.

Even as we boarded the ferry to our summer getaway, my stomach churned with guilt. I had removed my wedding ring and put it away. With the wind in my face, I felt that I would pay for betraying Aiden, but we were separated, and I couldn't forget the way he had reacted in my moment of need, could I? Somehow, Jacob's words altered my memory. I forgot Aiden's concern. What did Jacob tell him about me? How had this psychopath poisoned my husband's mind?

I didn't know what would come next. I didn't know if I would sleep with Jacob. All I knew was that he nurtured me when I needed someone, held me when I cried, wiped my tears. He was my escape.

"Don't worry about the real world," Jacob said on the ferry. "Anything is possible on Mystic Island."

Was it worth destroying my marriage to run away with him? I had to admit, the sexual tension had simmered between us for a long time.

On the ferry with Jacob, I'm exhausted, full of mixed emotions.

"So, we're really going to do this?" I say, as Mystic Island comes into view.

Jacob grins down at me. To anyone looking through the ferry's glass windows, we are a couple. When he slides the wedding ring onto my finger, I laugh, shaking my head. "You're bold."

"It's a small island. Provincial. People talk if you come as an unmarried couple."

"Let them talk. We're grown-ups."

"But you can be anyone you want to be. We could play pretend."

"Pretend," I echo.

"Let's pretend it's just you and me in the world. Mr. and Mrs. Winthrop."

I look up at him and smile. "Okay. For a little while, I'll play the game."

"I was hoping you would say that."

The force of his charisma eclipsed my judgment. I was empty inside, depleted, and at that moment, my husband seemed very far away.

CHAPTER THIRTY-NINE

I remember now. The letter I wrote last summer, when Jacob and I were here on the island. Aiden and I had already separated. Jacob asked me to divorce Aiden and marry him, and I believed it could be possible. I believed maybe I could marry Jacob and live happily ever after in this beautiful fantasy world.

He asked me what I would say, if I could write a letter to Aiden. To say good-bye. I wrote that our marriage was over, that I'd met someone. A man who wouldn't waffle, who wouldn't be unsure of our relationship.

But I didn't send the letter. I burst into tears and dropped the paper on the floor. *That was a mistake,* I said. I reached down to grab the page, but Jacob put his arms around me. *Don't be afraid of change. I'm here with you.*

He must've kept the letter, which I never intended to send. *I threw it into the recycling bin,* Jacob said. *Would you like me to retrieve it for you? Have you changed your mind about sending it?*

No, I said, relieved. *Go ahead and recycle it.*

But he didn't. He kept it, and he gave it to Aiden. He intercepted Aiden's emails to me. Not only that, he replied to them.

I meant what I said, he typed from my email address. *Please get on with your life. We can't undo what happened.*

It was all a lie, just like my marriage to Jacob. Every moment, every kiss, every intimacy. A complete fabrication. *But I slept with him. Everything we've done . . .*

I run to the bathroom and vomit into the toilet. I dry heave until I'm spent. My mind tumbles like a tiny boat caught in a giant wave. Had Jacob been planning this whole charade all along? But why?

I have to find a way to contact Aiden. But the minute I pull up the Web browser again, the Internet cuts out. It's gone, just like that. The rain pummels the roof, the wind screaming in from the sea.

I run back to the house. The rooms look menacing now. Jacob created this world with the things I love—my seashells on the windowsill, this view of the ocean, my lecture notes, and my books. All a facsimile of the truth, like the abandoned shell of the Dungeness crab, perfect on the outside but hollow inside.

In the bedroom, I empty my purse again. *Lingerie, Print ticket, Get you know what . . .* I was preparing for my summer on the island with Jacob. A man who wasn't my husband. The condom is still in the drawer—but this time, when I hold it in my hand, I see Jacob handing me the condom from a full box. *We'll use these until you're ready,* he said. As if he was certain I would end my marriage to Aiden. I put everything back into my purse, drop the condom in the garbage.

I take the wedding photograph off the shelf. The formality becomes apparent in the way Jacob and I dance together. I'm leaning back, away from him. My wedding dress fans out as he spins me around, and I'm smiling, but not at him. From this distance, I'm looking off slightly to my left, over his shoulder. I recognize Linny, smiling and clapping. Aiden is standing next to her. The groom.

I can't breathe. I have to get out of here. Now. But there is no boat off the island before tomorrow. I stuff some clothes into my backpack. In the bathroom, I grab my toothbrush, a small bottle of lotion. That image of Jacob in the shower, the anticipation running through me—it was the nervous excitement a woman feels when she's about to sleep with a man *for the first time*. Not for the fiftieth time or the hundredth time. I felt the anticipation of discovery. But now, my heart blackens with guilt. Of all things, I should have remembered Aiden. I should have been there for him. Every extra minute I spend here is a new blight on my soul.

Back in the bedroom, I pack a few of my most precious seashells, but not all of them. I can't let Jacob know I'm gone for good. I need a head start. But how will I escape the island? I have to leave most of my belongings behind. I don't even know what's mine and what Jacob planted here to fool me. In the kitchen, I write a note, *Out for a ride.* I put on my rain gear, strap on my backpack in the garage, and take off on my bicycle. My heart is in my throat on the ride south on the only route—the main road. The whole way, I recite an internal mantra, *You're okay. You're alive.* I'm hoping Waverly's telephone works, that she can call the authorities.

I'm a mile from the house when Jacob's truck comes hurtling toward me, bouncing over potholes. My heart plummets. To the right, nothing but forest. It would be stupid to take off into those woods in the cold, with the rain shooting sideways in the wind. Where would I go? To the left, more forest. I won't get far on foot.

Jacob pulls up alongside me and rolls down the driver's-side window. "Where are you going?"

"Just into town for a few things." Somehow, I manage to

smile. I want to kill him. He motions me over to kiss him. I have to pretend, but I want to throw up.

"Get in, I'll take you home."

"I'm okay—I'll go on my bike."

"You won't make it back in the storm."

"I'm okay," I say, trying to sound confident.

"Get in. The wind is picking up."

I look down the road, but I can't outpedal him. I couldn't outrun him. *Breathe, think.* I get off my bicycle. He hoists my bike into the bed of the truck. He opens the passenger-side door. The hinge squeaks. I hesitate for a long moment, looking into the truck, down the road. *Run. Don't get into the car. No, don't run. He'll know. He'll catch up. You're still weak. He's faster, stronger.*

"Hurry up, get in," he says.

I slide in and sit down, putting my backpack on the seat between us. Thankfully, he doesn't ask me why I'm carrying a backpack.

He gets into the driver's seat and presses a button to the left of the steering wheel, locking all the doors. I look forward through the windshield, the glass spotless, scoured by Jacob's incessant compulsion to keep surfaces clean.

"Where did you go off to?" I ask on the bumpy drive home.

"Nancy needed help fixing a leak. Van's AWOL."

"He's on a dive in Colombia," I say.

Jacob glances sidelong at me. "He told you that? When?"

"I visited him on the boat, remember?"

"Oh, yeah. The guy gets around."

"What about us? A trip to the mainland tomorrow?" I'm surprised I sound so casual.

"The ferry won't be running for a while."

"What?" My voice comes out high-pitched.

"Eighth breakdown this year. They need to replace that damned boat."

"How does a ferry break down?" I keep my voice measured. But I want to throw the backpack at him, scream, jump out of the truck, run forever.

"Something about the drive motor. Tugboats towed the ferry into the harbor. It stalled a distance out. There were maybe a dozen people aboard at the time."

"So it could be days."

"At least." He pulls into the garage. I could make a run for it now. And then what? He would come after me. He would be relentless. I've got to think. He turns off the engine as the garage door slams shut. We plunge into momentary darkness, and then the overhead light flickers on.

We're inside the house now, taking off our shoes. My clothes hang heavily on my body, my skin clammy. I shove the backpack in the closet in the bedroom, take a deep breath, and lean back against the closed door. My heartbeat gallops. The floor creaks in the hallway. I can hear him breathing on the other side of the door.

"You okay?" he says.

"I feel a little sick. I might be coming down with something."

"I'll make you some ginger tea. Good for digestion." He goes into the kitchen.

Breathe, you can do this. Think. Jacob doesn't *want* to kill me, or I would be dead by now. What he wants is to be my husband, to live this lie of a marriage. Until I can make my escape, I have to pretend to be Jacob's loving wife.

CHAPTER FORTY

"You look pale," Jacob says, handing me tea.

"I need to rest. You're too good to me." I'm a basket case of fear and nerves. The wind howls across the island, rattling the windows.

"Do you have a fever?" His voice is cautious, worried. He touches my forehead. It's all I can do not to slap his hand away. "You're not too warm. You're probably just tired."

"Exhausted," I say. "I got caught in the rain."

"You make a habit of doing that. On our second date, we got caught in a storm. We hung out under an awning, then we went for dinner in Belltown."

"Probably somewhere romantic." *No,* I'm thinking, *I was with Aiden that night, not you.*

"Il Bistro on Pike Street, I think it was. Great food."

Aiden and I ran into Il Bistro to get out of the rain. Later, I related the story to Jacob. "We'll have to go back there," I say.

"We will. For now, I'll make you some soup."

"I'm not all that hungry." I get up on shaky legs. "I think I'll just go to bed."

But I can't sleep. I lie awake late into the night. Jacob's rhythmic snores fill the room. He came in here to be with me again, and I did not protest. I did not want to arouse his suspicion. A faint glow emanates from the night-light in the hall. As I quietly lift myself out of bed, Jacob shifts . . . my heart jumps. *Please don't wake up.*

He turns away from me, his breathing soft and regular. I tiptoe to the bathroom, close the door but not all the way. I don't want to make a sound. I quietly open the bottle of sleeping pills and empty the contents into the pocket of my pajama bottoms. I slide the bottle into the back of the drawer. I open the door to the bedroom and gasp. Jacob is standing right there, his hand against the doorjamb.

"What are you doing?" he says, scratching his head.

"I had to pee. I didn't want to wake you."

"I'm glad you did." His hands travel under my pajama top. I don't move. His touch tortures me now.

"I'm not feeling well," I say, slipping away from him and into bed.

"Sorry, I know." He comes back into bed, and soon he is snoring again. I watch the clock tick away the minutes. I close my eyes, not expecting to sleep at all, but I drift off now and then, and in the morning, I'm up early. I put on my robe and slippers, and I go into the kitchen to make coffee. The pills are still in my pajama pocket.

When Jacob gets up to make a fire, I take two mugs from the cabinet and pour the coffee, turning my back to him. I reach into my pocket for the pills.

"You want honey?" I say. "The usual three spoons?"

"Maybe stop the honey. It's not healthy."

"Honey has antibiotic properties. It's your one indulgence. You're so good about everything else."

"You've persuaded me."

I let out a breath of relief, scoop in the honey, adding the pills as I stir. My fingers shake. The spoon rattles against the side of the mug. The pills break into pieces, but what if they don't dissolve? How many pills have I dropped in? I lost count. What if they don't knock him out? What if he tastes them? I stir the coffee vigorously. He feeds the fire. I take a tiny sip from his mug. The coffee has a slightly bitter taste. I stir in the milk. What if I accidentally kill him? What's an acceptable overdose?

My hands tremble as I give him the mug. I'm aware of the contaminated liquid inside, as he adds another log to the fire.

Jacob gazes at the flame through the glass door of the woodstove. He sips his coffee, stops, and looks into the cup. *He knows. He knows what I've done. He knows that I know I'm not married to him. He's going to hurl the mug across the room. I am dead.*

He says, "Hmmm," and keeps sipping.

I nearly collapse with relief. I can't say anything, can't let on.

He puts the mug on the coffee table and sits on the couch, patting the cushion next to him. *He didn't drink enough. What if he doesn't finish?*

As I sit next to him, it's as if our two coffee mugs are at center stage beneath a spotlight. He knows what I'm up to. He must know.

"How are you feeling this morning?" he says.

"I'm a little better," I say.

"Last night . . . I'm sorry. I should have been more understanding."

"It's okay," I say.

"Are you sure?"

"Mmm-hmm."

"Give me your feet," he says. My heart beats in time with

the wall clock. The refrigerator hums too loudly. What if he leaves his mug untouched?

I place my mug on the table. Mine is blue. His is white. I can't get the mugs mixed up.

I put my feet in his lap. He massages them. I resist the urge to kick him in the face. I keep my breathing deep and even. *Come on, drink the coffee.* He eventually sits back and takes his mug from the table, watching the fire diminish. "Feels good to let go," he says. "Doesn't it?"

"Let go of what?"

"The past. Things better left behind."

I'm not going to argue with him, not now. The last time we were here, on the island, I decided to go back to the mainland, to try again with Aiden. Jacob was furious. He threw the soap across the bathroom when I told him. *He made the dent in the door.* But a couple of months later, he called me. *I miss you,* he said. *I'll take friendship with you, if that's what we have.*

We met for a drink. I was surprised by how understanding he was. *Kyra,* he said, *I hope it's been obvious from the start that I really care about you. That all I want is for you to be happy. For you to be with a person who loves you, and who is willing to put you first.* I told him that I wished him every happiness, too. When I started to gather my things, he said that Aiden had asked him about us. I had stopped moving then, sat down, and taken his hand. I remember pleading. *Please don't say anything, Jacob. He knows that you were there for me, but I haven't told him that you were the man I was with during the summer.*

He looked down at my hand. *You know that I would do anything for you. Aiden may be blind to some things, but he's going to be suspicious if we don't spend time together, like we used to.*

I know, I said. *Let's just give it time.*

A few weeks later, Aiden said he'd been talking with Jacob about a dive and I knew I couldn't put it off any longer. I decided to allow us this one outing all together. We were either going to slip back into our familiar dynamic, or I was going to tell Aiden the truth afterward.

Maybe he already knows, I thought. *Maybe Aiden knows what I did and he understands. And maybe he forgives me.*

So we went on the dive, all three of us. On the drive up to Deception Pass, we hiked at Ebey's Landing. As I stumbled down the cliff into Aiden's arms, I was wearing my wedding ring again, the one with the orca engraving, not this impostor ring.

Jacob's ring glints in the light as he raises his mug to sip the coffee. "Tastes weird today."

Time screeches to a stop. He's onto me. "I noticed," I say smoothly. My voice gives no hint of the panic inside me. "I need to clean the coffee pot. I'll run some vinegar through the machine."

He nods, distracted, takes another gulp. He puts the mug on the table and snuggles against me. "I need a nap," he says, yawning. "Damn, it's still early."

"You didn't get enough sleep last night." I try to peer into his mug. Did he finish the coffee? How much did he drink?

"Come back to bed with me." He pulls me close. How long is this going to take? What if the pills don't work? We sit this way for a while, for far too long. Finally, he hoists himself to his feet, swaying a little. "Whoa, maybe I'm getting the flu, too."

"You don't feel well? Are you okay?" A sudden wave of guilt washes over me. He seems somehow vulnerable. What if he falls asleep and never wakes up? But this man has lied to me every day since we got here. Every minute.

He gives me a quizzical look. *How long is he going to stay conscious?* I follow him to the bedroom. He's staggering. He flops onto the bed on his belly. His eyes are closed, his breathing labored.

I prod him. He doesn't move. He's still breathing, but he appears to be out cold. I reach into his pockets. The truck keys are not there, where I've always seen him keep them. They're not in the dish in the hallway. They're not in the kitchen, next to his wallet. They're not anywhere. I check his mug. He drank less than half his coffee. The pills must be stronger than I thought. But how much time do I have before he wakes?

CHAPTER FORTY-ONE

I grab my backpack from the closet, slip out into the hall. Jacob's drawing jagged, uneven breaths. The truck keys are not on the ring of keys on the entry table by the telephone. Where are they? No dial tone again, either. Who could get here in time, before he wakes? What would he do? Throw me off a cliff? Bash my head in with the ax?

I go into the garage, taking my time closing the heavy door, so it doesn't make a sound. The truck is locked. *Where are the damned keys?* I hear a noise and the door to the hallway swings open. Light floods into the garage. I crouch by the wetsuit hanging on the wall, hiding behind the truck.

"Kyra? Looking for these?" The keys jingle in his hand.

How did he wake so quickly? He knew about the pills in the coffee. I don't answer. *Please, go away.*

"Where are you?" he says.

I hope he can't hear me breathing. He's between me and the garage door opener.

"Seriously, did you think I wouldn't be onto you?" he says.

Again, I don't answer.

"You shouldn't drive. You could lose your way or, who knows, steer into the ditch. In that wind, a tree could fall on the truck."

Still, I say nothing. The blood rushes in my ears.

"You were in my office," he says.

My heart nearly explodes in my chest.

"You shouldn't have logged into my computer."

Still, I say nothing.

"Look. Everyone has disagreements. All married couples have ups and downs. We'll get through this."

We're not married! I want to scream. *We never were.* "How did you get me out of rehab and all the way here?"

"We came by boat, like I said."

"Where was Aiden?"

"I don't know where he was. Why are you bringing Aiden into this?"

"You lied to me—"

"I was protecting you. Poor Aiden. He got the worst of it."

"You didn't answer my question. How did you get me out of rehab while Aiden was still in a coma?"

"It wasn't difficult. I visited you quite often, but then, you don't remember."

"They wouldn't have let you take me! I wouldn't have let you!"

"You shouldn't work yourself up. You're not feeling well."

"Why did you bring me here?"

"Come in and I'll make you some hot peppermint tea."

"You've been telling me lies. Everything is a lie. Tell me the truth."

"I've always told you the truth. I have nothing to hide from you. If we're going to keep our marriage on a solid foundation—"

"We do not have a marriage."

"You're under stress. But I'm taking care of you."

"What do you mean, taking care of me? You're a liar and a kidnapper."

"Kidnapper! That's a strong accusation."

"You brought me here under false pretenses."

"I did not. I was hoping you would remember us. You started to remember, didn't you? I was going to tell you everything, when the time was right. You jumped way ahead of me."

"You were going to tell me everything, really? When, Jacob?"

"When you finally remembered you love me. You were getting there. You *are* getting there."

"I was never in love with you."

"Of course you were."

"None of this is real."

"You have your dream life here in the wilderness with your seashells and your books, away from technology. It was what you always wanted."

"Away from technology. That's convenient for you, not me. You've kept me away from my real life."

"This is your real life—you even have your things from before."

"How did you get my belongings? The books and shells and boxes of stuff?"

"We stopped by your house. But the important things were already here."

"Clothes I bought last summer, when I was here with you. When we had our affair."

"You are my wife. It was what I wanted, and what I want—"

"What you want, you always get," I say. "Isn't that right? You couldn't stand knowing that I was with Aiden. You had to kidnap me."

"That's a harsh word," he says calmly. "You were always mine."

I take a deep breath. "How did you get away with this?"

"Good old Uncle Theo came in handy."

"Did you . . . pretend to be Uncle Theo? But how . . . ?"

"I couldn't pretend to be Aiden. The staff at the center knew where he was. In a coma. I don't know why he didn't just stay asleep."

"Uncle Theo . . ."

"Would you like to call him? I know you feel disconnected from family here. But I doubt he'll remember you."

I look around for a way out. If I try to open the heavy garage door manually, Jacob will be upon me. But he's not coming toward me, not trying to grab me and drag me back into the house. "How did you get me out?"

"You agreed to come with me, and they signed you out."

I'm still crouched behind the car. The garage is cold. "I'm going back to the city." Even I recognize that this is wishful thinking, but a part of me hopes he can still see reason.

"Why? You love it here. Look, you surprised me when you wanted to give Aiden another chance. He didn't deserve you. I had to make another plan."

"I have to get back to him. What did you do to him? Did you tamper with his oxygen?" My voice trembles. I look around for something to use as a weapon. The garden tools are on the other side of the garage.

"With his gas mix, you mean. His *air*. Who's been planting these ideas in your head?" He's coming toward me, running his hand along the hood of the truck.

"Did you try to kill him on the dive?" I crouch behind the bumper. Our dusty scuba tanks sit on a shelf right next to me.

"Kyra, there are so many ways a dive can go wrong. It's so difficult to pinpoint the *cause* of an accident."

"You did something to his pressure hose, or his tank valve, didn't you?" Slowly, I pull my scuba tank to the edge of the shelf.

"It was an accident. Ask anyone. They'll tell you. No way to prove it wasn't."

"What about Van? His allergic reaction? Did you have something to do with that?"

"Kyra, Kyra. Do you think I am so cruel?"

"I do now. Did you? Was that your doing?"

"Van should watch what he eats, and he should keep an EpiPen around, don't you think?"

"You have to let me go. This was a mistake."

"Don't say that."

He's too close now. As he steps around to my side of the car, he reaches for me. I lift the scuba tank and swing it with all my might, with all the force of my body. The tank crashes into his head—I hear a horrible cracking sound, and he crumples to the floor. Blood trickles down the side of his head. He's moaning, pressing his hand to the wound.

I hit the button to open the garage, and as the door rises, I grab my bicycle, but it won't move. It's locked to Jacob's bicycle. Double locked. "What did you do?" I scream.

He's still moaning, holding his head.

"Give me the keys to the truck," I say.

"You can't . . . drive. You'll hurt yourself."

"I know how to drive. Give them to me."

"Come and get them."

I'll never be able to wrestle the keys away from him. I grab my backpack and run out into the wind. I take the steps down to the beach two at a time, and when I hit the sand I break into a sprint. The tide is rising. I look over my shoulder. He's not coming for me, not yet.

I keep running, and when I reach the final curve of shoreline leading to Doug Ingram's secluded beach, the tide laps against the embankment. I stop to catch my breath. A voice calls to me on the wind. I can't make out the words. It's Jacob. He's still far away, a mere speck on the beach, but he's gaining. His wound slows him down, but in the end, I won't be able to outrun him. I wade into the icy surf, my feet going numb. The dark current yanks at my legs, but I push my way forward, gasping as I stagger onto Douglas Ingram's beach. I collapse on the sand, gasping for breath. This can't be happening. There is no boat tethered to the dock. Douglas Ingram is gone.

CHAPTER FORTY-TWO

I climb the rickety, steep wooden stairs to Doug's house. The staircase sways from side to side. Some of the planks are soft, rotten. A rock tumbles past me, down the embankment. I keep climbing, hoping the railing won't give way. At the top of the steps, the log house comes into view through the trees. I run through the garden to knock on the door. There's no smoke rising from the chimney, and nobody answers. I knock again, frantically. My backpack is too heavy, pulling at my shoulders. It occurs to me that this is all I have in the world. My backpack and a crazy assailant who believes he is my husband.

I cup my hands to the window and peer inside the living room. Everything is neat and tidy, but Douglas is not at home. *Nobody has to lock their doors here,* Jacob says in my head. But the door is locked. Maddeningly locked up tight. The windows, too. In the back of the house, there's an unlocked door leading into a dank storage room. I lock myself inside, my heart pounding. The storage room leads into the house. I call for Doug, no answer. On a table in the hall, I see it. A telephone plugged into the wall. The line makes a crackling sound.

"Thank you," I breathe to the universe. I call 911, and a man's voice comes on the line.

"911, where's your emergency?"

"I'm on Mystic Island, at Douglas Ingram's house on Windswept Bluff. I need help. My husband is coming after me. I mean, Jacob Winthrop. He's after me. My name is Kyra Munin-Finlay."

"Stay on the phone. I'm sending help."

Through the trees, I see Jacob staggering to the top of the steps, holding the side of his head. "I have to go. I have to hang up. He's coming. I can't stay on the phone." He'll easily break a window or a door and find me cringing in a closet.

"Help is on the way, ma'am."

"You know where I am?"

"I do have your location."

I hang up, dash out of the house, and sprint up the driveway toward the main road. Help will not come fast enough, not out here. I don't know how long I've been running before Jacob catches up.

"Kyra, stop!" He's almost upon me now. He grabs at my backpack and pulls so hard he nearly knocks me over backward. I wriggle out of the straps and dash away. He's slower than usual, blood still seeping from the wound on his head, and his face is pale and glistening with sweat.

"Kyra, stop," he says, breathless. "Wait."

"Leave me alone!" He grabs my jacket, but I shrug out of it, sending him reeling backward. I keep running, my lungs screaming.

"I just want to talk to you."

"Go away!" I shout.

"Stop." Jacob catches up and grabs my arm, spins me around to face him. His face is distorted into a grimace. "What the hell do you think you're doing?"

"Don't touch me."

He yanks my arm, nearly dislocating my shoulder, and throws me on the ground with such force the wind is knocked from my lungs. Then he picks me up and throws me again.

"You're not going anywhere."

"Why are you doing this?" I stagger toward the driveway. He shoves me down.

"I've given you everything, and it's not enough for you?" His face turns a deep shade of red. His mouth is set in a thin line. He strides toward me, grabs my shoulders so tightly his fingers dig into the bone. I cry out in pain. "Let go of me!"

"Turn around. We are going home."

I struggle to escape from his grip, but he doesn't let go. "You're crazy!" I shout between sobs.

He shakes me by my shoulders, so hard I'm afraid my brain will fall out of my skull. "Stop, stop!" I say, but my knees weaken. Stars dance in front of my eyes, tiny pinpoints of light. He's shaking me; he swings a fist at me, the blow so hard on my cheek he must have cracked the bone. The forest blurs. I feel my body falling in slow motion.

There's a rumbling sound in the woods, approaching along the driveway. I'm on the ground, curled into the fetal position. My head hurts. I can't move. Jacob is kicking me, yelling at me from far away. "Get up, you bitch! How dare you leave me?" But I can't get up.

The truck pulls up behind us. Through my half-closed eyelids I see him, Doug Ingram. The boat is hooked to the back of his truck. He gets out and strides toward Jacob. "Hey, what's going on here? Get away from her!"

"Doug, be careful!" I shout.

Through a haze, I see him dash up to Jacob. The two grab

each other, tussling, swinging around and around. Doug Ingram is strong for his age, but not strong enough. I want to warn him, tell him to run, but my tongue thickens, and the words won't come. He swipes at Jacob, catching him square in the jaw. Jacob takes a step back, rights himself, and with one blow he knocks Doug to the ground. *Oh, Doug. Please be okay.*

I muster all my strength, stagger to my feet. My ribs are throbbing. "Leave him alone!" I shout. Jacob stands in the driveway, towering over Doug. I can't get past him. I turn and stumble toward the house, through the forest to the wooden steps. If I can get back down to the beach—

Jacob is upon me again, grasping my shoulders. "Come home now," he spits at me. His face is red, flushed. Blood seeps from his swollen lip, where Doug punched him.

"Get off me!" I back down the rickety steps. Behind me, the sea roars in a fury. The wind whips my hair into my face.

He lunges for me, and I step to the side. He trips down the stairs and grabs the railing, but the rotten wood gives way. In an instant, he's plunging down the cliff, yelling, flailing, reaching for something to hold on to, but he finds nothing. He seems to fall forever in slow motion, unable to gain a foothold. When he reaches the bottom, he's motionless, his body lying at an odd angle on the rocks.

With a deafening groan, the stairs below me start to give way, sliding down the cliff. I climb to the top and collapse onto flat ground. Someone's calling my name. *Kyra, where are you? Kyra?*

CHAPTER FORTY-THREE

Aiden and I ride the ferry into Friday Harbor. We're huddled together in a booth by the window, watching the turquoise ocean race past the boat. He is holding my hand, his grip not yet as firm as I remember. He was in a coma for months, and his body is still recovering. But he's the man I married, the man in the wool sweater with the scent of soap and pine.

My cheek is still sore where Jacob hit me, but the swelling is gone now, leaving only a faint yellow bruise after all these days. He cracked a rib when he kicked me, and I still can't sneeze or laugh without a stab of pain, but otherwise, I'm remarkably well. Physically, at least. Mentally, that's another story. A new nightmare plagues me now. Instead of a suffocating diver rising below me, I see Jacob coming for me, punching me, pulling my hair . . . I wake up gasping, and Aiden holds me close.

As soon as he woke from the coma, he asked for me, insisted on seeing me, but I had checked out of rehab. Jacob brought him the letter, which devastated him. It was easy for Jacob to check me out of the rehab center as my uncle. I was tabula rasa, unable to remember anything new for more than five minutes. Over and over again, he reminded me that he would take care of me. He whisked me away to the new life he had already created on the island, the life he planned to share with me after Aiden's death at sea.

"He expected me to *want* to stay with him," I say.

"I know," Aiden says regretfully. He doesn't ask, *Would you have wanted to move to Mystic Island with him? For good? If you had remembered our fights, our separation?*

"I would never have wanted to be with him," I say. "The affair was long over."

"You weren't cheating on me," Aiden says. "We were separated."

"But it never felt right to me . . . being with him."

"I drove you into his arms," Aiden says, taking my hands in his. "I never should've introduced you to him." The first time I met Jacob, I was visiting Aiden at his office. Jacob stared at me as if struck by lightning. *You remind me of someone,* he said.

"Nobody's to blame," I say, looking out the window again. The ghosts of our reflections stare back from the glass.

We're quiet for a time.

"I hope you like the house," Aiden says finally. He squeezes my hand.

"If I loved it when we bought it, I'll love it now, too," I say, smiling at him. Snippets of our marriage come back to me, but there are still gaps. I hope someday to fill them in, and until then, Aiden tells me what I need to know.

"You said you dreamed of the house," he says.

"I was in a bright yellow Victorian." I touch the stubble on his cheek. The wool of his sweater smells familiar, comforting. "It was a memory, but Jacob wanted me to believe it wasn't."

"The extent of his charade is what floors me," Aiden says,

wrapping my hand in both of his hands, bringing my hand to his chest. "Nobody could ever believe . . . It's too bizarre. He created such a complete world."

A little time has made me angrier, at Jacob, at myself. But I also learned enough about Jacob to know that he wasn't a monster. "It wasn't complete. He made mistakes. He didn't think he was doing anything wrong. He thought he could create this perfect life with everything I loved."

"He held you hostage."

"My lost memory kept me hostage."

Aiden looks at me, and I see a range of colors in his dark eyes. "He fooled everyone, but most of all me. I put you in harm's way. I was starting to suspect something was wrong. Something about the way you replied to me. The wording. Then after you agreed to meet me, you stood me up."

"I didn't even know about your messages." The authorities confirmed my suspicion: Jacob used an Ethernet cable to route the Internet through his computer in the cottage before any information reached my computer in the house. I was still in shock that such a deception was not difficult for a programmer to orchestrate.

The ferry slows as we approach the harbor, a density of buildings crowded along the shore. When the boat docks, Aiden drives us up the hill and along the winding roads of downtown Friday Harbor. Even though San Juan Island is similar to Mystic Island in its terrain, this house is closer to civilization, with reliable Internet and cell phone service, more frequent ferry runs, and a thriving community in Friday Harbor, including a network of writers and artists, two grocery stores, a few bookstores, a couple of theaters, and medical clinics.

Aiden drives along the east coast of the island, through balmy air and forest until we reach a narrow road leading down to the shoreline. There, facing the water, drinking in the light through a plethora of windows, is the house from my dream—an old yellow Victorian sitting on a bluff overlooking the strait.

EPILOGUE

I cherish mornings, when the day is still new. What I love now are the things I always loved. Morning tea, decaffeinated again, walks on the beach with Aiden before he leaves for the new software company he started here on the island. He stopped working for Jacob some time ago.

I'm starting up my research again. I found the Tompkins anemone where I never expected to find it, attached to the underside of a dock in Friday Harbor, in plain view. A rare, elongated, luminous sea creature right in front of my nose.

I'm volunteering at the Whale Museum, and occasionally I go out on a research vessel with two marine biologists studying a pod of resident orcas. I may consider teaching again at San Juan Island College. One step at a time. Like our marriage.

We love each other, that much is clear. But for all our faults—Aiden's impulsiveness, my uncertainty—our decision to marry was sacred and I will never forgive myself for thinking otherwise. And I don't think he will forgive himself, either.

A soft, salty breeze flows in, warmed by the sunlight of spring. Robins and chickadees flit between the trees. The rhododendrons blossom in splashes of bright pink, red, and purple. After the nighttime rain, the sparrows and nuthatches drink droplets of water off the softly rustling leaves.

A familiar truck appears through the trees, creeping down the winding driveway. When I open the door for Douglas Ingram, I'm taken aback. If it weren't for his beaten-up truck, I wouldn't recognize him. He's cut his hair short, and he cleaned up, shaved off his beard and mustache. He looks ten years younger now, and he's in a new plaid flannel coat, pressed jeans, new boots. "Morning, Kyra."

I hug him, although I can't pull him close. My growing belly is in the way. "I'm so glad you made it." He even smells clean.

"Congratulations," he says, looking down at my billowing maternity shirt.

"Thanks. We're lucky." I rest my hand on the curve of my abdomen.

"Nobody deserves it more." He follows me out to sit in the cedar recliners on the deck.

"What brings you here?" I say.

"I'm on my way to Bellevue."

"Bellevue! I thought you weren't going to—"

"I'm not going into any old folks' home. No way, no how, but I figured it's time to do a little traveling. Before I can't anymore."

"You're going to visit your daughter."

He nods and smiles. I can see the excitement in his eyes, and trepidation, worry, fear. But mostly excitement. "Can't let too much more time pass. My memory's not so good."

"Neither is mine," I say, and we laugh.

I shield my eyes against the sun. I rest my hand on his

arm. "I never got a chance to properly thank you. With everything that's happened. I ended up leaving the island so quickly, and there were the interviews with the authorities, and then Aiden showed up—"

"Hey, no worries."

We're both silent for a minute, and then I say, "How are Van and Nancy?"

"They're . . . Van and Nancy," he says, chuckling softly. "They were shocked to learn about Jacob. Nancy, especially. She knew Jacob as a kid, and he was good to her. She said in hindsight, she should have seen the signs. His terrible father. How Jacob always wanted his way, created elaborate fantasy worlds for himself, never really cared if anyone else went along."

"But how could anyone have predicted?" I say. "It's not like, when you're a kid, you point at a friend and say, *He's* going to grow up weird and kidnap someone and make her believe she's his wife."

"Hindsight's twenty-twenty," Douglas says. "I know that myself."

"We can't change the past," I say.

"But we can shape the future."

"Touché," I say. We smile at each other, an unbreakable connection between us now. We will always share those frightening moments at the top of the cliff on Mystic Island.

He follows my gaze toward the figure of a man walking along the beach, a broad-shouldered silhouette heading back this way from his long walk. Every time I see Aiden, my heart still leaps with anticipation. I wave to him, and he waves back.

"That your husband?" Douglas says. "The real one?"

"That's him," I say. "I would love for you to meet him before you go."

I'm in the newly painted room on the second floor. Aiden comes up behind me and wraps his arms around my waist. His lips touch the nape of my neck, and he settles against me. Our bodies fit so well together. "I like the color," he says. "Saffron?"

"More like straw." I lean against him. I can feel the softness of his flannel sleeves on my arms.

"Golden glow," he says.

"Goldfinch."

"Sun shower. We could call her that. Sunflower."

"Heck no."

"How about Daffodil?" He rests his hands gently on my belly.

"We're not naming her after the color of her nursery."

"Whatever you say. I still like the name Daffodil," he says. "Daff for short."

"No way," I say, laughing at his silliness.

"You have a better idea?"

"I'll think about it. I'm sure I will."

He takes my hand. I can feel the tremor in his fingers. He's still in physical therapy. "When's our next appointment with the doc?"

"In two weeks." I'm saturated in happiness, although the shadows still follow me. They may never completely disappear, but I've learned to hold them at bay. I'm five months along, past the point of danger. Smooth sailing from here, we hope. We don't talk about the timing, about what we will do if we see Jacob's eyes in our child's face.

Instead, I keep focusing on the light, on possibilities, on what is good and true. None of us is bound by the past. We can make our own future as a family. Our child will embody the best of her parents. She will become a decent, caring person, guided by love. This, I have to believe.

ACKNOWLEDGMENTS

I'm grateful to my amazing agent, Paige Wheeler; my fabulous editor, Tara Parsons; and the brilliant people on the Touchstone team, including but not limited to Susan Moldow, David Falk, Meredith Vilarello, Kelsey Manning, Jessica Roth, Charlotte O'Donnell, Etinosa Agbonlahor, Isabella Betita, and Joshua Cohen. Thank you for believing in this book.

Where would I be without my intrepid writing and brainstorming buddies? Thank you to Susan Wiggs, Sheila Roberts, Kate Breslin, Elsa Watson, Lois Dyer, Michael Donnelly, Elizabeth Wrenn, Sherill Leonardi, Randall Platt, Patricia Stricklin, Dianne Gardner, Anita LaRae, and Christa LaRae. Rich Penner, our lengthy "what if" discussions helped me imagine the possibilities. Huge thanks to Marilyn Lundberg for advice regarding the therapy scenes. Stephen Messer, your computer expertise kept me from falling wildly off track. A note of gratitude to Paige Wheeler's interns and her office manager, Ana-Maria Bonner, for valuable feedback on the manuscript. Thank you to my family, Joseph, and my friends for your support and encouragement. To my appreciative readers, who've posted such wonderful reviews of my first novel of psychological suspense, *The Good Neighbor*, and who have contacted me to say how much they love my work—thank you from the bottom of my heart.

ABOUT THE AUTHOR

Born in India and raised in North America, A. J. Banner graduated from high school in Southern California and received degrees from the University of California, Berkeley. She tried various professions after college, including a stint in law school and a memorable job at a veterinary clinic, since she loves animals, but eventually she returned to writing.

Her first novel of psychological suspense, *The Good Neighbor*, was the #1 Kindle bestseller for 34 days, remained in the top five on the Kindle bestseller list throughout the following month, and was in the top 50 in the Kindle Store for over 145 days in a row. *The Good Neighbor* was named by *Harper's Bazaar* as a book that could be the next *Gone Girl*.

A longtime fan of Agatha Christie, Daphne du Maurier, and *Alfred Hitchcock Presents*, A. J. feels at home writing stories with unexpected twists and turns. She lives in the Pacific Northwest with her husband and five rescued cats.

THE
TWILIGHT
WIFE

A. J. BANNER

This reading group guide for *The Twilight Wife* includes an introduction, discussion questions, ideas for enhancing your book club, and a Q&A with author A. J. Banner. The suggested questions are intended to help your reading group find new and interesting angles and topics for your discussion. We hope that these ideas will enrich your conversation and increase your enjoyment of the book.

INTRODUCTION

Kyra Winthrop is recovering from a harrowing diving accident, but her memory still isn't perfect. Luckily, her doting husband, Jacob, patiently recounts her past to her, filling in the gaps left by an unusual form of memory loss. So when Kyra begins to remember details that don't align with what she knows to be true, she must fight through her murky memory, her isolation, and her own intuition to discover what—and whom—she can trust.

TOPICS AND QUESTIONS
FOR DISCUSSION

1. Why do you think A. J. Banner chose to make Kyra a marine biologist? How does Kyra's intellectualism help ground her to reality? If you were to lose your memory, what are the parts of you that would stay, the way Kyra's memories of marine life stayed? In other words: What about you do you think is indelible?

2. Kyra pieces together, almost completely under her own direction, what happened on the fateful dive on which she lost her memory. At what point did you start to suspect that what happened wasn't quite what she had previously believed?

3. Sylvia says, "Smells can evoke memories in powerful ways. The smell goes to the olfactory bulb, which is directly connected to the parts of the brain involved in emotions and memory" (p. 57). What smells bring you most vividly to the past? Are there smells you can't stand because of the memories associated with them? Or are there smells you seek out to remind you of somewhere, sometime, or someone?

4. In trying to make sense of her world, Kyra learns about anterograde amnesia (difficulty storing new memories) and

retrograde amnesia (difficulty retrieving old ones). Which, if you had to choose, would you prefer to have? Why?

5. Kyra narrates, "Just because someone talks about murder, doesn't mean they intend to actually kill someone" (p. 69). What do you think she means by this? In what circumstances do you believe you might have to consider killing someone? Would you do it? If so, how? Remember, it's just a conversation starter!

6. Nancy says, "Couples get married for all kinds of reasons" (p. 82). For what reason did Van and Nancy marry? For what reason did Kyra get married? What other reasons are there?

7. There are two marriages profiled on Mystic Island, Van and Nancy's and Kyra and Jacob's. How do the two marriages contrast? How do the members of the couples interact with each other (for instance, Van and Kyra, and Nancy and Jacob)? Would you feel comfortable hanging out with Nancy, if you were Kyra?

8. Kyra says, "We're shaped by our past. The past makes us who we are" (p. 93). And Jacob replies, "It influences us, but it doesn't make us. We can do anything, *be* anyone" (p. 93). With which of these two statements do you agree most wholeheartedly? Why?

9. Van once describes Kyra as "a woman with secrets" (p. 125). What secrets was she keeping before she lost her memory? Does she have secrets at the end of the book?

10. During the dinner party at Van and Nancy's, Nancy says, "The only way to protect ourselves is to stay offline" (p. 157). Do you feel safer when you're connected digitally? Or when you're out of touch with the electronic world? What are the pros and cons of each?

11. At the inn, Waverly collects lunch boxes, and Jacob's mother collected plants. Kyra collects information about sea life. What do their collections say about them? What do our collections say about us?

12. There are a lot of different homes in *The Twilight Wife*— Jacob and Kyra's home on Mystic Island, the cottage in back of the house where Jacob writes, the old yellow Victorian on the bluff. What is the significance of home in the novel?

13. Mystic Island might sound like paradise to some and a nightmare to others—discuss who in the room would choose to live such an isolated life, and who would rather be closer to civilization.

ENHANCE YOUR BOOK CLUB

1. Read *The Soul of an Octopus* by Sy Montgomery, one of the books that appears in Jacob and Kyra's living room, to shed some light on the passion for marine life that Kyra retained even through her memory loss.

2. Kyra runs into a lot of people who knew her only briefly the previous summer, like Rachel Spignola and Doug Ingram, yet they all shed a little light on who she was. Take slips of paper and assign buddies, then take turns writing down a one-to-two-sentence description of who the other person is. What do you learn about yourself and each other?

3. As Kyra explores the island, the places she visits and certain objects also evoke memories—seashells, the contents of her purse, photographs, and the local shops, the inn, and coastal tide pools. Which places and objects evoke the strongest memories for you and why?

4. Have every member of your book club share with the group what their favorite element of the natural world is. Why does each person connect with that place or animal or phenomenon so strongly?

A CONVERSATION WITH A. J. BANNER

What significance does the title hold to the narrative? Is Kyra a twilight wife? What connotations does the word *twilight* have for you?

The word *twilight* suggests falling away into darkness, the strange, dreamlike in-between time, when day isn't quite finished and night hasn't quite begun. Kyra hovers in that limbo, not entirely herself without her memory and plunging into a terrifying night as her life unravels. However, she also finds beauty and hope in twilight. She remembers magical nights when she walked the beach and discovered unusual marine species beneath the moonlight. And night always becomes day again. Darkness leads to dawn. She discovers her own inner strength and reclaims her life.

How and when did you first come up with the conceit for the novel? What sparked the initial idea that became the book?

My ideas come from mysterious, deep thermal sea vents. I can never pinpoint the exact origin of a concept. But I do recall having an idea, some time ago, to write a story about a woman who suffers a head injury during a scuba diving accident, and when she awakens, she can no longer recognize faces. She suffers from prosopagnosia. I thought she could discover that the people around her weren't who they claimed to be. But the problem with this approach was, she would still recognize voices and mannerisms, so she would need to also have lost her memory. Even more problematic: I learned that once a person loses her ability to recognize faces, this ability rarely, if ever, returns. On the other hand, memory is more elastic—it can return. I was still enamored with the idea of a diving accident, and I held on to the idea of memory loss. I live in the rural Pacific Northwest and loved the idea of setting the novel on a remote, rainy, shadowy northwest island, which became integral to the plot.

Kyra and Jacob discuss the nearshore, the volatile confluence of sky, land, and water. How did you learn about this term, and what significance does it hold for you?
At the seashore, I feel most at home and somehow closest to the universe and timelessness. When I read about the nearshore in a marine biology textbook, I thought, *This is what I love, this place where sky, ocean, and land come together.* I loved the term—it seemed magical—and it seemed appropriate for Kyra, as she stands at a confluence in her life, at the junction of past, present, and future, where everything in her life is volatile and in flux.

Kyra begins to suspect that the people in her life are holding back important information. Is there ever a time when holding back could be a good thing for another person? Or do you believe that full disclosure is the only way to go?
This is a complex issue. I think the answer depends upon the situation and individual preference. For example, I recently read about a man with terminal cancer who didn't want to

know his prognosis. He seemed calm and content until a doctor told him point-blank that he was dying of cancer. The man became very depressed, rapidly deteriorated, and died. Other people might want the whole truth all the time. On the other hand, if a young child's dog is killed by a car, will the parent give the child all the horrible details about the dog's injuries? Perhaps not.

Your first book, *The Good Neighbor*, also deals with deception and uncovering the truth about those we love. What makes these themes so compelling to you?
As a writer, I find a variety of themes compelling, but the idea of deception is universally fascinating. If a character needs to uncover a dark truth about the people closest to her, or even herself, wouldn't that keep you turning the pages? I've always loved mysteries, from Nancy Drew and the Hardy Boys to Agatha Christie, and psychological suspense is merely an extension of that fascination. Haven't we all known someone who wasn't quite who he or she appeared to be? In fiction, deception raises the stakes for the main character, who may find her concept of reality and her very life at risk.

Kyra asks, "Did we seem happy?" How can you tell when a couple seems happy together? Is there anything about the way that Jacob and Kyra interact that makes them *seem* unhappy? What do you think of the appearance of happiness versus real happiness in a marriage?
I hope it's impossible to tell, in the beginning of the book, whether Kyra and Jacob were truly happy together. This is part of the story question that creates tension—*were they happy or weren't they?* I doubt any marriage is ever always

happy. But in our culture, I believe we expect to enjoy some fundamental stability or satisfaction in marriage. People can hide deep, personal secrets never shared with the outside world. For Kyra, the question is, what was wrong and what were her intentions before she lost her memory?

Did you invent the type of amnesia that Kyra suffers from, or is that form of memory loss actually possible? What research did you do to write so realistically from the perspective of someone who can't trust their own recollections? What was the hardest part about the process of writing an amnesiac character?
Ha, you caught me! I made up the form of memory loss to suit the kind of story I wanted to tell, but from what I've learned, forms of amnesia can be complex and indefinable. The brain remains a mystery. The story of the man who lost his memory and started speaking only in Swedish, a language he had never learned—it's true! I read about his strange life and death. It's entirely possible to lose both anterograde and retrograde memory, and it's entirely possible for memories to return. But because I've never heard of anyone with Kyra's form of memory loss, I can't say whether it's actually possible.

Were there any interesting details about marine life that you learned while doing research that didn't make it into the book? Can you share with us?
I learned so many fascinating facts about sea life, I thought I might want to drop writing and become a marine biologist. Just kidding, but seriously, I love the research. Did you know that over nine out of ten coiled (spiral) seashells today are dextral? This means they coil to the right. There are a few sinistral specimens—shells that coil to the left—but they

are rare and sought after by shell collectors. To learn the reasons for the abundance of right-coiling shells, read an engrossing book called *Spirals in Time: The Secret Life and Curious Afterlife of Seashells* by Helen Scales. She also notes that nobody knows how many mollusk species (she spells it *mollusc*) exist in the world, but estimates run from 50,000 to 100,000 known and named species.

What symbolism did you see in unearthing the marker for *Thymus citriodorus* in the old garden? Why did you choose a garden as the safest place for Jacob's mother?
Spoiler: the garden was the safest place for Jacob's mother because her abusive husband was allergic to lavender, but also, it was a place where she could focus on the positive, on growth and possibility, on nurturing herself. In the same garden years later, Kyra unwittingly unearths a key to unlocking her own past, and an indication of what her future could hold.

What are you writing now?
I'm writing another novel of psychological suspense, also set in the rainy, remote Pacific Northwest and featuring a woman in jeopardy, who begins to question the sincerity and motives of those closest to her. Hmmm, this is becoming a theme in my novels, isn't it? But a fun and intriguing theme for readers, I hope! I'm conducting research into the way a small-town detective (not the main character) might investigate a death that may or may not have been murder.